# The Birdcage Murders

## Karen Baugh MENUHIN

Copyright © 2022 by Karen Baugh Menuhin

Published by Little Dog Publishing

All rights reserved. No part of this book may be reproduced or used in any manner without written permission of the copyright owner except for the use of quotations in a book review.

This is a work of fiction. Names, places and incidents either are the product of the author's imagination or are used fictitiously. Any resemblance to actual persons, living or dead, events, or locales is entirely coincidental.

*Photo credits*
Shutterstock 1037950540 by matrioshka;
Embroidery – Birdcage

First paperback and ebook edition June 2022

ISBN 979-8-8379764-3-8

*Kim and Wendy Palin,
with love.*

# CHAPTER 1

*February 1923*

'Diamond dust?' That was unexpected. I'd never heard of such a thing.

'He was killed by diamond dust?' Swift sounded as surprised as I was.

'Yes, it perforated an ulcer in his stomach. He died within minutes,' Detective Chief Inspector Billings' tone was harsh; a stocky man with a broad nose, wide cheek bones, a pugnacious jaw, and hair more grey than black. 'According to the pathologist, it's one of the most evil means of murder he's come across.'

We were seated in front of Billings' desk in Scotland Yard. We'd received telegrams yesterday requesting our presence with no explanation as to why. I'd been at home in the Cotswolds, and Swift had been in the Scottish Highlands. He'd called me, and I'd agreed to meet him at Kings Cross station this morning, then driven him directly here. On arrival we'd been escorted straight to the DCI's cluttered office.

1

Swift had been elated at the summons; he'd given up Scotland Yard a couple of years ago to marry Florence Braeburn and join her Scottish Clan, and he'd missed the force ever since. Billings' account had quashed his ebullient mood. The tale was a grim narrative recounted in stark terms.

'How did it happen?' I leaned back in my chair, causing its rickety joints to squeak in protest.

'And why?' Swift's angular face was cast in sharp relief by winter sunshine filtering through a grimy window. The office was a workaday place of drab green walls, scuffed lino, and oak bookcases overflowing with boxes and folders. The desk was in better order: a wire basket filled with typed forms and scrawled notes, pens and pencils in a brass pot, and a plain black telephone at Billings' elbow.

We waited for his reply. He ran a thumb against a thick red file lying between his hands on the desk. Motes of dust escaped to drift upwards.

'Ezra, the fourth Lord De Ruyter, was dining with his mistress at Brundles Club four nights ago—'

'It must have been Ladies' Night.' I cut in, because I was a member of Brundles and ladies were mostly noticeable by their absence.

Exactly.' Billings' eyes flashed irritation at the interruption.

'Lennox.' Swift reprimanded with a frown.

'I'm simply stating the fact,' I countered.

'Quiet,' Billings rapped, and carried on. 'Ezra De Ruyter and his mistress, Lillian Lamb, were eating at a table in the Strangers' Room with seven other diners. At nine o'clock, the dessert trolley was wheeled in and one of the women suddenly leapt up with her sleeve on fire. Her husband tried to put it out, as did three other male diners. They failed. The steward poured a champagne bucket of iced water over her arm and that put an end to it. About ten minutes later, Ezra De Ruyter started coughing up blood, then fell face first onto the table.' He let out a sigh of disbelief and shook his head. 'I thought I'd heard it all, but diamond dust is a new one on me.'

I wondered how anyone could be careless enough to catch their sleeve on fire. 'Was the lady burned?'

'No,' Billings replied.

'Had she staged it?' Swift slipped his notebook from his jacket pocket and opened it on the desk.

'Probably,' Billings replied dourly.

'What was the dessert?' Swift began writing.

'De Ruyter had custard with cream and brown sugar,' Billings answered.

'Really?' It sounded unlike Brundles' usual fare. 'Was that on the menu?'

'No, he had it on his doctor's advice. It was supposed to soothe his ulcer after he'd stuffed himself,' Billings replied sourly, showing little sympathy for the victim.

'Was the custard the vehicle for the diamond dust?' Swift made rapid notes in a neat hand.

'We think so.' Billings was noncommittal. 'But we don't have actual proof of how it was administered.'

A knock sounded at the door. We all looked up.

'Sir?' A constable entered carrying a tray of tea and biscuits; steam rose from the teapot's pewter spout. 'Sarge said you'd be wantin' some refreshments.' He placed the tray down on his boss's desk. 'And he said there's a bloke with a dog in the hall dressed in a black tailcoat and wearin' a bowler hat.'

'The dog or the man?' I enquired.

'The man.' The constable grinned as he picked up the teapot.

'Greggs,' I remarked. 'He's my butler. He's in charge of Mr Fogg.'

'You got a butler?' The constable stopped mid pour to stare at me.

'He's a toff,' Billings said. He didn't make it sound like a compliment.

The constable looked my country tweeds up and down with comic disdain. 'Oooh, that explains the peculiar rig-out then.'

'Can we please get on?' Swift was poised with his pen in hand. He had dressed in a sharply pressed grey suit with highly polished shoes, his dark hair neatly brushed. He'd been as eager as a schoolboy before we'd entered Billings' office, then reverted to the diligent detective as soon as we'd sat down.

'How did they discover the diamond dust?' I helped myself to a piece of shortbread because the constable had cleared off without passing them around.

Billings wrapped a large hand around his cup. 'The pathologist saw something glittering in the blood around

De Ruyter's mouth. He scraped off a sample and sieved it, then did the same with the stomach contents. Both samples were peppered with minute shards of diamond.' He drained the cup and put it back with a clatter on its saucer. 'The report states…' He reached into the wire basket to pull a sheet of typed paper toward him, and ran a stubby finger down it as he read: *'Particles of an unknown matter were discovered in samples taken from the mouth and stomach of the deceased, one Ezra De Ruyter (Lord). The particles were later confirmed to be pulverised diamond – source unknown. Upon detailed examination, there was no evidence to indicate further ingress into other organs, suggesting the material was of recent ingestion. The post mortem revealed particles in the oesophagus and throat, but the greater preponderance were observed to be embedded in the lining of the gut. The regular peristaltic action of the stomach had caused particles to pierce the victim's peptic ulcer which resulted in a catastrophic haemorrhage leading rapidly to death. Cause of death; exsanguination.'*

Nothing was said for a few moments. Swift continued making notes. I ate another piece of shortbread. Billings stared at the red file on his desk; he seemed morose, I don't know why.

'How long would it take the diamond dust to perforate the ulcer?' Swift asked as he wrote.

'The pathologist wouldn't give a firm answer,' Billings said.

'They never do,' Swift replied wryly.

Billings grunted in accord. 'The ulcer was large and

inflamed. He speculated the perforation would take around fifteen to twenty minutes, and once the ulcer haemorrhaged, death would follow quickly.'

'What time did he start coughing up blood?' Swift asked.

'Half past nine,' Billings said. 'The time was stated by more than one witness.'

'What if he hadn't had an ulcer?' I finished my tea and placed my cup on the tray.

'That's where it gets nasty.' Billings glanced up. 'The shards of diamond would have worked their way into De Ruyter's internal organs, shredding tissue until internal bleeding and infection killed him. If he hadn't had an ulcer, it probably would have taken him ten to fourteen days to die. He'd have been in agony throughout.'

'Somebody hated him,' I remarked.

Billings muttered agreement.

Swift looked up from his notebook. 'Is this connected to the Birdcage Murders?'

'Of course!' I exclaimed as the penny dropped. 'De Ruyter inherited a fortune after his uncle and cousin were killed in an explosion.'

'The case was never solved.' Swift straightened up. 'It happened before the war…twelve years ago, wasn't it? I heard about it when I joined the force. Ezra De Ruyter was the primary suspect.'

'Yes.' Billings' gaze returned to the red file. 'It was the press who christened it the Birdcage Murders. I was a junior officer at the time, just a grunt, but I was part of the team. We were certain Ezra De Ruyter was behind it. That he'd caused the deaths of all those people – including his own family – for nothing but greed.' He slammed his hand down on the file, a cloud of dust spurted out. 'We couldn't prove it and he's been living high on the hog ever since...' He let out a sigh of frustration. 'Now we've got to re-open the case and the whole sorry episode will be dragged back through the mud by the bloody press.'

'I haven't seen anything about it in the newspapers,' I remarked.

'We've kept a lid on it, but they've got wind of it now and we can't stop them.' Billings' frown deepened. 'They're going to run the story in tonight's *Evening Standard* and they'll have a bloody field day...' He paused and leaned forward to point a finger at us. 'No-one's to know about the diamond dust, and I mean *no-one*. That piece of information is vital evidence and it's not to get out.'

'We won't talk,' Swift assured him.

'And you wouldn't have told us about it, if you thought we would,' I said blithely. I was more interested in the Birdcage Murders. 'Why wait twelve years after the event to kill De Ruyter?'

'Somebody must have learned something new.' Billings shrugged. 'Something that finally proved his guilt, but whoever did it should have come to us. Now we're going to have to track them down and hang them for it.'

'There was a family party.' Swift was still chasing facts. 'The son was about to be married and the Birdcage was being presented as a wedding gift. Eight people died. I don't recall the names...' He raised his pen from the page and looked expectantly at his old boss.

'Lord Frederick De Ruyter and his wife, Agnes.' Billings spoke quietly as Swift recommenced writing. 'Their only son, Xavier; his fiancée, Daphne Clifton; the bridesmaid, Nancy Stanford; the groom's best man, Lionel Moore; a butler, Grimes; and the maid, Fannie Johnson. She survived the blast but died a day later from her injuries.' He listed them as though they were a litany engraved in his memory. 'The fiancée's parents should have been present, but the father was ill. Ezra De Ruyter wasn't there either because he hadn't been invited.'

I recognised the Clifton name because a Lennox had once married a Clifton in the long-distant past. Twelve years ago I'd just gone up to Oxford; I was only eighteen but I hadn't forgotten the sensation it caused at the time: everybody was talking about the horrific details. 'There were diamonds in the bodies...'

Billings nodded, his face grim. 'The De Ruyter family had made a fortune trading diamonds in Antwerp. De Ruyter's grandfather decided to move to London; he was given British citizenship and ennobled. You can deduce the level of their wealth from that,' he said dryly. 'The family invested in property in the city, but they were still keen on the sparkles. The Birdcage was an heirloom, a solid gold automaton decorated with precious gems. Lord Frederick sent it for restoration; the mechanism was rebuilt and fifty matching diamonds of one carat each were fixed into the base – as I said, they were fond of the sparkles.' He shook his head as though it were nonsense. 'The Birdcage was delivered to the house on the eve of the party. Apparently Frederick had decided to hand it over before the big day as a private gift. That was the story anyway, I thought he just wanted to make sure it worked before showing it off in public.' He sighed quietly, then continued.

'I went with my boss to interview Fannie Johnson before she died. The Birdcage had been wheeled in after dinner and presented to the young couple. They all made a big hoo-ha about it and wound the key. The bird tweeted and twirled, and then the cage exploded.'

His gaze returned to the file, a grim expression on his face. 'The bodies were riddled with diamonds, gems, and fragments of gold. We ran the operation by the book: followed every lead, covered every motive, interviewed the servants, tradesmen, the victims' friends, and anyone who'd handled the Birdcage. The investigation ran for three solid years until war broke out. We were forced to stop when our best men were sent to the front.' His voice rose in irritation. 'It was one of the most notorious cases we'd handled. We knew it was Ezra De Ruyter, we'd eliminated all the rest, everything pointed to him, but we just couldn't nail him.'

'Someone has now,' I said.

'Is that why you called us here?' Swift asked, his sharp face keen. 'To help find out who killed De Ruyter, and if it was related to the Birdcage Murders?'

'No.' Billings quashed Swift's enthusiasm with a single

word. 'You're here because I want someone inside Brundles Club. None of the toffs will talk – they think De Ruyter deserved what he got, but one of them poured diamond dust onto his food.' He turned in my direction. 'You're a member, Major Lennox, I saw your name on the list. You and Swift can sniff around, find out what the staff know and what the members saw – see if you can get any of them to open up.'

'I assume you've already carried out interviews?' Swift asked.

'Of course we have.' Billings rapped a reply. 'And taken statements and fingerprints, but the crime scene was ruined. A doctor was among the diners and he declared De Ruyter's death to be natural, so the staff cleaned everything away on the night.'

'Who else was present when De Ruyter died?' Swift turned to a fresh page of his notebook.

A loud rap on the door interrupted us, and the constable came back in. 'Sorry, guv, the chief's got a bee in his bonnet about them reporters asking questions an' what they're going to put in the papers tonight. He's wanting you in his office.'

'Now?' Billings pulled his cuff back to check his watch.

'Yeah, right now.' The constable picked up the tray, ready to leave.

'Damn it, I shouldn't have let you divert me onto the Birdcage murders.' Billings stood up. 'You can find out at Brundles; it won't hurt to make them repeat themselves – it might even shake them up a bit. But, let me remind you

– you're to gather information about De Ruyter's death and *nothing else.*' He jabbed a finger at us. 'You're my eyes and ears in Brundles – no dabbling in the Birdcage murders. Do you understand?'

'Yes, absolutely,' Swift agreed instantly.

'Fine,' I said. 'A couple of days eating and drinking at Brundles sounds just the ticket.'

# CHAPTER 2

'It's a case, Lennox!' Swift was almost euphoric. 'They've let us in on a case.'

'We've been sent to spy, Swift,' I replied dryly.

'It's not spying.' His ebullience was undiminished. 'It's consulting.'

'He treated us like rank amateurs.'

'Billings is a hard man, it's just his manner, but he wouldn't have dragged us all this way unless he had confidence in us.'

'And he only told us half the story.'

'He was interrupted, and he confided in us about the diamond dust.'

I almost expected him to start skipping. We were walking along the main corridor, a wide, echoing place with worn floorboards and yellowed walls. The rapid tap of typewriters clattered from somewhere upstairs, overlapping the low tone of steady voices and abrupt interruptions from shrill ringing telephones.

'Greggs?' I could see him sitting on a slatted bench

beside a balustraded staircase. My little dog spotted me and left my old butler's side to race up the corridor and leap about my feet. I bent to give him a reassuring fuss as he yipped with excitement.

'Greggs?' Swift echoed, reaching him first.

The old fellow snorted, then woke to peer around in mild confusion. 'Ah, sirs. I had to move from my previous seat, and now I am here.'

'So you are,' I agreed.

'Why did you have to move?' Swift asked, ever the policeman.

'Mr Fogg...*ahem*...relieved himself against a fire extinguisher.' He focused on the little dog, who was standing now with his tongue hanging out, entirely unabashed. 'I did not wish to cause an incident in a police station, sir, so I... erm...'

'Skedaddled,' I said.

'Took evasive action,' Greggs corrected me haughtily.

Swift laughed.

'We're going to Brundles,' I informed my old butler.

He rose to his feet in a dignified manner, then paused to smooth his waistcoat over his paunch and straighten his bowler hat. 'I understood we were to lodge at The Reform Club, sir.'

'Change of plan. There's been a murder at Brundles. Come on,' I told him as we headed for the front doors.

'A murder, sir?'

'We'll explain when we reach the club. It's past lunchtime.' I tried to hurry him along.

Greggs refused to be rushed. 'Do you and Inspector Swift intend carrying out an investigation at the club, sir?'

'We're just spending a couple of days asking questions, old chap,' I assured him. 'Then we'll go home.'

Swift cut in. 'Our instructions are to be eyes and ears.'

Greggs stopped in his tracks. 'You mean you're going to spy on members of Brundles, sir?'

'No, no, it's merely a reconnoiter,' I explained in a soothing tone. 'And you can relax, the staff will look after us – treat it as a holiday.'

'Yes,' Swift joined in. 'Put your feet up for a day or two, enjoy yourself.'

Greggs looked dubious and trailed along behind, his sense of rectitude ruffled. We exited into a gated and guarded courtyard. The sun had dissolved the early morning clouds to leave wispy white strands in a cobalt blue sky. I took a breath of fresh cold air, pleased to leave the stuffy confines of Scotland Yard; a severe building in red brick and white stone, with unadorned windows and green front doors. The place held the same institutional aura as the Royal Flying Corps; I'd enjoyed the flying, but never liked the constraints of regimented order.

My Bentley was parked between a Black Maria van and a Crossley.

'Flying Squad,' Swift informed me with pride. 'The Yard initiated it in 1919.'

'They're not using aeroplanes then,' I remarked as I went to crank the car into life.

'It's designed for speed around the city,' he began an earnest explanation until the Bentley's engine kicked into life and drowned him out. He shut up and went to help Greggs and Foggy clamber into the rear before taking the passenger seat.

I revved the engine, then remembered where we were, so throttled back and drove sedately to the gateway. Uniformed guards waved us through with studied indifference. I crawled the car between stone pillars to find a huddle of men in macintosh coats and trilbies – two of them carried cameras with flash bulbs.

'Reporters,' Swift hissed. 'Don't say a word.'

'Why on earth would I?' I replied.

The men in macs stepped forward as though to surround the car; they were too slow, I put my foot down and roared past them, heading for St James's Square. It wasn't terribly far, just along Whitehall and into Cockspur Street, then a couple of turns before pulling up outside Brundles' classic facade. The club had been an elegant mansion before its formation, a house of white painted stone, slender pillars below tall windows and black iron railings forming a guard each side of the imposing portico.

Two footmen dashed down the stone steps as Foggy leapt out of the car and ran straight through the door held open by a man in a top hat and caped coat. We hopped out and left Greggs to organise the unloading.

'Swift,' I said, sotto voce, 'best not to mention you're ex-police.'

'Lennox, I'm not going to lie,' he objected.

'I'm not telling you to lie, but there's no need to bandy it about, that's all,' I warned, and trotted up the steps to enter the comforting confines of Brundles Club.

I hadn't visited the place for a few years and it had been redecorated in the meantime; velvet curtains in the club colours of navy and gold, thick dense carpets, and flocked wallpaper abounded.

'Ah, Major Lennox.' A deep voice rang out.

That brought me to a halt. 'Rossetti?'

Swift and I waited as an elegant figure emerged from an office located unobtrusively beyond an ornate archway. I knew who it was, and he'd have seen us arrive from his window overlooking the square.

'Indeed it is I,' Rossetti announced. 'I wish you good day.'

'Greetings,' I replied guardedly.

'And your guest?' Rossetti raised black brows in Swift's direction. A tall chap, Rossetti was perfectly poised and notoriously clever; he'd been Master of Brundles ever since I could recall. He spoke with a refined English accent, but his Italian predecessors had left their mark: olive skin and thick black hair swept back in dignified style. He cut a svelte figure in an immaculate tailcoat over a pristine dickie, I guessed him to be ten years older than Swift or I, putting him around forty.

'This is Swift,' I introduced him.

'We're here to—' Swift began.

'He's from Braeburn, the clan produce Braeburn Malt.'

I cut him off. 'He's come down from the Highlands for a few days to discuss whisky and that sort of thing.'

'You are to be congratulated, sir, Braeburn Malt is one of the finest.' Rossetti bowed stiffly in Swift's direction, then turned to address me. 'Major Lennox, I assume you've heard talk concerning the recent demise of Lord Ezra De Ruyter.' Rossetti fixed me with his dark eyes. 'As you know, Brundles abhors notoriety and we understand that you have recently helped the police in a number of murder enquiries.'

'That is pure circumstance, we were just…erm…' I spluttered, having been caught on the back foot. I shouldn't have been surprised by Rossetti's remarks, I knew how quickly word spread among the clubs.

Rossetti disregarded my babbling. 'The Board has threatened to prohibit more police intrusion, including any persons connected with the constabulary.'

'You can't exclude the law.' Swift instantly bristled.

'We can if the law has no legitimate reason to be here,' Rossetti rebutted.

'I'm sure Brundles doesn't object to giving the police full cooperation.' I tried a tactful tone. It didn't work.

'We have acceded to every demand the police have made. Three times their "team of experts" have trawled through the club.' Irritation grew in Rossetti's voice. 'Our members have been interrogated, as have the staff – including *me*, and now I have just been informed that we must anticipate the press on our doorstep.' He narrowed his gaze. 'Major Lennox, I hope you are not here to pry.'

'No,' I lied.

'Or you, Inspector Swift?' He turned to Swift.

'Ex Inspector…but…I…' Swift corrected him, then stuttered to a halt as he realised Rossetti knew exactly who he was.

I bit back a curse and decided to come clean. 'We're simply here as a conduit, Rossetti,' I told him.

'Scotland Yard has asked us to observe matters. We will be professional and discreet,' Swift added.

'The Board has specifically stated—' Rossetti took a supercilious air, but Swift cut in.

'Ezra De Ruyter was suspected of orchestrating the murder of his own family,' Swift asserted. 'Why did this club accept him?'

That scored a hit. Rossetti glowered. 'Lord De Ruyter was a member of Brundles before the tragedy. The Board imposed a suspension for several years while awaiting the outcome of the official investigation, but as nothing was ever proven, Brundles had no grounds upon which to exclude him.'

I'd had enough of standing in the foyer. 'Look, better the devil you know, Rossetti, and we'll avoid treading on toes. Which rooms are we in?'

I half expected him to declare the club fully occupied – the usual excuse made when excluding errant members. I was prepared for the rebuff when Foggy ambled over from wherever he'd been. He sat at my feet to look up at me, then Rossetti, who gazed down at him.

'This is your dog, Major?' Rossetti enquired in a quieter tone.

'Mr Fogg. He's a golden spaniel.' It was perfectly obvious, but I thought it worth mentioning.

Rossetti slipped his hand into his tailored waistcoat and pulled out a dried biscuit. 'Welcome, little dog,' he murmured and offered it to Foggy. He took the morsel with good manners, then lay down to chew it on the thick carpet. Rossetti's face softened as he watched, then stiffened as he straightened up.

'Very well, Major Lennox, your party may remain, but I assure you there is nothing here that the police do not already know.' He closed his lips firmly.

Swift was inclined to contest the remark, but Rossetti had already turned his attention to a hovering footman. 'The first quarter chambers, two plus one.'

This obviously meant something to the man as he immediately rushed off toward the front entrance, presumably to direct Greggs and the luggage. Rossetti clicked his fingers at another chap, who stepped forward with a nervous bob of the head.

'Show the gentlemen to their chambers, Pinner.'

'Aye, Master, I'll do that, quick as can be,' Pinner agreed eagerly. He looked up at us with a friendly grin: a sparse fellow with thin brown hair, a face creased with wrinkles, and a crump-back which rather spoiled the line of his smart navy and gold uniform.

'Also, the little dog.' Rossetti indicated Fogg, who immediately hopped up onto his back legs in the hope of more treats. 'Mr Fogg is an honoured guest.'

'Ha, we like our doggies here.' Pinner's eyes lit up.

'Come along then, Mr Fogg.' He went off toward the stairs; Foggy wagged his tail in delight and gambolled after him.

Dogs clearly had their uses. I wondered what they'd make of my cat.

# CHAPTER 3

'This way, sirs.' Pinner was quick, but ungainly in movement, his arms and legs seemingly over-proportioned to his bent body. 'The Master has put you in the best rooms. He'd have put you at the back if he'd have really taken against youse.' He turned to grin at us as we were halfway up the stairs leading to the second floor. 'Barks worse than he bites, does the Master.'

'He seems fond of dogs,' Swift remarked.

'You're right there, sir, he likes animals better than people, and I can't say I blames him.'

We arrived at the top of the stairs, and walked a short way along the passage, this was papered in burnished gold damask of stately design. Pinner stopped outside a mahogany door; the brass knob and fingerplate spotless and shinning. 'Now, this 'uns yours, Major Lennox, and your butler has the adjoinin' room.' He threw open the door to allow my entry. 'An' yours is next, Inspector Swift.' He indicated with a waved hand. 'If you follow me, it's just along here.'

'How do you know I was an Inspector?' Swift demanded.

'Heard the Master say so, and he knows who's who. Got his ear to the ground, that's part of 'is job,' Pinner explained as they continued down the passage. 'The rooms are all ready and fires are lit; we keep them like that so's members can feel right at home the minute they arrive…'

The footmen appeared with my luggage. I followed them into the spacious bedroom and waited as they parked my trunk and whatnots in front of the large wardrobe. Greggs arrived as they went out; he was carrying a wicker hamper, and puffed across the carpet to place it on a desk beneath tall windows.

'Well done, old chap.' I went to help.

'If you would allow me, sir,' he insisted. He opened the lid and Tubbs jumped out. A rotund black cat with stumpy legs, blue eyes, and ridiculously long whiskers. I'd adopted him as an orphaned kitten and he'd never quite grown into the standard feline form. I probably should have called him Misfit, although Mischief would be more appropriate. He took a slow look about the room before sidling up to the telephone and knocking the receiver off its hook. Then he pushed the penholder with a soft black paw until it tumbled to the floor. Satisfied with his endeavours, he jumped down to saunter over to the blazing fire and curl up for a snooze. Foggy went to lie next to him in companionable warmth.

Greggs replaced the telephone and crossed over to the

trunk to begin the unpacking. 'Greggs, Pinner can do that…'

'Certainly not, sir. It is my duty.' He adopted an air of martyrdom.

'Right, fine.' The room was rather grand and furnished in gracious style, unlike the Brundles of old. Plushly upholstered wing chairs stood before the hearth, a dark blue rug covered the floorboards, and heavy curtains in navy and gold framed the tall windows. Matching fabric hung about the four-poster bed, with similar wallpaper adorning the walls.

'William Morris,' I remarked darkly. I knew about the designs of William Morris because I'd recently married, and my wife, Persi, or Persephone, to be exact, had decided my old house needed sprucing. She'd shown me any number of pattern books and asked me which I liked, to which I'd replied, 'none', and then she'd carried on regardless.

'Indeed, sir.' Greggs slipped a tweed waistcoat onto a hanger. 'William Morris is quintessential Arts and Crafts and is destined for m'lady's parlour.'

'Really,' I muttered without enthusiasm.

'There are to be fabrics in a similar style. The colours are cream and red and the theme is Strawberry Thief.' He forgot his feigned weariness and became animated with enthusiasm. 'Lady Persi asked my opinion, and we passed considerable time with swatches and samples. Her Ladyship intends carrying out much of the work herself, with Tommy's and my help.'

'Hum.' I turned grumpy. The changes unfolding in my old home had come as a bit of a shock. 'Well, no-one is to touch my library.'

'That is perfectly understood, sir,' he replied as though repeating a mantra, then bent over the trunk to extract shoes.

Persi and I had honeymooned in Switzerland before returning home to my house, The Manor at Ashton Steeple. I'd described it to her in detail, because she'd never actually seen it – a visit prior to marriage would have scandalised the neighbourhood. I'd done what I could to make her feel comfortable, and even offered her carte blanche to add a few women's touches here and there. She'd taken me at my word, and Greggs had instantly joined forces with her, aided by Tommy, our bootboy. The Manor had rapidly become a jumble of buckets, mops, paint pots, and now pattern books. I'd actually been quite pleased when the telegram arrived from Billings yesterday requesting I go to Scotland Yard.

Swift walked in without knocking. 'Lennox, come to my room will you? I've asked Pinner to find a roll of wallpaper.'

'Why does everyone have an obsession with wallpaper?' I complained.

'We can write on the back of it, it will be our event board,' he explained as he waited impatiently. 'Pinner said he wouldn't be able to find a blackboard, so I've asked for a roll of wallpaper. My room can be our centre of operations. I've already cleared some pictures off the wall, we can pin the paper up and write everything on it.' He was on a mission, in full police mode.

'Fine,' I replied. 'But not until we've had lunch.'

He turned mulish. 'Lennox, Billings will expect us to report back. We have to get on.'

'Yes, and we can start in the room where Ezra De Ruyter was killed.'

'Oh.' He paused, then grinned. 'Right, of course.'

We left Greggs to his endeavours and trotted downstairs with Foggy at our heels. I'd never been to the Strangers Room before, and sought directions. A waiter offered to show us the way; it was further than I'd expected.

We passed through the splendid dining room, crowded with men of varying ages, mostly in city suits, but a few fellow countrymen in tweeds and boots, along with the usual eccentrics.

'Why didn't you know where the Strangers Room was?' Swift asked.

'Because I've never brought a guest to the club before.'

He digested that. 'So, members with guests have to sit in the Strangers Room.'

'Yes, it's fairly standard.'

'Does that mean I can't eat in the dining room?'

We were tailing the waiter down a short flight of stairs heading toward the rear of the building.

'You may do so if Rossetti indicates it's acceptable, but non-members aren't supposed to roam around the club without their sponsor,' I said. Knowing this would spark his socialist tendencies, I tried to explain. 'It's not about privilege, Swift, there are rules. I wouldn't be allowed to wander around Scotland Yard on my own.'

'It's not the same…' He frowned. 'Do you mean I can't go anywhere without you?'

'That's what I've been trying to say,' I replied in mild exasperation. 'Billings asked us to come here because he saw my name on the members' list. It's the reason we're *both* here.'

He mulled the meaning of that in silence.

'Which table would be your preference, sir?' The waiter had come to a halt in a daintily decorated room. There was nobody else in it.

We had the choice of five circular tables, each with two chairs. I was inclined to sit nearest the fire, but asked, 'Where was Ezra de Ruyter sitting when he died?'

The waiter's plump cheeks flushed. 'I'm afraid Master Rossetti has given orders that the subject is forbidden, sir.'

'We're here to investigate on behalf of Scotland Yard,' Swift instantly announced.

'The Master mentioned Scotland Yard had sent two gentlemen.' The waiter sounded apologetic. 'But he was very specific that the staff should not discuss the matter, sir.'

'Fine,' I replied. 'Couldn't just sit us at De Ruyter's table, could you, old chap?'

He hesitated, looked over his shoulder as though someone might be watching, then walked over to a linen covered table by the wall. 'If you would care to be seated here, sir.' He pulled out a chair and indicated I sit down.

'And the lady would have been here?' Swift asked as he took the chair opposite.

'I could not possibly say, sir,' the waiter replied, and left precipitously without even offering to spread napkins on our knees.

'They can't do this, Lennox...' Swift began.

'Patience, Swift. Rossetti will either open up, or shut us out. It's the way it works, and he's more likely to cooperate if you don't go about it like a bull at a gate.'

His face sharpened in irritation, then he let out a long sigh. 'What if he won't let anyone talk to us? Billings won't ask us to help again.'

I can't say that worried me; it had been a complete surprise that Billings had asked us to do anything at all, but I knew Swift was hoping this was a route back into working with Scotland Yard.

'Would you like to change places?' I switched tack. 'Then you can see things from De Ruyter's viewpoint.'

His face lit up. 'Yes, good idea, and we can make a map of where everyone was sitting that night.'

'Assuming we had that information,' I said as we swapped seats.

'We can make a start.'

It was generally understood that gentlemen allowed ladies to face the room. It said much about Ezra De Ruyter's manners that he hadn't done so.

I gazed about as Swift settled himself. The room was pleasant enough with thickly padded chairs upholstered in pastel shades. Walls had been papered with a matching floral design in dusky pink, pale yellow, and light blue. Large windows in deep bays gave a view onto a walled garden, bare and sunlit in cold winter guise.

The waiter returned with a tray bearing a wine bottle, glasses, warm bread and butter. He placed them in front of us as we gave him our order for the set lunch. He nodded in a tightlipped manner and scooted off again, just as the ormolu clock on the mantelpiece struck two. Swift checked the time against his wristwatch.

'Did Pinner tell you anything?' I asked.

'No. He was quite chatty until I asked about De Ruyter's death, then he made excuses and left.'

Fogg was sniffing the air. I took the hint and cut a chunk of butter to spread over the bread. I shared it with my little dog, then reached for another slice.

'De Ruyter's murder is wrapped up with the Birdcage Murder,' I said. 'We can't investigate one without the other.'

'We're not investigating anything, Lennox, we're merely seeking information pertaining to the night of Ezra de Ruyter's murder.' Swift was pedantic.

'You just told the waiter we were investigating,' I reminded him.

'Yes, but that was to give us some authority,' he blustered.

'And you're planning an event board.'

'Because it's efficient,' he prevaricated. 'It will help us visualise the information we gather.'

'It still sounds like spying to me, Swift.'

'We're not spying,' he said through gritted teeth.

'Why don't you telephone Billings and ask for the names of the suspects?' I suggested. 'It's a ridiculous waste of our time to search them out.'

'Absolutely not. This is a chance to prove our resourcefulness.' Swift leaned over his notebook and proceeded to sketch the outline of the room – a rectangle and the two bay windows. He drew five circles to represent the five tables, then wrote EZRA DE RUYTER (Victim) in the place he occupied. 'Ezra was here…you're where Lillian Lamb was sitting…' He noted her name and wrote (Mistress) after it. 'We need to know where they were all seated, particularly the lady who set her sleeve alight.'

'She created a diversion,' I stated, 'to allow the murderer to pour diamond dust into the custard.'

'Obviously.' He turned over to a fresh page to continue his notes.

'Surely De Ruyter would have noticed diamond dust in his pudding,' I said, because I thought the whole thing sounded extraordinary.

'Custard is swallowed without chewing, and it was sprinkled with sugar, which would account for any grittiness.' Swift didn't look up as he talked. 'I think it's feasible.'

'The killer had to know he was going to request custard…' I buttered the last slice of bread and ate it. 'What does diamond dust look like? Would it sparkle?'

He shrugged. 'I don't know, I've never seen any.'

'They use diamond edged tools for grinding.' I picked up my wine and sipped it, it was excellent.

'Yes, and for sawing stone.' He'd stopped writing and was gazing at the empty bread basket.

'Swift, it really shouldn't be difficult to pin-point the killer – it must be someone who passed the dessert trolley during the diversion…Actually, all Billings needs to do is compel them to talk and he'd have the whole thing settled.'

'If it were that easy, he'd have done it already,' Swift said dryly.

I would have argued but lunch arrived. Swift closed his notebook to slip it back into his jacket pocket.

'How's Florence and Angus, and the clan?' I turned the subject away from murder to save the waiter's discomfort.

'They're all fine.' Swift suddenly smiled. 'Did I mention we have a telephone over at the castle now? They had to sink a cable under the loch to connect us. And we've just expanded the schoolhouse on the mainland, two of the local ladies are training alongside the teachers. Florence is on the school board, and we go over as often as the weather allows.'

Settling into a new life in the isolated castle and gaining acceptance with the close-knit Braeburn clan had caused Swift much anxiety. He'd had a couple of disastrous episodes, particularly with the clan's whisky distilling enterprise, but had persevered and was now bringing new work and fresh hope to the community. 'We take Angus, he's a sturdy little chap; he'll be two this year, he's walking really well now, and he's fearless. As soon as he sees the boat, he points and wants to get in…'

He carried on talking in an animated fashion as I ate lemon sole drenched in butter with green vegetables and a side dish of new potatoes. On the rare occasions I'd stayed in London, I'd favoured the Reform because it had the best cuisine, but the food at Brundles had improved immeasurably. In fact the whole club had become really rather sumptuous; I assumed it to be part of the post-war recovery, as everywhere seemed to be doing the same.

'Are you listening, Lennox?' Swift asked suddenly.

I looked up. 'Yes, erm…mostly.'

He muttered something under his breath. 'Florence said Persi had plans to decorate.'

Florence and Persi had become firm friends despite the distance between the Cotswolds and the Highlands.

'The Parlour,' I admitted. 'It's to be William Morris and strawberries.' The waiter removed our plates and refilled our wine glasses. 'I don't know why she wants to decorate it, nobody has used the room since my mother died.'

'It'll be somewhere for her to sit with visitors. Florence has a music room she uses when there are ladies staying. They knit or sew, and talk about babies and women's things. It's quite normal.'

'Hum.' He was probably right, and it meant Persi wouldn't be expecting me to join in. Marriage had brought great joy into my life, but I was still trying to adjust to Persi's presence in the house, and her plans.

The waiter returned with our pudding, vanilla sponge lavishly smothered in custard.

'Custard?' I made a show of eyeing it warily.

'It wasn't in the custard, sir.' The plump waiter spoke in an undertone as he placed the dishes in front of us.

'What wasn't?' I replied.

'Whatever killed the gentleman, sir.'

I could see apprehension in the chap's eyes. Billings had said the diamond dust was a closely guarded secret, so the staff must be completely in the dark about what caused De Ruyter's death. 'Can you be sure of that?'

He looked quickly about, although there was nobody else in the room. 'Chef had a spoonful before it was sent to table, sir, just to check it was how his Lordship liked it. Chef's been right as rain since…'

'Were the police told that?' Swift asked.

'Yes, sir.'

'What happened after Lord de Ruyter died?' Swift had barely started his pudding. I ate mine before it went cold.

'The Master told us his Lordship had suffered a haemorrhage.' He shook his head. 'After the guests left and the ambulance took the body away, we were ordered to come in with buckets and scrub everything clean. It was a horrible mess, what with the blood…' He stared at the table as though blood were still visible. 'Everyone said it was his ulcer – he was always making a fuss about it, but nobody expected anything like that. The laundry had to rub the tablecloth with lye to get the stains out…and then the police arrived the next day and said it was murder.' His eyes darted around the room again. 'We're all worried one of us will be accused of poisoning his food, but I swear it wasn't anybody below stairs.'

'We heard there was an incident involving one of the ladies?' I'd finished my pudding and decided to join in.

'I wasn't there, but I heard talk of it, sir.' He poured more wine into our glasses; his hand shook as he manoeuvred the bottle.

'Where was she sitting?' Swift asked.

'Right over there, sir, with her husband.' He pointed to the furthest table in the bay window.

'Did Lord De Ruyter go to help her?' Swift continued.

'I don't think so, he was a large gentleman, and didn't usually move for anybody, sir.'

'Who was the lady?' I asked.

He hesitated, his face quivering with nerves. 'It...it was Lady Estelle Clifton, sir, but please don't mention I said anything...' he stuttered, then turned abruptly and hurried away.

'Clifton!' Swift exclaimed. 'The girl who was going to marry Frederick De Ruyter's son was Daphne Clifton.'

'Yes.' I'd been mulling what I knew of the family since Billings mentioned her name this morning. 'Lord and Lady Clifton are immensely wealthy – actually, she's the one with all the money, but he is one of the most influential men in the country.'

'They aren't above the law,' Swift instantly replied.

'No, but it explains why everyone is treading so carefully. Their lawyers are notoriously aggressive; they won't hesitate to protect their clients.'

'How do you know all this?' Swift demanded.

I didn't answer.

'Toffs' network?' He guessed correctly. 'Well, this is a murder case, Lennox. Lady Clifton is linked to the Birdcage Murders, and she could be directly involved in De Ruyter's death. Wealth won't protect anyone from justice being served.'

# CHAPTER 4

'Let's go to my room, we can set up the event board and write the details on it.' Swift placed his napkin next to his empty plate.

'We haven't had coffee yet,' I objected.

'They can send some up,' he replied and set off.

I swore under my breath and followed him out. Foggy trotted along at my heels, clearly enjoying himself.

We strode through the dining room, aware of the staff's furtive glances in our direction, and up the stairs. Pinner was in the corridor, and rushed to open Swift's door when he saw where we were headed.

'That were a quick lunch, sirs.' Pinner stood aside to allow us entry. 'Up to scratch, was it?'

'Excellent,' I assured him. 'Couldn't rustle up some coffee, could you?'

'I can, sir, straight away.' His face wrinkled into a grin.

'Did you find any wallpaper?' Swift turned to ask him.

'I left it on your desk, sir.' Pinner nodded in that direction. 'Lining paper, it is, I looked for it special. It's white on both sides, so you can use it anyway you wants – an' I found this, too.' Pinner dug in his waistcoat pocket and pulled out a small box of drawing pins. 'For fixin' it to the wall.'

'Thank you.' Swift smiled and headed straight to where a roll of thick paper lay on the leather topped desk.

'You're from Liverpool, aren't you?' I recognised Pinner's accent.

He chuckled. 'A long time ago, sir, but I'm not a scallywag – straight as a die, I am.'

'There were a few Liverpudlians in the Flying Corps – mechanics mostly,' I remarked. 'They were a resourceful bunch.'

'Oh, you was one them flyin' aces?' He sounded impressed.

'Just a pilot,' I said, then diverted the subject. 'I heard the Chef's worried about whatever caused De Ruyter's death.'

Pinner's grin dissolved. 'We're not supposed to talk about that, sir.'

'No, but we're certain it wasn't poison. Perhaps you could pass that message on, it may help ease his mind.'

'I'm only Chambers, y' know, I'm not Service…but, I can let 'im know.' He looked up at me. 'There's been a lot of bother about them coppers being here. They asked loads of questions, then they let drop it was murder.'

Swift came back to where we were still standing near the door, the roll of paper in his hand. 'We're willing to listen, Pinner, and we'll try to allay any concerns anyone has.' His tone was tactful and seemed to do the trick.

Pinner sighed. 'Aye, well, I'll put a quiet word round, but it's the Master you need to soften up. He rules the roost round 'ere and none of us would cross 'im.'

'Is he hard on the staff?' I asked.

'Can be where it's needed, but most times he's fair and straight. Brundles is a good place to work.' He nodded in emphasis. 'We're mates below stairs, nobody sniping or playin' nasty tricks, and that's down to the Master – he won't put up with no nonsense and we respect 'im for it,' Pinner explained. 'Now, I'd best be fetchin' that coffee for youse.' He bustled out, closing the door behind him.

Swift grinned and turned to me. 'That might open them up.'

I glanced at the roll of paper in his hand. 'And they'll want to come in here to see what you've written about them.'

'I'll be careful,' he said and returned to the desk.

I followed him. His room was almost identical to mine, except the shade of blue was lighter. Foggy jumped up onto the bed, turned around three times, then flopped down to snooze on the padded quilt. It was a cozy spot for a chill winter's day.

Swift had been cutting a length from the roll of paper with a penknife. The section was about a yard and a half long and two feet deep. He proceeded to pin it at eye level above the mantelpiece.

'We have two events, twelve years apart, with direct links connecting them both…' He took out a packet of coloured wax crayons from his inside pocket, picked the dark blue one and used it to draw two vertical lines to divide the length of paper into three sections.

'The first section will represent the night De Ruyter died, the third will depict the Birdcage Murders, and the middle will list the people who are linked to both events,' he explained. 'Billings said the murder was four nights ago, which would be February 1st 1923.' He crayoned the date at the top of the first section, then wrote Strangers Room below it and a thick line underneath. 'The Strangers Room is a rectangle with two bay windows overlooking a walled garden.' He made an outline of the room, just as he'd done in his notebook, labelled the entrance and fireplace, and drew five circles, each with two small squares positioned around them. 'These are the tables and chairs…' He extended his index finger to point to the places we'd sat at lunch. 'Ezra De Ruyter was here and Lillian Lamb sat opposite…' He wrote this in crayon. 'Lord and Lady Clifton were diagonally across from them, seated at the table in the furthest bay window.' He swung his hand to the top right of the drawing and marked their names appropriately, then stood back, folded his arms and stared at his creation.

'Swift, why are you carrying crayons?'

'I bought them for Angus at York railway station while I was waiting for the London train.'

'Not part of your detecting kit?'

'No, but I'll add them to it.' He was entirely serious, he seemed ever prepared for hunting down murder, whatever the circumstances. He stopped pondering and moved over to the third section of the board. 'This represents the evening of the Birdcage Murders...' He hesitated, his hand hovering in the air. 'Damn, I don't know the date.'

'Just write the title.'

'I will but—'

A knock at the door interrupted us.

'Come in.' Swift lowered his arm and put the crayon on the mantelshelf.

It was an unknown chap neatly attired in the club's livery of navy and gold.

'Coffee and biscuits, sirs.' He spoke with a Scottish accent; a tall, sparse man with dark hair, and deep lines etched around nose and mouth. He placed the tray on a table under the window. Fogg woke up at the word 'biscuits' and jumped off the bed to go and watch him.

'I wouldn't recommend letting your wee doggie have a macaroon, sir, they're filled with chocolate,' he said slowly and precisely.

'Actually, he prefers steak,' I replied, strolling over.

'Then he is indeed fortunate, sir. Chef added a dish of sliced beef with his compliments.' The Scot carefully lifted a napkin to reveal said beef. Foggy's eyes lit up.

'Should I serve, sir?'

'Please,' I agreed.

He placed the dish on the floor for the dog to devour his treat. I thanked him and returned to helping Swift while the coffee was poured.

'Excuse me, sir,' the Scot said and placed coffee and macaroons on the mantelshelf in front of us.

'Couldn't help out, could you?' I asked the chap.

'I could, sir.'

That surprised me. 'Do you know whereabouts the dessert trolley was when Lady Clifton's sleeve caught fire?'

He raised a gloved finger to indicate a spot near to the Cliftons' table. 'I pushed the trolley in, sir. It was there.'

Swift's brows rose, then he reached for the packet of crayons and pulled out a red one. 'About here?' He waited, poised and keen.

'An inch more to your right,' the Scot replied.

'So, you were there,' I stated the obvious, as Swift wielded the crayon.

'Indeed, sir. I am the steward, Mr Browne.'

'Ah!' I recalled Billings mentioning the steward. 'You're the fellow who extinguished the fire.'

'Yes, sir,' he replied, his sombre expression unchanged.

Swift had drawn a small rectangle and labelled it 'Trolley', then turned back to Browne. 'Who else was there?'

Browne stepped closer to the diagram. 'Dr Moore was at the table in the other bay window.'

Swift switched to the blue crayon to note the name. 'Who was with Dr Moore?'

'Nobody, sir. The gentleman dined alone.'

'Then why did he eat in the Strangers Room?' I asked, because it was unnecessary without a guest.

'You must address that question to Dr Moore, sir,' Browne replied, then pointed to the table left of the entrance. 'Sir Humphrey and Lady Stanford were seated there. Lady Stanford was facing the room, Sir Humphrey

Stanford sat across from her.' He waited as Swift wrote their names each side of the circle.

I hesitated to speak, but my conscience was pricking. 'Browne, you are aware that Rossetti has forbidden the staff from discussing this?'

'Lennox,' Swift hissed in protest.

Browne didn't flicker an eyelid. 'I am quite aware, sir. Mr Rossetti and I are friends of long acquaintance, but I do not agree with his dictum. The police already possess this information, and my understanding is that you are here under their orders. I see no reason for members of staff to withhold such knowledge from you.' He looked at us, doleful eyes in a long face. 'The staff would like to be notified of events, sirs, and trust you may offer some enlightenment.'

I gathered he was looking for a quid pro quo.

'We know less than you at the moment,' I admitted, 'but we'll tell you what we can.'

Swift frowned at my rash promise but didn't argue the point. 'Who was at the other table?' He tapped the circle in the far corner, to the right of where Ezra De Ruyter would have been sitting.

'That would be Mr Richard Phillips, sir. He is an artist. He was seated opposite his companion.'

'Who was…?' Swift asked, blue crayon at the ready.

'Miss Gloria Thornton, sir. She is a well-known actress.'

Swift duly filled in the names. I'd never heard of Miss Gloria Thornton, but assumed there was something scandalous attached to her name, given Browne's reproving tone. I wondered what he'd made of De Ruyter's mistress, Lillian Lamb.

'Who else was in the room?' Swift's eagerness was barely suppressed.

I finished my coffee and picked up the last macaroon.

'Myself and Mr Rossetti, sir,' Browne replied.

'Rossetti?' I was surprised. 'Why was he there?'

'I cannot remark, sir,' Browne became guarded.

Swift was engrossed in his diagram. 'Do you know the whereabouts of everyone when Lady Clifton cried out?'

'I do, sir. The members and their guests were all seated in the positions you have noted. I was standing beside the trolley at that moment.' Browne pointed to the red square representing the trolley near the Cliftons' table, then moved his finger to the entrance. 'And Mr Rossetti was in the doorway.'

'Then what happened?' Swift held his crayon in readiness.

'Lady Clifton raised her arm – flames were clearly evident. The men rushed to help her, with the exception of Lord De Ruyter, and Mr Rossetti, both of whom remained in place.' Browne was even more pedantic than Swift. 'The gentlemen attempted to dab Lady Clifton's sleeve with napkins, to no avail. As already mentioned, I crossed to Mr Phillips' table, took up the ice bucket and used the contents to douse the fire.'

Nobody spoke for a moment. We stared at the diagram, imagining the actions on the night.

'There must have been quite a crowd around Lady Clifton,' I said.

'There were three, sir, along with Lord Clifton. I had to ease through them.'

'Did you see anyone near the dessert trolley? Anybody acting suspiciously?' Swift sounded like a typical detective.

'As I mentioned, sir, I had rushed to the far corner of the room.' Browne sounded mildly exasperated. 'I was unable to observe the actions of the other occupants.'

'If anyone had been seen acting suspiciously, Swift, the police would have already nabbed the culprit and we wouldn't be here,' I said.

I received a black look in reply.

'Who passed by the trolley, to your knowledge?' Swift continued, doggedly pursuing every detail.

'Sir Humphrey Stanford, Mr Phillips, and Dr Moore, sir.'

'Not Lord Clifton?' Swift demanded.

'No, sir.'

'Did any of the ladies move?' I asked.

'I believe not, sir,' he replied.

Swift drew dotted lines in red to indicate the movements of each man. 'So, they are the most likely suspects...' Swift picked out a green crayon and put a line under their names. 'In collusion with Lady Clifton.'

Browne looked uncomfortable at the word 'suspects'.

'I must leave now,' he announced, then gathered the coffee cups, Foggy's dish, and the empty plates to place on the tray. He moved toward the door, then paused on the threshold, a gloved hand on the doorknob. 'You are aware of Lord De Ruyter's connection to The Birdcage Murders, sir?'

'We are,' I admitted.

Browne nodded as though confirming his assumptions. 'We, at Brundles, do not wish to see our good names besmirched, sirs, but we would not tarnish ourselves by pursuing Lord De Ruyter's executioner, nor stain our reputations by association,' he said, then exited with a silent tread.

# CHAPTER 5

'Tarnish ourselves?' I went to sit in one of the fireside chairs. Browne's words had hit like a dash of cold water. The realisation of how black De Ruyter's reputation was, and how hunting his killer would affect our own reputations, hit home.

'Hell.' Swift sank into the other chair. 'We're not going to achieve anything. No-one will co-operate with us and the press is about to dredge up the Birdcage Murders. They'll accuse the police of incompetence, and Billings is in charge…Damn it, Lennox, he'll be hung out to dry.' He chewed his lip.

And so will we, I thought but didn't say. Typical Swift, he'd only focused on the police perspective. 'Swift, Browne's parting words were a warning worth listening to.'

'We're not giving up.' He jumped to his feet and returned to his event board. 'How many people in the Strangers Room were connected to the Birdcage Murders?'

I didn't reply to that. He turned to face me. 'Lennox?'

'Swift, do you truly want to hunt down De Ruyter's killer?'

'Of course.' He sounded perplexed.

'He deserved it, Swift.'

'That isn't for us to judge, Lennox. We're agents of the law, not the law itself,' he replied in heroic fashion.

I bit back a dry retort. 'The task is tainted – Billings has sent us to do dirty work.'

'Nonsense, he's treating us as… as though we just happened to be here and are passing on anything useful we hear…'

I cut in. 'So we *are* spies.'

'No…yes, but not the sneaking sorts.'

'What other sorts are there!' This was exactly what I'd objected to earlier. 'You said we would be consultants.'

'Lennox, you have to be realistic.'

'Damn it, Swift, our reputations are at stake…' I crossed my arms, trying to quell my anger. 'We'll be talked about, and it won't be polite – I'll be looked on as a bloody turncoat, and worse.'

'For heaven's sake, Lennox, you're helping solve a murder, not blowing up the houses of Parliament.'

'De Ruyter's reputation is black as the devil. Finding his killer is hardly going to cover us in glory.' I was becoming rather heated. 'You heard Browne…'

Swift was having none of it. 'We can't let killers go free just because they murdered a murderer.'

'It's not our responsibility to let anyone do anything,' I retorted.

'We've already discussed this…'

'No, we haven't, you've batted away my objections without listening to what I'm saying.' I raised my voice. 'It's our bloody reputations on the line, and it's important.'

'Look, if you want to go home…' Swift challenged.

'It's not a question of that.' I took a breath and moderated my tone. 'Swift, you said it yourself, no-one will co-operate with us. This whole case is bound to fail, and when it does, Scotland Yard will never approach us again.'

'And if we duck out now, they'll forget we ever existed.' His set his lips in a stubborn line. 'We only have to do our part – just make a few enquiries. Is that too much to ask?'

Foggy came to my side and put his paw on my knee. Harsh words upset him. I ruffled his fur in reassurance.

'Lennox, I'm not going to force you to pursue this, but you're a member here and I'm not. I can't do it without you…' He sighed. 'I'll let it go if that's what you want.'

'I'm not proposing we give up, Swift. It's just the realisation of what we've got ourselves into, that's all.'

'Fine.' He sound diffident. 'Why don't you discuss it with Persi?'

'No.'

'You've called home, haven't you? Just to say we've arrived safely?'

'Erm, not yet…' I frowned, was I supposed to do that? This was the first time Persi and I had been apart since we married, and I hadn't given it a thought.

'Well, you probably should,' he suggested. 'And I need to call Florence…'

'Oh, yes, right.' I gathered Foggy up. 'I'll leave you to it.' I returned to my room with my little dog under my arm, and put him down on the hearthrug.

'Sir?' Greggs emerged through the discreet door beside the fireplace.

'I'd better call her Ladyship,' I told him.

'Very good, sir. I have already informed the house of our safe arrival.'

'Excellent, well done old chap.' I looked about. 'Where's Tubbs?'

'Ah, I'm afraid he caused something of a commotion in the dining room, sir.'

'What sort of commotion?'

He took a breath. 'He stole a chicken leg from the plate of Sir Bernard Sykes and carried it under Viscount Marshall's chair, where he ate it. After that he joined Lord Emmerson's group to walk the length of their table, and then he was sick on the carpet.'

I grinned. I knew the misdemeanours of a small cat would be treated as light diversion by most members. 'Where is he now?'

'Asleep on the Earl of Albemarle's lap, sir, in the Reading Room.'

'No irreparable damage done then.'

'Indeed not, sir.'

I cut to the chase. 'What's being said about Swift and myself, Greggs?'

'Ah.' His chins wobbled. 'There are mutterings, sir.'

'I thought there would be.'

'Lord De Ruyter was a friendless man. The consensus regarding his demise is surprise that it had taken so long.'

'Do they think we should avoid searching for his killer?'

Greggs assumed an equivocal air. 'According to talk, the members are divided between two lines of thought, sir. There are those who believe you should refrain from meddling, for fear of uncovering the culprit, and there are others who believe you pose no threat to the, erm… outcome.'

'Right.' I'm not sure if that soothed my scruples. 'What about the staff themselves?'

'Very troubled, sir. No explanation regarding the murder was offered to them and they fear one of them may be made a scapegoat.'

I nodded. 'I can't give up, Greggs. Swift's keen to impress Scotland Yard, and I'm not going to let him down.' I walked over to the window and gazed down at a group of men huddled near the entrance to St James's garden. They were obviously Press, some held cameras. 'How long have the reporters been outside?'

'They arrived a short while ago, sir. The doorman has kept them from the front steps, but apparently they have the right to remain on the pavement.'

I peered out at the sun-washed scene. St James's Square was centred around a tree-lined garden enclosed by black railings and framed by broad paths and verges. The houses facing the square were mostly Georgian in style – tall, grand and imposing.

'What did her Ladyship say when you called her?' I turned the conversation to home.

'I spoke to young Tommy, sir. M'lady was attending to the chickens.' He had gone back into his room, for some reason, and was now talking through the open door.

'We don't have chickens.' I turned around.

'I believe we have now, sir.' He'd donned his overcoat and was pulling on leather gloves.

'What?'

'Perhaps you should telephone m'lady, sir?'

'Hum.' I particularly disliked talking on the phone. 'Where are you going?'

He placed his bowler hat onto his carefully combed hair. 'I have a rendezvous, sir.'

'Really, who with?'

'Miss Fairchild is currently in London and I suggested an outing to the theatre. We have seats for *The Mikado*.'

'Miss Fairchild does get about.' We'd encountered her some time ago in Braeburn Castle, where she'd arrived out of the blue. A pleasant lady of a certain age who believed she could commune with ghosts. I'd thought her a bit batty, but Greggs seemed keen.

'She is a most intuitive lady, sir.' He was brushing cat hair from his sleeve, but stopped and eyed me from beneath the bowler. 'You did say I should treat our stay as a holiday, but if you prefer I remain…?'

'No, no,' I instantly refuted. 'Can't let a lady down, old chap.'

'Indeed, sir, and I will return before dinner to lay out

your evening dress.' He nodded a bow. 'Please pass my regards to m'lady, when you telephone,' he said, then exited with a determined tread.

I sighed. Greggs was ever the stalwart old soldier, and it occurred to me that he was a far more effective spy than I would ever be.

I went to the telephone and stood next to it. Chickens? Why the devil would Persi want chickens? I picked up the receiver. 'Hello, could you connect me to Ashton Steeple 451, please.'

'Certainly, Major Lennox,' the club's switchboard operator replied promptly.

Quite a lot of static and crackling later, a boy's voice chirped on the line.

'Ello? There ain't nobody at home now 'cept me an' my auntie, she's the cook, but she's busy, so you'll have to talk to me.'

'Tommy?'

'Sir! Is that you? It's me, sir. M'lady is in the orchard. I've only come in the house to get a hammer. We're making nest boxes for the chickens, there's six of them. I'm allowed one for my own, she's black and—'

'Tommy will you—' I tried to interrupt.

'I was goin' to call her Esmerelda but now I think Nettie is better 'cause she keeps goin' in the nettle patch an'—'

'Tommy,' I tried again. Tommy was our bootboy and would chatter without pause. 'Where is her Ladyship?'

'I told you sir, she's in the orchard an'—'

'Right, right…Why have we got chickens?'

'On account of Farmer Alcott's wife, sir. Lady Persi said how much she liked the eggs, and then Mrs Alcott said maybe we should have some chickens of our own, and then she said they had some spare an' Farmer Alcott brought them over just after lunch.'

There had been no mention of chickens at breakfast this morning. 'When did her Ladyship have this conversation with Mrs Alcott?'

'It was last week, sir, but the chickens only arrived today. We're puttin' them in the walled garden, 'cause of the foxes. Mr Benson is fixin' the gates so we can open an' shut them, and Brendan's helping him. Then we're goin' to mend the shed and m'lady is wanting to put the nest boxes in, and I've got to go, sir.'

'Wait. What? Who's Brendan?'

'Brendan Alcott, the farmer's youngest son. He likes looking after animals, but he gets upset when they got to be killed on the farm, so m'lady says we should ask him to stay an' help Mr Benson on account of him being so bent an' old. I'm goin' now, they're waitin' on me. Bye, sir.'

I heard a clunk then the line fizzling as I stood looking at the receiver in my hand. I'd barely been away five hours and Persi had already acquired chickens and an apprentice gardener.

A rap on the door caused me to replace the receiver and turn about. 'What?'

'Sir. Message for you, sir.'

'Is it about chickens?'

'Erm…Don't think so, sir.' It was a young bellboy in a blue cap with a red band around the rim. He offered up a silver tray sporting a folded note. 'It was an outside telephone call, sir. The Master wrote it down and told me to bring it up to you.'

'Right, thank you.' I took the note. It was written on thick paper heavily embossed with 'Brundles' at the top, and the address, 'St James's Square' below.

'Will there be anything more, sir?'

'No.' I slipped him a thruppence.

'Thanks, sir!' He nodded a bow then left, shutting the door behind him.

The writing was precise and clear. I read it twice, then strode out and along the passage to Swift's room.

'Swift?' I called. 'Are you in?'

'Of course I'm in.' He was sitting in a chair by the fire, his arms crossed, and looking sour. 'I can't move about the club without you so I've been stuck here…' he began a minor tirade.

'Never mind that. We've had a message.'

'Oh.' He sat up, his testiness forgotten. 'Who from?'

'Lord Clifton. He'd like to talk to us.'

# CHAPTER 6

Swift's eyes lit up. 'Lord Clifton! When does he want to see us?'

I looked again at the note. 'Now.' I handed the paper to him. 'Rossetti took the message and sent it up.'

He scanned it quickly. 'Sir Heathcliff Lennox, c/o Brundles. Please attend Clifton House, Belgrave Square, at your earliest convenience, yours etc., Arthur Clifton,' he read aloud. 'It's addressed to you – it doesn't mention me at all.'

'It doesn't mean anything, Swift,' I assured him.

'Right. I'll get my coat, and perhaps I should bring…'

'We don't need any detecting paraphernalia.'

'Fine.' He was ready in an instant with buttoned-up coat, smart new fedora and neat wool scarf.

Foggy had followed me to Swift's room and was trotting alongside me as we walked down the corridor. Pinner was coming up the stairs.

'Look after Mr Fogg, would you old chap,' I told him.

'Will do, sir. He can come down to the kitchen with

me, he'll enjoy that,' Pinner grinned and picked the dog up.

'Shouldn't be long,' I replied as we trotted down the stairs. Fogg was used to coming with me on my jaunts, but I thought London streets would be too crowded for a small dog of country habits.

We reached the foyer, a few elderly members were ambling about; staff were hovering, waiting to assist should they be required. An atmosphere of after-lunch torpor permeated the place, although I still felt eyes slide in our direction as we passed by.

'Rossetti.' I nodded to him on approach. He was standing in the archway; ramrod straight and not a hair out of place.

'Major Lennox, Inspector Swift.' He made the barest bow in acknowledgment and watched us without any expression on his smooth face. I was pleased to walk out and into the crisp, cold air.

'Sir, sir!' A clamour broke out and the small crowd of reporters ran across the road in our direction. 'D'you know anything about Lord De Ruyter's murder? Did you see anything? We'll pay for a quote. What do you know about the Birdcage Murders? Do you think De Ruyter deserved to die...?' They carried on shouting. One took photographs, the flash bulb popping off, which irritated me.

We strode quickly into King Street; from there it was a short distance to St James's Place and the concealed passageway into Green Park. It was a pleasant stroll along a cinder path; Buckingham Palace lay in the far distance, people sauntered about walking dogs, pushing prams or herding children – an intrepid few even managed the whole caboodle.

We crossed the road into Grosvenor Place, then Chapel Street, and thence to our destination in Belgrave Square.

Clifton House presented a magnificent frontage in a genteel setting. We paused to gaze up at the stone-built mansion; five storeys high with rows of wide windows and myriad chimney pots trailing smoke into the bright blue sky. We stepped up to bang the knocker on the gleaming black door.

It opened instantly.

'Good afternoon.'

'Major Lennox and Inspector Swift for Lord Clifton,' I said.

The butler paused to look down his thin nose at us. 'I understood his Lordship's request was directed to Sir Heathcliff Lennox only.'

I eyed the man narrowly. 'Then your understanding is deficient.'

The remark ruffled him. Two spots of indignation rose in his pallid cheeks. 'Very well, sir. If you would like to follow me to the small library, I will inform his Lordship of your arrival.' He turned without waiting for a response and stalked off – he was so damned superior he should have been levitating.

We trailed behind, gazing about us, trying not to appear overawed by the palatial splendour; every inch of the place seemed to have been intricately and expensively embellished. Frescoes of cavorting deities covered the walls and ceilings, richly coloured rugs swathed marble-tiled floors, inlaid furniture in exotic wood stood in strategic spots, and gilded carvings crested doors and mirrors.

We were led to a small library furbished in a sedate shade of green with a multitude of book-lined shelves. The decor was a great deal easier on the eye than the kaleidoscope of colour in the reception hall.

'Wait here, please.' The butler went off with his nose in the air.

'This must be the most ostentatious house I've ever stepped foot in.' Swift sounded waspish.

'You don't have to live in it,' I remarked, staring at a painting of soldiers raising a war-torn flag on some foreign hilltop.

'You said his wife was the one with the money – she must have spent it all on fresco artists.'

'I don't suppose he could stop her,' I replied glumly. 'Persi does whatever she chooses, regardless of anything I say.'

'Is this about the wallpaper again, Lennox, because it's really not so bad.'

'No.' I told him about the chickens and Brendan, the new gardener.

'You're not jealous are you, Lennox?'

'No, that would be ridiculous, but it's my home.'

'It's yours and Persi's home now.'

'Fine...I realise that, but she just wants to change things.'

'Well, perhaps it's for the better.'

'What?' That stung. 'Swift, my house is perfectly comfortable the way it is.'

He rolled his eyes. I was about to offer a rebuttal when we were interrupted.

'His Lordship will see you now.' The butler had entered without a sound.

We formed a procession up a wide staircase, our footsteps silenced by the deep pile carpet. Portraits massed the walls: ladies with elaborately coiffed hair were flanked by military men in uniform, and interspersed by a few earnest political types. The upper landing was dominated by a more recent painting – a young lady carefully attired in a debutante's white frock. Her golden locks were crowned by a diamond tiara, and a look of mischievous delight played on her pretty face. We paused to read the name plate – 'Daphne Clifton' – the artist had signed it 'Richard Phillips'.

'The same Richard Phillips?' Swift muttered.

'Possibly,' I muttered in return.

The butler had continued along the corridor. We extended our stride to catch up as he thrust open a door and waited for us. We entered into a spacious sitting room dominated by a huge marble fireplace. The decor was lemon and white, and brightly lit by sunshine streaming through the windows.

'Sir Heathcliff.' Lord Clifton rose to greet us. 'And I believe you have brought Inspector Swift with you'

'Greetings,' I replied. 'And I prefer Lennox.'

'Ah, very well,' Clifton acknowledged graciously, and turned to Swift. 'Inspector.'

'Ex Inspector.' Swift was coolly polite.

I suddenly noticed there was another chap in the room. He was seated in a corner with a yellow notepad on his lap.

'That is my lawyer, Wallace. I have asked him to attend this meeting,' Lord Clifton explained, as though it were entirely normal to have lawyers lurking in the drawing room.

Wallace didn't move, he didn't even lift his eyes when we turned to look at him.

'Please be seated.' Clifton indicated a pair of small sofas. He was around my height, aged about 60, slim and immaculately attired in a light grey suit. He had the look of a Roman patrician with white hair swept back from a high forehead, pale blue eyes, and a classical profile.

We sat as directed. I watched the lawyer from the corner of my eye; he'd taken out a pen and begun writing.

'You wanted to see us?' I sat back and extended my feet toward the hearth.

'I did,' Clifton replied.

'May I ask why?' I enquired.

'I knew your father, we were in the same regiment, and members of Brundles, of course.'

'Ah.' That was a surprise. I'd known there were ancient family links, but had no idea of a more recent connection. I also realised he'd avoided the question.

'Your wife created a scene just before De Ruyter died.' Swift cut through the niceties.

'I hope Lady Clifton didn't suffer any injury to her arm.' I tried a smoother approach.

'Thank you, she is perfectly well,' Clifton replied, then hesitated before stating, 'Her actions were deliberate.'

That caused another surprise. I saw the lawyer's head jerk up.

'Why did she do it?' Swift asked.

Clifton closed his eyes briefly before answering. 'She believed we were to receive final proof of Ezra De Ruyter's guilt. You must know that he was suspected of causing the death of our daughter, Daphne…' His voice quavered at the mention of her name.

'Yes, we are aware of that.' Swift's tone softened. 'I'm sorry, this must be painful for you.'

'She was our only child,' he spoke quietly. 'Full of mischief, always laughing when she shouldn't. She was so vibrant, so alive… This house feels like a mausoleum without her.' His gaze swept around the room. 'I didn't like Xavier De Ruyter, he was a spoiled jackanapes, but Daphne fell for him and nothing her mother or I could say would change her mind…' He faltered and fell silent again, leaving the crackle of the burning coals to fill the void.

I let a couple of seconds tick by, then prompted him. 'Xavier was heir to Frederick De Ruyter's fortune?'

'Yes.' Clifton met my gaze. 'In time he would have inherited everything, that's why Ezra killed him…killed them all…and Estelle and I would have died with them.' He gave a shake of his head.

'I'm sorry…' I paused, searching for the right words. 'Were you unwell that night?'

'I was not,' he admitted. 'I fabricated an excuse. Frederick De Ruyter had been creating a song and dance about the damned Birdcage – insisting it was to be the centre of the wedding celebrations.' His lips pursed in irritation at the memory. 'He announced they would hold a family dinner to formally present it to the young couple some days prior to the wedding. He pretended it was a tradition, but I thought he just wanted to flaunt his wealth in front of us.' He turned toward the fire, his aristocratic profile lit in relief. 'The De Ruyters were brash, arriviste types, and my family is one of the oldest in England. There was a clash of cultures… I couldn't face the damned palaver, so I feigned illness and made our excuses.' He raised his voice suddenly. 'I was so angry – Daphne was joyful, and kind, she was a sparkling girl and the De Ruyters couldn't see it. They were more interested in their gaudy treasure. They couldn't see that Daphne was *our* treasure, and we were losing her to their idiot son.' He closed his eyes and quelled his temper. 'As it was, we held joint funerals for them instead.'

Clifton was not at all as I'd imagined him; no arrogant airs or condescending manner, just a man who'd lost a much loved child and never stopped grieving for her.

'The police carried out a lengthy investigation into the murders.' Swift had been discreetly making notes, but I could see he was affected by Clifton's anguish.

Clifton sat back. 'Scotland Yard were convinced Ezra was behind it. So were we.'

'Could you tell us what you recall of the event?' I asked quietly.

'You must have all the details.' Clifton attempted another evasion.

'But we'd like to hear your version, if you don't mind,' Swift asked in a respectful manner.

'Very well, but I can only tell you what we learned in the course of the investigation,' Clifton agreed. The lawyer, Wallace, coughed loudly. I took it to be a warning, but Clifton ignored him. 'I had seen the Birdcage before its renovation, Frederick had insisted on inviting me to view it, and apprising me of his plan to gift it to the young couple. It was quite large, almost three feet in height, and had flowers formed from gemstones attached to the bars. On the evening of the presentation, it had been covered in fine cloth and placed on a trolley in a side room. After dinner everyone was asked to gather in the family parlour. The butler wheeled in the trolley, Frederick De Ruyter made some sort of speech, removed the cloth, then offered the key to Xavier and Daphne. He invited them to wind the mechanism, this set the bird to sing and…well, you are aware of the consequences. The police informed us of the tragedy some hours later – this marked the beginning of their enquiry. I judged it to be quite chaotic at the start, and they were very slow to release the bodies. They subsequently explained that it had been necessary to remove the gold and diamonds embedded in the flesh.' His lips trembled, but he caught himself and carried on. 'This was evidence, apparently. The police requested statements from us, and there were many questions.' He shook his head at the memory. 'They interviewed the artisans who had handled the Birdcage; it had been sent to a reputable jeweller, Aaron Goldstein. He had been commissioned by Frederick De Ruyter to restore the automaton to working order. The police concluded that the explosive device was planted into the base shortly before it left Goldstein's workshop.' He stopped suddenly, realising that Swift was writing furiously, and waited for him to catch up.

'Thank you,' Swift muttered.

'Reynolds, one of Goldstein's men, fell under suspicion. He had financial troubles. He'd served in the army and been trained in munitions. He was deemed quite capable of building an explosive device and planting it in the base of the Birdcage. The investigative team believed Ezra de Ruyter paid him to do this, although they were unable to find definitive proof.'

'Where is he now?' I asked.

Clifton raised his brows at my question. 'Dead, of course. I understood you had some grasp of the facts.'

'Not entirely,' I replied, irritated that Billings hadn't told us.

Clifton's patrician face stiffened. 'Reynolds committed suicide while detained.'

'In a prison cell?' I was astounded.

'Yes,' Clifton replied sharply.

I swore under my breath. Swift reddened and bent over his notebook; he obviously knew about it. I hesitated, then tried to regroup.

'What type of explosives were used?' I asked.

'You do not possess that information, either?' Clifton's demeanour cooled; he shifted in his seat. 'I must apologise, gentlemen, I haven't offered any refreshments. Would you care for a drink?'

'No, thank you.' Swift's refusal was polite.

Clifton was prevaricating and we were in danger of losing his confidence. I decided to wrest what information I could from him. 'Were all of the diners in the Strangers Room related to victims of the explosion?'

'Yes,' Clifton replied as though it were self-evident. Swift wrote another rapid note.

'Who orchestrated the Ladies Night dinner?' I continued.

'That is the issue I have asked you here to discuss,' Clifton began but was interrupted by a woman's voice.

'It wasn't me – and I've already informed the police of that.' Her American accent radiated energy. 'Now, who do we have here?'

'Estelle,' Clifton's voice sharpened. He stood as the lady approached. We followed suit.

'Arthur, is this one of your clandestine meetings?' she demanded of her husband. 'And I see Wallace has elbowed his way in.' She cast the lawyer an arch look. He stiffened but said nothing.

'May I present Lady Estelle Clifton, my wife.' Clifton

made a formal introduction. 'This is Detective Inspector Swift, who is retired from Scotland Yard, and Hugh Lennox's son, Sir Heathcliff.'

She smiled up at me. 'Oh, so you're Hugh and Mary-Rose's son! We knew your parents before you were even born, and my goodness, haven't you grown into a fine young man! Both of you are just so handsome.' Her accent held the warmth of the American South. 'Call me Estelle, I insist.'

'Delighted to meet you.' Swift bowed, sounding genuinely pleased.

'Greetings.' I kissed the back of her hand. 'And it's Major Lennox.'

'But Heathcliff suits you so well.' She laughed. 'Except for the hair – the original Heathcliff was dark, wasn't he? I prefer your blond good looks and chiselled jaw.'

'I...erm.' There wasn't much I could say to that. 'I'm afraid I don't recall our meeting...?'

She laughed lightly. 'You were just a baby last we saw you. Your mother loved to be in the country, and we were city folks. Arthur sometimes met Hugh at the club when he came to town, but your mother and I kind of drifted.' She sat down in a cushioned chair nearest the fire. 'And now you're all grown up...and you've become a sleuth!' She turned to her husband. 'Have you set them on the track of the Devil's assassin?'

'My wife refers to Ezra De Ruyter as the Devil,' Lord Clifton explained, and then addressed his wife. 'I haven't set them on anything.'

'Well, you must!' she demanded. 'Or are they here to investigate me?' She was short and slim, with ash blonde hair trimmed to flatter her high cheekbones. A beautiful woman, despite the years, and elegantly dressed in flowing blue chiffon.

Clifton's expression remained stiff. 'We were discussing the Birdcage.'

'I'm not a fool, Arthur.' Her smile dimmed. 'And I know it makes you sad, but it was long ago. Daphne's gone, and we're left to live life as best we can.' Her resemblance to her daughter's portrait was striking: the same gleam of mischief in her blue eyes, although Estelle's were discreetly accentuated with a touch of shimmering make-up.

'It didn't end with Daphne.' Clifton watched her, his love writ in the softening of his face. 'Someone has now killed Ezra.'

She waved a hand in dismissal. 'It should have been done years ago.'

Swift leaned forward. 'Lady Estelle, your husband told us that you set your sleeve alight on purpose. That directly implicates you in Ezra De Ruyter's murder.'

'Well, in that case I confess – I did it.' Her blue eyes flashed with amusement and a glint of something harder. 'So what are you going to do about that?'

# CHAPTER 7

'You killed Ezra De Ruyter?' Swift was astonished.

Lady Estelle laughed. 'Many times, but only in my dreams…' Her lips trembled as her laughter died. 'That Devil took Daphne from us. She was our only surviving child – our very own angel. I will curse that man's name to my dying breath.'

I waited a moment before speaking. 'Could you explain what you meant when you said, "I did it"?'

The mischief returned to her eyes. 'I created the scene just as I was told. I'd no idea he was going to die then and there. I thought someone was going to jump up and wave evidence and point a finger at him, just like in those novels. Then the police would drag him off to the hangman's noose, while we all watched him squirm.'

Swift looked as bemused as I was. 'Who instructed you to cause a scene?'

'I don't know, it was in the note with the invitation.' She looked over at her husband. 'I didn't tell Arthur about it until afterwards. He was so mad at me.' She laughed, entirely unrepentant. 'He still is!'

Lord Clifton retained a dignified silence. Wallace had been fidgeting since Lady Estelle made her dramatic announcement, and was now waving his notepad in our direction.

'I think your lawyer would like a word,' I mentioned to Clifton.

He turned in his seat. 'Wallace, please be patient, would you.'

Wallace looked peeved and lowered his yellow pad back onto his lap.

'Lady Estelle,' I said. 'Could you explain about the invitation?'

'For you, my dear Heathcliff, I surely could.' Merriment bubbled in her voice. 'I received an envelope two weeks back. It was all written in capital letters, inviting me to Ladies' Night at Brundles – I had to have my husband attend me, of course.'

Swift had been writing rapidly, but paused to ask, 'What made you think it was connected to De Ruyter?'

'Oh, am I not being clear? My husband has always said I'm a flibbertigibbet, not that I have any idea what that means.' She turned to tease him with a bright smile, then back to us. 'It was the card. Such a pretty thing, decorated with a golden Birdcage and flowers on a black background. The other side had an image of Justice – you know the one – like our statue of liberty, except she's wearing a blindfold and holding a pair of scales in her hand.'

I glanced over at Swift: he was watching her with barely suppressed excitement.

'Do you still have it?' I asked.

'Of course I do. I've kept it hidden, where snoopers can't find it.' She looked over at the lawyer in the corner, who was studiously writing and refused to meet her eye.

'May we see it, Lady Estelle?' Swift leaned forward.

She smiled, perfect white teeth between pink tinged lips, before slipping a buff-coloured envelope from the pocket of her gown, and holding it out to me. 'Here, you shall have it, Heathcliff.'

I took the envelope with a polite thank you – actually I could have kissed her.

'I do wish you'd discussed this with me first, Estelle.' Clifton uttered a weary reprimand.

'You brought Wallace in without consulting me,' she countered, then softened her tone. 'We need a pair of fresh eyes on this, my dear, or we'll just go round in endless circles.'

Swift was practically twitching with excitement; the invitation was a new lead, unknown even to the police. He watched my every move as I studied the envelope in my hands. The closing flap had been carefully undone, rather than hastily torn open. I ran a thumb over the surface: the texture was coarse to the touch, it felt cheap and looked commonplace. The address had been written with black ink in block capitals: PRIVATE; LADY ESTELLE CLIFTON, CLIFTON HOUSE, BELGRAVE SQUARE. There was no stamp.

'Do you know how it was delivered?' I glanced at Lady Estelle.

'By hand, I suppose. I asked the staff, but none of them knew anything about it.'

I removed the contents – a card and a folded note – and passed the envelope to Swift. He took it from me, scrutinising it as closely as I had, then held it up to the light. Nothing unusual was visible

I studied the card. It was of standard size, the printed image exactly as Lady Estelle described: a golden Birdcage laced with colourful flowers on a black background. The bird inside was red and plump. 'Is this an accurate representation of the original Birdcage?' I held the card up for Clifton to see.

He leaned forward to gaze at it. 'I believe so.'

I'd become the centre of attention; even Wallace was craning to watch from the corner as I turned the card over to study the reverse.

Lady Justice was outlined in black against a white background, the words *'Justice will be Served'* were printed in italics across the top. Below was *'Ladies' Night, Brundles, February 1st'*. The card must have cost time and money in its design and execution. I wondered who had printed it.

Swift reached his hand out; I passed it to him, then unfolded the single sheet of notepaper. It was as cheap and common as the envelope, the message written in the same block capitals as the address. I read the words out loud.

'*Twelve years have passed, the time for justice has come. Attend Ladies' Night and play your part. On the stroke of nine, create a scene: let the candle light your sleeve and cry out, then await the Devil's undoing.*'

'It's ridiculous. Utterly theatrical.' Clifton was caustic.

'You haven't seen it before?' I asked, just to be certain.

'No, I haven't seen it before now and wasn't even informed of its existence until after the dinner.' Anger rippled in his voice.

'If I'd told you, Arthur, you'd have made such a fuss and refused to go.' Lady Estelle was unrepentant.

'Exactly, and that piece of nonsense should have been given to the police,' he replied sharply.

'Why didn't you inform them yourself?' Swift cut in.

Clifton's jaw tightened. 'I will not inform on my wife, she is answerable for her own actions.' He turned back to her. 'As it is, Estelle, you have made us complicit.'

'It has made *me* complicit, Arthur. And I had no idea he was going to die.'

'*Justice will be Served,*' Swift quoted from the card. 'It could mean anything, including murder.'

'No.' She turned to him. 'I was sure someone was going to reveal proof that he was guilty…'

Swift cut into her explanation. 'In the middle of a dining room? That's ridiculous, if anyone had real proof they'd have called in the police.'

'This was precisely my argument once I'd learned of it, Inspector,' Clifton said in support.

'Perhaps the person who sent it didn't trust the police

to handle it competently,' Lady Estelle retorted. I hid a smile. She wasn't easily intimidated, and she had a point, given Reynolds' death in a police cell.

'The invitation proves the dinner was orchestrated and someone had planned the murder,' I stated. 'Have you spoken to any of the other people who were there?'

She turned her blue eyes to me. 'I haven't had a chance. It was such a surprise when that Devil died, and afterwards I knew how it would look…' She broke off with a sigh. 'We don't even know what caused his death, the police won't tell us a darn thing. They've been here asking questions, but they wouldn't answer any of ours.'

'Estelle, the police cannot do their job unless they have all the facts,' Clifton said.

'Well, they won't get any from me!' She stood up and walked out, her head held high.

Clifton rose too. 'Gentlemen, I trust you will excuse us. This situation has opened old wounds, it is painful to revisit…' His voice wavered, he suddenly seemed weighed down by age and distress. 'I will leave you with Wallace; he has my permission to discuss the matter with you.' His Lordship followed his wife from the room, leaving us with the lawyer.

Wallace jumped to his feet and strode over to sit in the chair Clifton had just vacated. He straightened his tie and ran fingers through his thick brown hair before addressing us. 'Lord Clifton is an esteemed client of many years,' he began briskly. 'You can be assured I am acting in his best interests.'

'Why did he ask us here then?' I said, which caused a frown to crease his smooth face.

'Lady Estelle knows we'll hand this to Scotland Yard.' Swift held up the invitation. 'Why didn't she give it to them herself?'

'She will not co-operate directly with the police after their failure to convict De Ruyter,' Wallace replied. His accent was plummy London. He held out his hand toward Swift. 'Would you pass the invitation to me, please?'

Swift didn't move.

'Why didn't Lady Estelle give it to you?' I needled Wallace.

He gave an exasperated sigh and dropped his hand back into his lap. 'Because she doesn't like me,' he admitted.

At least that was honest.

'We will present it to the right authority,' Swift said, his face set in a determined manner.

'Look, gentlemen.' Wallace attempted a persuasive tone. He was around forty, and typical of most city lawyers – polished, clever and supremely confident. 'Lady Estelle concealed the invitation for understandable reasons, but it is tantamount to obstruction of justice. She's in danger of being prosecuted as an accessory to murder – it is vital we protect her. If you will allow me to handle this matter, I will ensure the invitation is presented in such a way as to exonerate her Ladyship. You must see the necessity of that.' He ended on a sharp note.

'Why did Lord Clifton ask us to come here?' Swift repeated the question I'd already posed.

Wallace sighed in exasperation. 'We were informed you were co-opted by Scotland Yard and had arrived at Brundles. That, and the fact Lord Clifton knew your father, Major Lennox, brought about the decision to interview you. We didn't anticipate Lady Estelle's action, but it is favourable and confirms our decision to contact you was correct.'

I didn't believe Wallace's slick explanation. 'Clifton wouldn't confide in us merely on hearsay and a remote acquaintance with my father.'

He shifted in his seat. 'I had a report raised on you both. It seems you have acquired experience in uncovering the guilty. We were quite impressed, actually.'

'So, you have your own team of investigators,' Swift was quick to realise.

Wallace nodded. 'My firm specialises in gathering information on behalf of our clients. We provide a discreet and detailed service.'

'Did you investigate the Birdcage Murders at the time?' I asked.

'We did,' Wallace replied.

'Could we see the report, please?' Swift immediately asked.

'It's in the hands of Scotland Yard,' Wallace replied.

'Is there a copy?' Swift asked.

'No,' Wallace said, I thought he was lying.

Swift's brows drew together.

'Which type of explosives were used in the Birdcage?' I demanded, because the lack of detail had been irritating me.

Wallace twitched his lips, annoyed at being forced to deal with ignoramuses. 'It was gelignite. Scotland Yard called in bomb-making experts. They tested the remains of the Birdcage; fragments of rubber, explosive, and splinters of magnetised iron were found burned into the base of the cage. They calculated that approximately two pounds of gelignite had been pushed into a bicycle inner tube and fastened at each end with copper wire. This was fitted around the clockwork mechanism in the shape of a horseshoe. A detonator was buried within the gelignite and wired to a magneto. The magneto was attached to the winding spindle. Once the key was turned, the magneto created an electrical current which triggered the gelignite.'

'What size was the De Ruyter's family parlour?' I was trying to imagine the extent of the explosion.

'Smaller than this,' Wallace indicated with a brief wave of the hand.

I was familiar with the aftermath of bomb blasts from my time in the war, and the impact explosives had on bodies when detonated in confined spaces. I shook the memories away and glanced over at Swift. He'd been taking notes, but had now stopped to focus on Wallace.

'What was the date of the explosion?' he asked.

'May twenty-fourth 1911.' Wallace sounded bored, which irritated me further.

I glowered at him. 'What else did you find during your investigation for Lord Clifton?'

'Nothing definitive,' Wallace replied. 'Reynolds could have provided the evidence needed to hang De Ruyter, but he died as a result of police brutality. It poisoned the relationship with the bereaved and ruined the official investigation.'

'Brutality?' I turned to Swift.

A shadow crossed his face. 'It wasn't "brutality". Reynolds wouldn't open up. One of the detectives lost his temper and threw a punch. They put Reynolds in a cell to let things cool down and he committed suicide that night.' His jaw tightened. 'Assault by police wasn't usual practice, Lennox, despite what people think. A full enquiry was held and the detective lost his rank.' He let out a sigh of exasperation. 'Wallace is right, without Reynolds they couldn't establish a link between De Ruyter and the murders.'

'Precisely, and Scotland Yard was excoriated,' Wallace added. 'The newspapers lambasted them for their complete failure, and now they're rehashing the story. This whole investigation is mired in controversy; it will ruin reputations, including yours, gentlemen, if you persist.' He stood up and buttoned his jacket. 'Now, please, I'd like the invitation.'

I also rose to my feet. 'As you said, we've been co-opted by Scotland Yard. We'll hand it to them ourselves.'

# CHAPTER 8

Wallace argued all the way to the front door, and when that didn't work, he threatened us with the sort of persecution only lawyers are capable of. We ignored the blighter and stalked out into Belgrave Square just as the sun sank below the rooftops. Swift was cock-a-hoop.

'This will make Billings sit up!' He grinned. 'I'll bet the Yard know nothing about the invitations.'

'Assuming there are more.' We were walking alongside the central garden in Belgrave Square.

'Of course there are,' Swift said. 'That dinner had been set up like a stage set.'

'Swift.' I turned to him. 'You should have told me about Reynolds and how he died.'

He had the grace to look shamefaced. 'I thought you may have read it in the newspaper reports at the time, but then I realised you hadn't. I apologise, Lennox.' He sounded sincere, then added, 'You could have mentioned your parents were friends of the Cliftons.'

'I had no idea, I'd only heard about the marriage connection.'

'What? You mean you're related to them?'

'It was three centuries ago, Swift.'

'Hm,' he grumbled, then said, 'They wanted to sound us out.'

'I know, but for what reason.' I'd been looking for a taxi and spotted one crawling along the other side of the gardens. I waved at it.

'To discover what we know, to judge who we might side with.' He sounded caustic. 'And to find out how useful we might be.'

'Just like Billings then,' I replied dryly.

The taxi made its way slowly towards us and halted at the pavement.

'Scotland Yard,' I instructed.

We slid into the back. The leather seats were rubbed smooth with use.

'The Yard! You summat to do with that toff what were murdered, then?' the cabbie asked as we set off very slowly toward the river.

'No,' Swift lied.

'Strange you comin' out of Clifton House, then goin' straight to Scotland Yard. Clifton was the name of one o' them what was killed.'

I realised that however large London was, word still spread with the same lightning speed as it did in the countryside.

'It's the Birdcage Murders all over again,' the cabbie continued, a navy cap pulled low over his forehead, his collar pulled up against the cold. 'In the *Standard*, it is, front page news. Bet there's a reward for information.'

'Thank you, driver,' Swift replied coolly.

'What makes you think there's a reward?' I asked.

'I dunno, but stands to reason, don't it? They're all toffs an' that's what they do, throw money round till they get what they want.'

'They're not all like that,' I muttered.

'Yeah, well I reckon they should reward the bloke what killed ol' Ezra.' The cabbie drove at a snail's pace; we'd have been quicker walking. 'Blew up his own family 'e did. I was reading about it before I spotted you pair.'

'Couldn't put your foot down, could you?' I tried encouragement.

'Nah, don't like goin' fast.' Which was probably a good thing as he kept twisting around to talk to us, then back to peer through the windscreen.

A cyclist veered across our path and carried on weaving through the traffic in suicidal style, which diverted the cabbie for a while, then he piped up again, 'That copper should never 'ave bashed the bloke what gave 'im the jellynite.'

'Was that in the newspaper?' I leaned forward to talk to him.

'Aye, it were.' The cab driver nodded his head. 'Good story it is, they'll drag it out for weeks, 'specially with them toffs bein' in it…You're a toff, ain't ye?' He twisted around again to address me. 'I can tell by your voice. You sure you're not summat to do with it?'

'Drop us off here, cabbie,' Swift told him firmly. We'd arrived at the corner of Scotland Place and could see a bevy of reporters near the gateway to the Yard. I paid the chap, we hopped out and strode quickly past the throng, then through the gates into Scotland Yard itself. We were delayed in reception while Billings was informed of our arrival; a few minutes later we were sitting in front of his desk.

'What have you got?' Billings cut straight to the point.

'An invitation to murder,' Swift announced and placed the envelope on Billings' desk.

He picked it up, opened it and extracted the contents, holding each piece by the rim to avoid fingerprints. Then he placed the items onto his blotter and scrutinised them under a magnifying glass. Finally, he carefully and slowly read each word. He glanced up at us, then reached for his telephone to call in two officers.

'Guv?' They arrived, eager with anticipation. Both were in standard plain clothes.

All three fired questions at us; we answered as best we could, including what little we'd gleaned from Browne at Brundles. Swift was made to read out his own detailed notes while one of the officers wrote every fact down on an official pad. I could see the exhilaration in their faces – the invitation must have been an entirely unexpected and important lead.

Swift completed his account and waited in his chair like a schoolboy on prize-winning day.

Billings dismissed the officers; they exited with rapid strides and eager grins.

'You've exceeded any expectations I had, gentlemen.' Billings leaned his elbows on the desk and regarded us with narrowed eyes. 'Well done.'

'I think we can put a lot of it down to luck,' Swift said modestly.

'Probably,' Billings agreed. 'This lead could prove crucial to the investigation, and I'd like to thank you both on behalf of myself and the Force.' He stood up and offered his hand. 'Hope to work with you again, Swift.'

Shock showed on Swift's face. He shook the proffered hand in silence.

'Lennox.' Billings turned to me.

'You're dismissing us?' I was as astounded as Swift.

'As I said, you've exceeded expectations,' Billings replied coolly. 'We'll take it from here.'

Swift remained in dumbfounded silence. I opened my mouth to argue, but then shut it again, realising the powerlessness of our position. We left Billings' office without a word and made our way out and onto the street. Dusk was giving way to night; the gas lamps were lit and frost had begun to form on the pavements.

'I suppose we should have expected that,' Swift muttered.

'It's utterly graceless.' I wasn't as understanding. 'We've come all this way at Billings' behest...'

'We're not a formal part of the investigation, Lennox, and Billings is right, we've given them a new lead, there's nothing more for us to do.'

There weren't any taxis around so we kept walking. 'There's a pub.' I nodded toward bright lights emanating from a bow-fronted free house; it was a tempting sight as the cold closed in. 'We could have a pint.'

'No.' He shook his head, despondency in every movement. 'I think we should go back to Brundles and pack…'

I was still furious at Billings' treatment of us, and had little patience with Swift's dejection. 'Stop being so damned gloomy. In the space of a few hours we've given the Yard more than they've achieved since De Ruyter keeled over.'

'You don't understand, Lennox.' He suddenly sparked with anger. 'I really hoped we'd be allowed to work alongside them…to act as consultants…' He bit his lip.

'Billings won't forget what we did today. He'll call us the next time he thinks we'll be useful.' I tried to commiserate.

It didn't help. He just shoved his hands in his pockets. We came to the pub; he was about to trudge by, but I grabbed him by the elbow.

'Drink, Swift,' I said and manoeuvred him inside.

The welcoming smell of spilled beer, stale tobacco and coal fires met us; it was instantly cheering. I left Swift to find a seat and went to the bar.

'Two pints of bitter, please.'

'Comin' up, dearie.' The barmaid beamed at me. I looked about as she drew the beer; it was a classic tradesmen's pub rather than the mirrored variety aimed at raffish city boys. Dark wood, pipe racks, a roaring fire, and smoke-stained ceilings. Five o'clock was traditionally teatime, so the place was almost empty.

I paid for the pints and found Swift in a nook by the hearth.

'Cheer up,' I said.

He didn't. He sipped his pint while staring at the fire. I felt the same despondency; the investigation was intriguing and the invitation had added crucial momentum to it. I didn't want to walk away from it.

'Lady Estelle couldn't have put the diamond dust in his dessert,' I began.

'Hm,' he grunted.

'But there's no proof it had actually been put in the custard, so it doesn't absolve her from suspicion.'

'If it weren't in the custard, how did he ingest it?' Swift countered.

'We'll have to find out.'

'We can't, we're off the case,' he intoned.

'Billings must have been pressured.' I sipped my beer.

'How?' He demanded.

'I've no idea, but if he intended cutting us out of the investigation he wouldn't have told us about the diamond dust this morning.'

We drank in silence for a while, mulling over the afternoon's events.

'The blast from the gelignite would have killed them instantly in a room that size,' I continued.

'Yes,' he agreed. 'The maid must have been standing near the door or she'd have been killed the same instant.' He finished his drink. 'We should go, Lennox. I want to call Florence and tell her I'm coming home.'

I realised I should call Persi, too, so I drained my beer and returned the glasses to the bar.

'Goodnight, dearie,' the barmaid called cheerfully.

We set off briskly through the streets to arrive at Brundles, our breath white in the cold air. The reporters had cleared off, and the doorman pulled the door open to let the escaping warmth greet us.

'Nice night, Major Lennox,' the chap said through his muffler. 'Inspector Swift.' He raised a gloved hand to the rim of his top hat.

'Thank you… erm, George, isn't it?' I had a vague recollection.

'It is, sir,' he replied jovially. 'Nice to be remembered. Your father always had a kind word to say. We were sorry to hear he'd passed away.'

'It was just after the war…' I replied. 'He always liked the club.'

'Aye, well, it's an exceptional place.' George nodded.

'Have a good evening,' I told him and stepped inside. Swift muttered something too quiet to be heard and followed me in.

The foyer was mostly vacant, it being the period when those with any sense were seated by the hearth in convivial company with a drink in hand. We made our way upstairs without encountering a soul, and entered my room.

'Ah, there you are.' Lord Clifton was sitting in an armchair waiting for us. Foggy was at his feet. 'I saw Pinner, he allowed me to accompany your dog.'

'Clifton, what the devil are you doing here?' I demanded.

'We've been removed from the case,' Swift launched into a tirade. 'Was that your doing?'

'Indirectly, I fear it was.' Clifton sounded contrite.

'How?' Swift demanded.

'Wallace took it upon himself to intervene after you refused to give up the invitation.' Clifton hesitated. 'In consequence, I telephoned the Chief of Police and asked him to reconsider his decision.'

'Does that mean the Yard will reinstate us?' Hope rose in Swift's eyes.

'I doubt the likelihood of that, at present.' Clifton chose his words carefully. 'But I would like you to continue with your enquiries on my behalf, if you would be so kind.'

That gave us pause and we contemplated it while removing coats, scarves, and the usual whatnots. I decided we needed a drink and went to the side table to pour three glasses of whisky from one of the decanters. I handed the tumblers round, then sat down to face Clifton.

'What do you expect us to do?' I asked.

Clifton's patrician face was emotionless, but his eyes held a look of determination. 'Discover as much as you are able.'

'What about Wallace?' I asked.

'I have asked him to refrain from further action,' he replied.

'You've fired him?' Swift sounded surprised.

'No.' Clifton's lips twitched with a suppressed smile. 'Wallace has his uses, but my wife dislikes him and has asked me to exclude him from this case.'

'He had no right to interfere. We should be working with the Yard. We could have achieved far more.' Swift wasn't mollified.

'Could you?' Clifton replied dryly.

That shut him up.

'We will do what we can,' I said.

'We can't accept money,' Swift cut in.

'I understand.' Clifton nodded without smiling. 'And if you could keep me abreast of your findings, particularly as regards Lady Estelle, I would be most grateful.'

'Within reason,' I replied. I wasn't prepared to make promises on unknown outcomes.

Clifton finished his whisky in one, then rose to leave. 'I bid you both a very good evening,' he said in formal tones. 'And your dog.' He bent to ruffle the fur on Fogg's head. 'I gave him his evening meal, by the way.' He pointed to an empty dish under the desk.

'Thank you,' I said sincerely.

We bid him a polite good evening and waited until he'd made his exit.

'We're not rich people's puppets,' Swift said.

'Swift…' I swallowed a sigh. 'We're back on the case.'

'Yes, but Clifton might have done it deliberately.'

'Done what?'

'Used Wallace to cut us off from the Yard.' He was quite serious.

'Why?' I was sceptical.

'Because he wants us to keep him directly informed.'

I knew his objections were fired by his socialist suspicions. 'Look, Swift, Clifton could be useful, and we need his authority to carry on, but we're not going to answer to him.'

'Oh,' he looked at me. 'So we're not working for Clifton.'

'No, he just thinks we are.' I turned toward the door. 'Shall we go to your chamber and fill in your event board?'

Excitement suddenly gleamed in his eyes. 'Right, yes, we could.'

I grinned. We gathered Foggy, the whisky decanter and tumblers, and decamped to his room next door. He went straight to the mantelshelf to shuffle through crayons, found the red one and raised it to the top of the third section.

'The date was May 24th, 1911.' He wrote it in capitals, then "Birdcage Murders" beneath it, and underlined them both. 'Right, so Billings gave us the list of victims…' He stopped to pull out his notebook and flicked through to the correct page. 'Read them out, would you, Lennox?' He handed it to me.

'Fine.' I went to stand next to him. 'Frederick and Agnes De Ruyter and their son Xavier.'

I waited as he noted the names of the dead.

'Daphne Clifton and her bridesmaid, Nancy Stanford. Lionel Moore, who was to be best man. The butler, Grimes, and the maid, Fannie Johnson.'

Each was listed one below the other to fill the third section of the board.

'That's all eight,' Swift said.

'Yes,' I agreed and took another sip of whisky.

'Clifton said all the people dining in the Strangers Room were connected to the Birdcage victims.' He moved to the first section and stared at it. 'Browne gave us the names of the diners, but we don't know the relationships between those who were in the Strangers Room and those who died in the explosion.'

'Well, just write the ones that are obvious.'

'Fine.' He moved to the centre section. 'Ezra De Ruyter was related to Frederick, Agnes, and Xavier De Ruyter.' He wrote them in close formation. 'Lord Arthur Clifton and Lady Estelle Clifton were related to Daphne Clifton… Sir Humphrey Stanford and Lady Stanford were related to Nancy Stanford… Dr Moore was related to Lionel Moore…and…we can't connect the rest.'

I poured more whisky from the decanter. Foggy was snoozing in front of the fire.

Swift tapped the crayon against his teeth as he gazed at the names. He'd shed his jacket and rolled up his sleeves. The room was comfortably warm; the fire had been kept blazing during our absence, the curtains drawn, and the room tidied. Brundles was essentially a bachelor's paradise.

'The only people to pass by the trolley were the three men: Phillips, Moore, and Stanford.' Swift pointed a finger at each. 'Lennox, we should make a proper list of suspects.'

'I thought we already had?'

'No, I only underlined them in green, look.' He pointed to their names in the first section.

'Then you've done it.'

'But it's not a proper list.' He really was ridiculously pedantic.

I took another sip of whisky. 'You can't put specific details on the event board – they'll be seen.'

'I know.' This was obviously a dilemma for him.

'We could make notes?'

'Yes, and then we won't lose anything.'

'Right.' I pulled my notebook from my jacket pocket. The binding was dark leather; Persi had bought it for me on an outing. I sighed. I was beginning to miss her.

I found my pen, unscrewed it, blotted the nib and wrote the three names, then paused 'Browne wheeled the trolley in,' I recalled, 'he could be involved.'

'But he was keen to help, and he was the only one who was.'

'I'll put him on my suspect list with a question mark next to his name.' I did so. 'I'm going to draw the invitation.'

'Oh, good idea! I'll do the same.'

We sat and worked in quiet concentration – it felt like prep school. My Birdcage was wonky, so was the figure of Justice, although I made a fine rendition of her sword.

'What was written on the card and notepaper?'

Swift flicked back through his notebook and read out: *Justice will be Served,* above the image of Justice, and below was, *Ladies' Night, Brundles, February 1st*. The Message was: *Twelve years have passed, the time for justice has come. Attend Ladies' Night and play your part. On the stroke of nine, create a scene: let the candle light your sleeve and cry out, then await the Devil's undoing.*'

'Whoever set this up knew Lady Estelle referred to De Ruyter as 'the Devil,' I said when I'd finished.

'And the layout of the room, and that candles were used on the tables.'

'Places like this always have candles, what else would they use?' I replied.

'We use oil lamps in Scotland.'

'Why?'

'It's easier to find than beeswax, not that it's relevant. Will you please focus, Lennox.'

'I am focused,' I replied, stung. 'What next?'

'We need to interview them, of course.'

'We're hardly going to do that before dinner,' I replied. 'We should add details about Reynolds and the gelignite.'

'I already have.'

'Right, well I'll just make my own notes then.' I jotted down what I could recall while he stared at the event board.

A knock sounded at the door interrupting the companionable silence.

'Come in,' Swift called.

It was Pinner. He held my cat in his arms. 'Master says he's yours, Major Lennox, sir.' The man grinned. 'Been a little rascal downstairs with the gentry, but he's put a smile on most of their faces.' He placed him gently onto the bed.

'Pinner,' I addressed him. 'Are any of these chaps staying at Brundles?' I indicated Swift's diagram.

He came to squint up at it. 'The doctor all but lives 'ere, sir. Says it suits him now he's retired.'

'You mean Dr Moore?' Swift asked.

'I do, sir.' Pinner nodded. 'Fond of his food is Dr Moore.'

'Would you ask him if he'd like to join us for dinner,' I said.

'Now there's a funny thing,' Pinner replied. 'Because he's already mentioned he'd like a word with you.' He looked toward Swift. 'The both of youse, I mean.'

'Keep a table for eight o'clock, would you,' I said.

'Certainly, sir. I'll tell Service. And Lord Clifton had a word with the Master, so now he says you'll be eatin' in the dining room, an' you can bring the dog an' cat if you wants.'

'Thank you.' I gave him a grin, then picked up my notebook and added a name to the list of suspects: Rossetti.

# CHAPTER 9

'Does this mean I can move around the club on my own without you acting as a guard?' Swift asked as we took our seats in the dining room. We'd both changed into formal rig, with stiff shirt fronts and white bow ties.

'One step at a time, Swift,' I told him. There were a number of other diners, talking quietly with convivial ease. This room, too, had been spruced up since my last visit. Walnut paneling lustrous under fresh layers of lacquer, candlelight glowing from gilded chandeliers. Gold brocade curtains drawn across lofty windows, tables laid with spotless linen, cabriole chairs of comfortable proportions, and a thick red carpet muffling footfalls, stilling the atmosphere of immutable permanence.

Fogg went off to rootle under tables for any stray scraps – Tubbs had decided to stay with Greggs, who had returned as promised to lay out my evening wear. By the look of his soppy grin, he'd already arranged another assignation.

'Why are you a member of two clubs?' Swift suddenly asked.

'My father put me down,' I said. I didn't like to explain that a gentleman wasn't considered a gentleman unless he was a member of a club. It was the way of our world, like Eton, Harrow, and Oxford.

'It's utterly archaic that clubs don't allow women in except on special occasions.' Swift had been looking about.

'Members of these clubs hold the reins of this country,' I told him. 'Politics is a nasty, back-stabbing game – why would anyone want to involve women in it?'

'That's just an excuse for misogyny; women are as capable as men, they should be included.'

'Lady Astor sits in the House of Commons. Progress is being made, Swift.' I withheld from saying more. I sympathised with his sentiment, but had a greater understanding of how the establishment worked. Husbands went home and talked to their wives, who had opinions of their own, and those opinions shaped decisions. It wasn't direct, but few men wanted ladies exposed to the ruthless bear pit of power-broking – it was the balance we'd struck and it had sustained the country for centuries.

'Ah… Now there's a couple of likely looking sleuths.' A booming voice interrupted us; it came from a rotund chap in a well-worn dinner jacket. He skirted tables to head in our direction, beaming broadly as other members turned to watch. 'Holmes and Watson, I presume.'

'Dr Moore?' I stood up to greet the man.

'Spot on, old boy.' He grabbed my hand and wrung it robustly.

Swift rose too. 'Inspector Swift.'

'Ha! You're the ex-copper. Word gets around, you know, no hiding anything here.' Moore chortled and turned back to me. 'Lennox, I'm an old friend of your uncle, Charlie Melrose – fine man – never see him in town nowadays; heard he's taken to rusticating in the sticks. Shame. There's a lot to be said for the city.'

'Would you care to join us?' I suggested. Browne had followed in Moore's wake and was now hovering behind the vacant chair at our table.

'Gladly, gladly. Browne here will help me.' He was seated and made comfortable by the glum steward. We nodded to the chap in acknowledgement, both of us wary of speaking, given Browne's inclusion on our suspect list. Moore ordered a bottle of Puligny-Montrachet for the table, and Browne went off to fetch it. The doctor seemed the friendly sort; hair and eyebrows curly white, his features plump, with a rosy nose.

'Dr Moore.' Swift was coolly professional. 'We'd like to see the invitation you received to Ladies' Night.'

The old man's mouth dropped open in astonishment. 'You know about that?'

'As you said, there's no hiding anything here,' Swift rejoined.

'Well, De Ruyter deserved it and I'm glad he's dead.' Moore's tone was unapologetic.

'What made you so certain he was guilty of the murders?' I watched him, his expression a mixture of defiance and grief.

'Everyone was certain, but they never had the proof to convict him...' His eyes glistened with tears. 'He murdered my boy – I hope he's rotting in Hell.'

Browne reappeared with the bottle of fine white Burgundy and proceeded to pour generous glasses for each of us. It was first-class stuff, Moore obviously knew his wine.

We sipped in silence, letting the old man recover himself.

'Could we see the invitation, please?' Swift asked again.

'Oh, very well.' Moore patted his jacket, then pushed thick fingers into his waistcoat pocket, before discovering it in his wallet. 'Ah, here's the blighter.' He tugged out a folded and creased envelope, paused to gaze at it for a moment, then handed it to Swift.

It was virtually identical to Lady Estelle's, the same envelope, the same block capitals, only the address was different: PRIVATE: DR RUPERT MOORE, C/O BRUNDLES, ST JAMES'S SQUARE.

'There's no stamp. Do you know who brought it here?' I asked him.

He shook his head, his white curls gleaming in the candlelight. 'No, but well considered, young man,' he commended. 'I raised the very same question myself. Didn't tell them what was in the envelope, of course, kept that hush-hush. Desk clerk told me it was left by hands unknown in the postbox by the entrance.'

'What about the doorman?' I continued.

He beamed at that. 'Aha, a real sleuth's question! George would have noticed a stranger bearing a missive, wouldn't he? But I'm ahead of you. I questioned him, and he said no stranger had posted anything outside the club that day. That means it must have been left in the dead of night.'

'Which date was that?' Swift was quick to ask.

'Couple of weeks before Ladies' Night. Don't know exactly, one of the staff might remember.' He waved a plump hand in the direction of waiters moving unobtrusively about the room, then leaned in to eye us. 'How many of the others received invitations? I'll bet they all did, and one of them's blabbed, haven't they.'

'I couldn't say,' I evaded the question.

Browne arrived to replenish our glasses. Moore had already finished his.

Swift had been examining the envelope, but slipped it below the table when Browne approached. I glanced up at the steward; I thought he'd caught a glimpse of the manoeuvre, but his rigid expression gave nothing away.

Once the coast was clear, Swift extracted the contents and placed the papers onto the white linen cloth. The collection was identical to Lady Estelle's invitation: a cheap envelope, the black card decorated with the gold Birdcage, and a folded message – he opened it, read it, then passed it to me.

'*Twelve years have passed, the time for justice has come. You must play your part. On the stroke of nine, assist the lady in distress, then await the Devil's undoing.*' I read it carefully, then returned it to him for safekeeping.

'Couldn't fathom what on earth the message meant.' Moore's cheerful demeanour had returned. 'Though it certainly piqued my interest. There's something Italian about the whole show – theatrics, menace, and murder – it could be a plot by the Borgias!' His eyes gleamed. 'But I've been racking my brains over what killed De Ruyter and I haven't been able to pinpoint it.' He looked under wiry brows from one of us to the other, his glass held firmly in his hand. 'The police were tight-lipped; they finally admitted it was murder, but not the method – what do you chaps know of it?'

'We weren't told,' Swift lied smoothly. 'May we keep this, please?' He indicated the invitation.

'Doubt I can stop you – but you mustn't give it to the Old Bill,' Moore warned. 'They didn't catch that Devil when he killed my boy, and I'm not going to help them catch his dispatcher.'

Swift nodded and slipped the envelope into his dinner jacket pocket. 'How closely did you pass the dessert trolley when you went to help Lady Estelle?'

'Ah, so that's how it was done – his custard! Haha, very good, very good. But it wasn't poison. I examined the body, his stomach ulcer haemorrhaged. What caused it? Ground glass? Can't be, it's rarely deadly, the stomach acid can deal with it. So, what was behind it, eh? You must have some ideas?'

'There's nothing to be gained by speculation.' Swift sidestepped the topic. Moore was clever and we needed to be careful what we said to him.

Three waiters arrived with our entrée and we remained tight-lipped as they placed our plates in front of us. Discs of smoked salmon topped with thin slices of tomato and sprinkled with shavings of cheese, with something dark dribbled over it in an artistic manner – the chef must have been foreign because it certainly wasn't the usual English fare.

'Grub's up.' Dr Moore tucked his napkin under his chin, then picked up his knife and fork. 'Food here is on a par with the Reform, y'know.'

'There's not much of it.' I observed the small portion.

'It's about the combination of flavours, Lennox,' Swift replied dryly. 'It's fashionable in the city now.'

I couldn't imagine how food could be fashionable, but the first forkful proved him right about the taste – it was excellent, and there was even a hint of whisky in the brown drizzle.

Foggy had been somewhere distant in search of forgotten morsels, but returned at the first clink of our cutlery.

'Good heavens, a dog!' Moore paused mid bite. 'Now, he's a handsome fellow. Hello little doggy.' He lowered a hand over his chair to stroke the top of Fogg's head.

'Mr Fogg – he's mine,' I told him between mouthfuls.

'Says a lot about a man, a dog does.' Moore cleared his plate before Swift or I were halfway through, then started spreading butter on a warm bread roll.

'Did anyone stop at the dessert trolley, or tamper with it in any way?' Swift returned to his questioning.

'Didn't see if they did.' Moore finished his bread roll, and broke another in half.

Our plates were cleared away, the glasses were replaced, and a deep red wine poured. We were served Beef Wellington, crispy roast potatoes, green vegetables, and gravy. It was sublime. Fogg sat and watched us; we all passed down tender morsels to him.

'We understand you wanted to talk to us?' I began.

'Yes, I mentioned it to Pinner.' He pointed a fork at us. 'You shouldn't be dabbling in this can of worms. It'll do you no good and I doubt you'll want your good names sullied with it.'

'We're aware of the nature,' I replied without expansion.

'Could you tell us what happened the night De Ruyter died?' Swift prompted Moore.

'Thought you'd heard it from the others,' he mumbled through his food.

'We'd like your version, please.' Swift was amiable; I guessed he liked the old man. I did too and would have preferred to spend the evening in convivial conversation rather than discussing murder and loss.

Moore sighed. 'Very well, if you're determined...' He turned to indicate the expanse of the dining room. 'I usually eat here, not the Strangers Room, but I went along because that was what the invitation indicated. I didn't have a lady with me, my wife's long dead and I'm too long in the tooth to play the swain. I sat where I was shown. Rossetti was directing us. I thought it odd at the time but there you are. Then De Ruyter arrived with that woman.' He leaned forward as though imparting a secret. 'And we all know about her! The most beguiling gal I've ever laid eyes on. Lillian Lamb, her name is, she's kept in comfort by De Ruyter. He liked to parade her round town, but he'd never brought her to the club before – even I was shocked. I thought bringing her to Brundles would be the last straw and they'd suspend his membership for good, or they would if he didn't own the place.'

'What?' I exclaimed in surprise.

'Ezra inherited the freehold, thought you might have known that.'

'We're finding out, that's the purpose of investigating,' I replied.

'Haha, touché!' Moore chortled. 'Well, the De Ruyter Trust owns swathes of London. Ezra wasn't allowed to get his mitts on any actual governance but he received the largess, and he could have influenced matters if he weren't too fat and idle to bother.'

'It explains how he kept his membership here,' I said, glancing at Swift. I could see he was itching to make notes.

'Hm…' Moore took another swig of wine and plonked the empty glass down on the table. 'Anyway, back to the night of his deserved demise – I sat there goggling at his effrontery and wondering what was going to happen next. *Justice will be served*, those were the words going round in my head. Then the Stanfords came in and that opened my eyes even wider. Then the Cliftons! They were escorted straight to the table in the window. Next was Dickie Phillips, he's an artist you know – he brought that actress, Gloria Thornton – now she's an eyeful, not in the same league as Lillian Lamb, but a beauty nonetheless.' He stopped talking to slice up a roast potato.

'Did anyone speak at all?' I asked

'No, nary a word, just a few nods and bows to the ladies, then we all sat waiting to see what happened next. You could have cut the atmosphere with a knife – I half expected drums to roll and an executioner to arrive. Ridiculous, of course, but it still sends shivers down my spine to think on it.'

'Did it continue like that throughout the meal?' Swift asked him.

'No, the staff came and went as usual, the bustle broke the tension. Wine was ferried in, then dinner, much like this, but they served fish as it was Friday. But then, as the clock ticked on, the tension crept back up again. Only De Ruyter and his woman were unaffected…' He paused, his cheeks flushed with wine. 'De Ruyter must have thought it deuced odd. There we were, each of us bereaved by his hand, all seated in the same room watching his every move, yet he carried on as though he didn't have a care in the world. And so it went until the clock struck nine.' He stopped talking to tuck into his meal.

We ate in silence musing over the story. I cleared my plate at the same time as Moore and leaned back to enjoy the wine. 'We don't have a clear picture of what happened just before Ezra died,' I said. It wasn't entirely true, but the Doctor was obviously a good observer and I wanted him to expand on his story.

'You heard about the hullaballoo with Estelle?'

'We did,' I confirmed.

'Ah, well, after that we resumed our seats, but everyone's eyes were darting from face to face. De Ruyter carried on, still oblivious.' He paused as waiters arrived to whisk away our plates and replace them with dessert — a pastry confection with layers of chocolate fondant, mushed raspberries and thick cream. I tucked in, thinking I should have come here more often in my bachelor days.

'Then what happened?' Swift prompted Moore.

'Pudding was served, we ate, nobody talked,' Moore said as he plunged a fork into his fondant. 'I was expecting someone to leap up and point the finger at De Ruyter, and I doubt I was the only one, but on it went. We finished dessert, Browne cleared the plates away and was asking me if I'd like any coffee, when Ezra began coughing. He put his hand to his throat, then blood flew from his mouth all over Lillian Lamb. She jumped up and grabbed a napkin, trying to wipe it off her face. He held his hand out to her, but she stepped away from him. He tried shouting, but that just produced more blood. We sat frozen in our seats, his eyes swivelling about, bulging in terror — he must have realised nobody was going to help him. Then he groaned like a fiend and collapsed across the table.' He sighed. 'Rossetti moved first—'

'Rossetti was still in the room?' Swift asked to confirm the fact.

'Hadn't budged from the doorway,' Moore said. 'Strange, hardly ever see him in the evening, but once he stepped forward we all got up and surged towards De Ruyter. I called out, reminding them that I'm a doctor, so they moved aside. De Ruyter was near death – I was shocked, it wasn't what I'd expected, not after that invitation...' He shook his head again. 'Well, he choked his last. All the evidence indicated a perforated ulcer, and that's what I told them. Nobody was sorry to see him dead, not even his mistress. She stalked out and we didn't see her again.' He became subdued. 'I'd expected to see proof of De Ruyter's guilt, and how he'd arranged the explosion – and I wanted to watch him hang.' He snatched up his glass and drained it. 'Now, you've wrung me out. I'm off to the smoking room for a brandy and a cigar. I'll bid you goodnight gentlemen, and your little dog.' He bent to ruffle Fogg's head once more, then left, swaying as he wove through the tables.

# CHAPTER 10

The room sounded with the murmurings of men's voices and the chink of cutlery on china. Our table was cleared, and Dr Moore's place setting removed. Brandy was offered; we both accepted.

'He didn't tell us how the artist, Phillips, was involved.' Swift swirled his brandy glass in the palm of his hand.

'We didn't ask,' I reminded him. 'And we were right, Rossetti is clearly part of it.'

'As is Browne.'

We both glanced at the Scotsman watching us from near the entrance.

'Dr Moore called De Ruyter *the Devil*.' I took a sip of brandy; it held a comforting warmth.

'I read the *Evening Standard* while you were dressing,' Swift replied. 'They re-ran the whole story on the Birdcage murders. Apparently Lady Estelle was overheard calling him the Devil and the press picked up the reference.'

'So the term's a familiar one…' Pinner had asked me if

I'd like to take a newspaper and I'd declined. 'Was there anything else worth reading in it?'

'No, it was mostly speculation and sensation.'

'It's a clever murder, Swift. It's almost impossible to pinpoint how De Ruyter ingested the diamond dust, or even when. According to Clifton, everyone in that room was connected to the victims, so they all had a motive to kill him.'

'The murderer sent the invitations to gather the suspects together, and hide among them,' he stated.

'Or they're all working together.'

'Which may be why Ladies' Night was chosen.'

I shrugged. 'We have so few facts, it's just guesswork at the moment… If we could tie the diamond dust directly to somebody it would help.'

'Or find whoever printed the cards and the client who commissioned them.' Swift slipped his notebook out and began writing with quick strokes of his pen.

'Not here, old chap,' I told him.

He glanced up, then put pen and book away with a wry grimace. 'Fine, but I'll need to tell Billings…'

'He's sacked us.'

'Yes, but he may want to reinstate us if we give him Moore's invitation…' His reaction was predictable. 'And we can't withhold evidence, Lennox.'

'Don't be hasty, Swift. Wait until morning.'

'But, we…' he began, then sighed. 'I'm going to write my report and telephone Florence before bed.'

'Excellent. Good night.' I raised my brandy glass to him.

'Right…do I need an escort?'

I looked about. Browne had gone and nobody else was taking an interest in us. 'No, I think we've passed muster.'

He went off. I remained in quiet contemplation with my brandy and my dog. What if De Ruyter wasn't guilty? They were all so certain, and yet nothing was proven – and his death proved nothing either – apart from how comprehensively he was despised.

Fogg yipped and put a paw on my knee. I knew what he wanted, and St James's garden was only across the road. I finished my brandy, left the glass on the table, and walked Fogg to the front door.

It took mere minutes to arrive at the garden's elaborate gateway with my little dog running ahead of me. I told him to be quick about it as I was in evening dress and it was freezing.

Flickering gas lamps painted the square in nighttime colours of dark and amber glow. Houses, looming and silent, enclosed the square beneath a starlit sky. Bare trees with black boughs and white frosted tips threw shadows across the expanse of quiet garden. I trod across the lawn to pause and gaze up at a statue dominating the centre. It was a man on horseback togged out in Roman style. The plaque read: GVLIELMVS III. William the 3rd. I recalled my history, he was the Dutch prince who overthrew King James 2nd in 1680-something, and married his daughter, Mary. William died after his horse stumbled over a molehill and threw him to the ground. Perhaps the statue was a metaphor for how the mighty are fallen, or maybe William was a well-loved sovereign, despite his unorthodox rise to the throne…although neither theory explained why he was dressed as a Roman General.

A shadow moved among the trees.

Fogg stopped running to cock his head to one side. I waited. A man took a step forward, a black hat pulled low over his face, his hands buried deep in coat pockets.

'Rossetti.' I recognised the stiff stance.

'Major Lennox.' His tone was soft and without deference.

'Neutral ground,' I observed.

'You are persistent, Major.' He remained in the shadows cast by the trees.

'I've barely begun.'

'Is this delving really necessary?' he demanded. 'The man deserved his death. He should have died twelve years ago.'

'There's no proof De Ruyter was guilty,' I replied.

'The police failed us…'

'That's not reason enough to kill a man.'

'So you're going to rake over the past – for what? To show how clever you are?' He hissed anger through clenched teeth. 'You and your Inspector are prying into the lives of the afflicted.'

'It's not prying. Clifton has asked us to intervene. He wants to protect his wife.'

Silence followed. I waited, wondering if he had moved away, but then he spoke again. 'Lord and Lady Clifton are rich—'

I cut in, riled by his attitude. 'That's utterly irrelevant. Don't any of you understand – suspicion will hang over you all for the rest of your lives, just as it did for De Ruyter. There will never be an end to it.'

'It's a small price to pay for justice that was not exacted,' he rapped back.

'You may think so, but the police will search for the truth, and so will we.'

'The police failed. You think you and your Inspector can perform this miracle?' Rossetti scoffed.

That gave me pause: what the devil did we think we could achieve? I moderated my tone. 'I have no idea, but there must have been a trigger, something that proved De Ruyter's guilt.'

'You are a fool, Major Lennox.' He walked toward me, into the light cast by the moon.

'Perhaps.' I tried a milder approach. 'We need cooperation and facts, Rossetti. What did you see during dinner?'

'Nothing untoward.' His answer was assured.

My temper snapped. 'Everything was untoward.

He swore in exasperation. 'I am aware that you and the Inspector believe a substance was secreted into Lord De Ruyter's dessert. I saw no such action. The only instant my attention was distracted was during the ruction caused by Lady Estelle.'

'Did anyone hesitate near the trolley?'

'No, Major Lennox, and you will mislead yourself if you persist in believing Lord De Ruyter's food was adulterated.'

He was utterly convincing, and yet I was certain he was lying. 'The invitation stated justice would be served. That implies poison, or worse.'

'What is worse than poison?'

I clamped my lips together. The guilty would know about the diamond dust, the innocent would be ignorant of it, and I was achieving nothing. I switched tack. 'How are you and Browne connected to the Birdcage murders?'

He let out a long sigh, his breath white in the cold dark. 'Surely you know this. The police have the information.'

I cursed Billings again for failing to pass on details of the case. 'I'm not the police and I'd appreciate hearing your story,' I asked with as much tact as I could muster.

'What good does it do?' He almost spat the words.

My temper flared again. 'How the hell do you think De Ruyter's killer is going to be uncovered if you don't co-operate.' I let that sink in, then said, 'Or are you part of it?'

Rossetti's eyes remained hidden under the hat, but I could see tension in his stance. 'Very well, for what little it will gain you. My father was Grimes, the butler.'

'Thank you,' I replied. 'Why did he change his name?'

'He was an immigrant, one among thousands. He knew he had to be an Englishman to find a job. Someone told him Grimes was a good name and he adopted it. He learned the language and began as an under footman and ultimately became Lord Frederick De Ruyter's butler. Soon afterwards he married my mother and rented a home where she and I lived. He was too fearful for his job to admit he had a family. He was granted one day off each month, which is when he would come to visit us.'

I was nonplussed at the revelation. 'It's perfectly acceptable for butlers, or anyone in service, to have families.'

'Is it?'

I hesitated. I knew of many cases where married servants were well provided for by their employers – but it was true, there were others who'd found themselves on the street when they declared their intentions to wed. I sighed. 'What about Browne?'

'Fannie Johnson was his daughter.'

'Was she married?' They had different surnames, so there had to be a reason.

'No, and neither was her mother,' Rossetti said dryly.

'Ah.' That was unexpected. Browne seemed the puritan sort.

'She refused, despite Browne's pleadings. Her name was Astrid Jönsson; she was Swedish and had strange ideas about individuality, and freedom.' Irritation crept into Rossetti's voice. 'When Fannie was ten, Astrid returned to Sweden to settle before sending for the girl, but she died before she could do so. Browne raised the child himself.'

'I'm sorry, it must have been hard.'

'Astrid took hallucinatory drugs. She was an unstable woman. Truly, her departure was better for them both, although Browne has never accepted this.'

'He said you were close friends,' I recalled.

'We still are.'

'We know about the invitations. May we have yours?' I was polite in the asking.

'No.'

'It's us or the police,' I warned him.

He turned on his heel. 'Let us return to the warmth, Major Lennox; your dog has need of his bed.'

Foggy had gone to stand in the gateway, his nose pointing toward the welcoming portal of Brundles across the way. We walked side by side and entered the foyer in silence; he headed for his office, and I the stairs, without another word.

Greggs had not gone out and was pootling about my room. 'Ah, sir. Mr Tubbs has completed his toilette and partaken of supper.

'Excellent,' I commended him. 'I thought you had another assignation with Miss Fairchild.' I went to the fire to rub some warmth into my freezing hands.

'I do not have "assignations", sir.' He turned stuffy.

'A rendezvous, then.'

'We have agreed to rearrange our evening. Miss Fairchild has a certain theatre production in mind, and tomorrow is to be the opening night.'

'What's the production?' I undid my bow tie and moved to toss it onto the bed. I disliked formal dress – it felt like a damned straightjacket.

Greggs came over to retrieve my discarded togs. 'A play by Mr Noel Coward, sir. Seemingly light and comic, but Miss Fairchild believes he is an astute observer of the human condition. It is called *The Young Idea*.'

'Oh.' The title didn't sound very inspiring. 'Don't happen to have heard of the actress Gloria Thornton, have you?'

'Indeed I have, sir. A lady who excels at her craft, although I believe she is finding parts harder to come by.' He placed my jacket and whatnots in the wardrobe.

'Why?'

'There are fewer roles in the theatre for the mature lady, sir.'

'She was at Ladies' night when De Ruyter died.'

'So I believe, sir,' he replied from the wardrobe. 'She was his inamorata, some years ago.'

'What? How do you know that?' I stopped in the middle of donning my dressing gown.

'Miss Fairchild mentioned it. We were discussing the tragic events of the Birdcage murders, and the recent demise of Lord De Ruyter.'

'Really! What else did she say?'

'Nothing of relevance, sir.' He finished ordering the wardrobe and headed in the direction of his room. 'I imagine m'lady will be anticipating a telephone call.'

'Yes.' I tied the belt of my dressing gown. 'I imagine she will.'

'Good night, sir.'

I wished him the same and he went off, closing the door behind him.

I contemplated going to tell Swift the latest disclosures, but decided he'd had enough excitement for one day.

Persi answered on the third ring. 'Hello?'

'Greetings.'

'Lennox!' She sounded joyful. 'Oh, how lovely to hear your voice. It feels as though you've been away for days, and it was only this morning. I miss you already.'

I'd begun in starchy tone, which was my usual reaction to speaking on the telephone, but softened with the warmth of her voice. 'I've missed you too. I called earlier. Tommy answered, but all he could talk about was chickens.'

'Yes, he's thrilled. We have six. They're rather comical—'

I cut in. 'You could have mentioned you'd ordered them.'

'I did, last week, over breakfast,' she replied blithely. 'You probably weren't listening. Anyway, I allowed Tommy to choose one for himself and he immediately picked the smallest, but it's a nervous little thing and is being bullied by the others.'

'Well, that's the nature of chickens.' Avian pecking orders weren't uppermost in my mind. 'And he told me about the new gardener – Brendan.'

'Oh, Brendan's been such a help. Benson's arthritis was too painful for him to come out into the cold today, so I insisted he stay in the kitchen with Cook,' she explained. 'Brendan and Tommy set to work in the walled garden, mending the gates and the potting shed. We were worried the foxes would get in…'

'But Persi, *who is* Brendan?'

'He's Farmer Alcott's youngest, he's sixteen…'

'Sixteen?'

'Yes, and big for his age, but very gentle. He's a lovely boy and he adores animals. Tommy has put himself in charge and Brendan does whatever he orders. It's quite funny to watch them together,' she replied, then laughed again. 'Were you feeling jealous?'

'No, no, of course not,' I spluttered, then tried a sterner tone. 'But finances are limited, Persi, you know we really can't take on any more staff.'

'He's only helping when we need him.' She was dismissive. 'Tommy's chicken tried to fly onto the shed roof, but fell and hurt its leg. The boys have fixed a splint around it, but it still limps and it's made the bullying worse. I think we need a cockerel to keep them in check.'

'Persi.' I was exasperated. 'Have you really thought this through? Foggy will chase them, and someone will have to feed them, and collect the eggs…'

'Oh don't worry, my love, Tommy and I will do that.' She was utterly impervious to my objections. 'How is Jonathan? He must be so excited to be back at Scotland Yard.'

'But…' I began then gave up. 'Yes, Swift's in fine form. We saw Billings this morning.'

'What was it about?'

'A chap called Ezra De Ruyter died…' I gave her a distilled account of what we'd learned. 'Diamond dust was a complete surprise, even Billings hadn't heard of it.'

'Good heavens, how fascinating. Death by diamond dust is almost mythical.' She sounded excited. I supposed macabre means of murder were the sort of thing to enthral forensic archeologists. 'There was a Sultan…

oh, what was he called?' She paused. The crackles on the line sounded louder in the lull. 'Bajazet of Turkey! His son was rumoured to have put diamond dust in his food. And there was Pope Clement the seventh – his death was blamed on poisonous mushrooms, but he had a food taster, so it wasn't awfully convincing. Later on, they found out his physicians had fed him ground up gems which lacerated his innards. And Henrietta, the Duchess of Orleans, was rumoured to have died after diamond dust was sprinkled on her strawberries, but Voltaire wrote a scathing account; he argued razor sharp granules would be impossible to swallow.'

'So, it's well-known in history?' I was amazed.

'I wouldn't say it's well-known. Diamond dust was confined to the immensely wealthy. And it was almost impossible to prove; they simply had no means of detecting tiny particles in festering corpses. De Ruyter's death will be fascinating to modern-day pathologists.'

'Hum.' I didn't share her passion for mouldering bodies. 'If diamond dust is relatively unknown, how would anyone learn about it?'

'A few reference books discuss it, and Voltaire, of course. I'd try the London Library in St James's Square.'

'You're awfully clever.' I was impressed. 'You don't happen to know where diamond dust could be found, do you?'

'Wherever they cut diamonds, my love,' she laughed. 'And it's used in tools, of course, and the ancient Egyptians were thought to have added it to cosmetics.'

'Really? Are you sure?'

'Well, they're all dead, so no, I can't be sure, but ancient Egypt is terribly fashionable since the discovery of Tutankhamen.'

'Ah, yes, Tutankhamen…' I stuttered. Persi was supposed to have been in Egypt, helping excavate the lost pharaoh, until I'd swept her off her feet last year.

'Now, I really must go and see how Tommy's chicken is. Sleep well my darling.'

'Persi wait…'

'Yes?'

'I…I do think of you.'

'And I love you, Lennox,' she told me tenderly. 'Good night.'

I replaced the receiver and wandered over to the bed. Foggy had already draped himself across the quilt and Tubbs was curled up at his side. I manoeuvred around them and sank onto the pillows, my mind on my home and my wife. I loved Persi profoundly, but couldn't find the words to express my feelings. I'd tried different terms of endearment, but she'd objected to being called 'old stick', and everything else had sounded stilted. It was Valentine's Day soon, perhaps I should buy her a gift. I wondered where I could find a cockerel in London…

# CHAPTER 11

Swift strode in with an eager air. 'Lennox, two more invitations were pushed under my door this morning!'

Dawn had not yet broken. I'd chivvied the fire into life, switched on the lights, and barely finished dressing.

'Rossetti and Browne,' I guessed.

'Oh…how did you know?'

'Rossetti was in the garden last evening.' I tugged on my tweed jacket.

'What did he say?'

I gave him a concise account of the conversation.

He sat on the arm of the fireside chair. 'Rossetti's father was Grimes the butler, and Fannie Johnson was Browne's daughter… strange Browne didn't tell us that.'

'He provided enough information to satisfy us, then tried to scare us off the case.' I pulled on my shoes and tied the laces. 'Either they're all involved or they're covering up for the culprit.'

'I thought we'd already agreed that.' His sunny good

humour was undiminished, which was unsettling so early in the morning.

'Yes, but they're running rings around us, Swift. They're drip-feeding us details while trying to undermine our efforts.' I hadn't slept well and was in tetchy mood. The early hour and lack of breakfast didn't help either.

'Well, what do you expect them to do? Throw up their hands and surrender?'

'No, but it's unsettling. This is the world I live in; people I have connections with. I feel like an outsider, and Persi is changing the house…' I shut up, feeling like an idiot for expressing my disquiet.

'It's not a conspiracy against us, Lennox, they're just protecting themselves, and Persi is doing her best to help. I did the same when I moved to Braeburn; they thought I was interfering, but it was just my way of trying to show I could be valuable in some way.' He was sympathetic, and I was quite aware of the problems he'd had when joining the Braeburn clan.

'I know, and I'll adjust.' I pulled myself together and turned to focus on the case. 'Persi knew about diamond dust.'

'Really?' His eyes lit up. I told him about the Sultan, the Pope, and Voltaire's doubt about the Duchess Henrietta's death by diamond dust.

'They must have got the idea from history books,' I said.

'Or a forensic archeologist,' he joked. 'Come on, we need to get a move on. We have all this new evidence to pass to Billings, and I'll have to include it in my report—'

'Swift,' I cut in before he started obsessing again. 'What messages were included with the invitations?'

'I'll show you. They're in my room.' He headed for the door.

'Wait.' I glanced over to my little duo on the bed. Tubbs was curled amidst the bedcovers. Fogg opened his eyes, his long spaniel ears spread out each side of his head, then he closed them again.

'They're sleeping,' Swift said and went out.

'That's because it's still dark outside.' I followed him along the corridor, the thick carpet soaking up our footsteps. 'Why did you leave the invitations in your room?'

'Because I want to put the information on the event board,' he said, eagerness in his voice.

Pinner came along in the opposite direction, his gait made lopsided by his crooked back. 'Now, you're early birds!' He greeted us cheerfully. 'If you're wanting breakfast, they'll start serving in half an hour, and I'll bet there's not a soul downstairs even then.'

'We'll be there shortly,' I assured him.

'Aye, well that's grand, and while you're gone, I'll bring some grub for the little 'uns, and give your chambers a good tidy up.'

'Excellent,' I told him. Swift had disappeared into his room.

'The invitations are there.' He nodded toward the now familiar envelopes, which lay on the mantelshelf with a scattering of colourful crayons.

I picked them up and sank into a chair to study the

contents. Both were exact copies of Estelle Clifton's and Dr Moore's; only the instructions were different. Rossetti's stated: *Put the Devil in his place and set all the ladies to face him.* Browne's read: *Wheel in the dessert as the clock strikes nine.*

'There's nothing precise about the scheme.' I stared at the papers in my hand. I'd expected specific instructions, but these were quite vague.

'I agree. I'd thought there would be a seating plan, at least.' Swift was busy with his crayons.

'But the murderer couldn't be sure who would actually attend, and if any one of them went to the police, too much detail would give the whole show away.' I held up one of cards printed with the Birdcage and twisted it in the firelight to see if there were any indents or marks hidden on it. There weren't.

'The killer just assumed that everybody would play their part, or the invitations are just a smokescreen to confuse and confound.' Swift had stopped writing and was gazing at his work.

'By the way, Greggs mentioned that the actress, Gloria Thornton, had once been De Ruyter's inamorata.'

That made him turn around. 'What? When?'

'I didn't ask, but I assume it was prior to Lillian Lamb.'

'Oh.' He hesitated, crayon in hand, then added 'ex inamorata' in brackets below Gloria Thornton's name.

I was finding the whole thing confusing, and I was hungry. 'Breakfast, Swift.'

'We must go and see Billings...'

'Invite him to join us here, then his chief won't know he's seen us.'

'We're not pariahs, Lennox,' he replied, then considered it. 'But, you're right, it would be more discreet if we spoke to him here.' He crossed the room to the telephone. I stood up to peruse the event board with hands in pockets while he explained to Billings in unnecessary detail what we'd discovered.

'He'll be here in twenty minutes.' Swift came over to join me.

'Lady Estelle and her sleeve could have been a sideshow,' I said.

'If that's true, then Browne is the most likely one behind it. He could have added the dust to the custard even before he wheeled it into the room.'

'Billings said it would take around fifteen to twenty minutes for the dust to perforate De Ruyter's ulcer,' I reminded him. 'What time did De Ruyter die?'

'Half past nine.'

'Then he can't have added the dust on the way to the Strangers Room, the time doesn't allow it…' I shook my head. 'It's all supposition, Swift.'

'Exactly, it's early days – the investigation has barely begun.' His enthusiasm was unabated. 'Come on, Lennox.'

We found a waiter at the bottom of the stairs. 'Please show Chief Inspector Billings to the Strangers Room when he arrives,' I instructed.

'Certainly, sir.' The chap bowed neatly.

'And bring breakfast, would you,' I added.

'Right you are, sir.' He went off.

'Why the Strangers Room?' Swift was suspicious.

'He's not a member,' I replied and turned in that direction.

'Ha, of course!' His chirpiness was quite annoying, but then it suddenly dissolved. 'Rossetti said he wouldn't allow any more incursions by the Constabulary.'

'Clifton's support will have put a stop to that nonsense.'

'Right.' He gave a grin. 'You don't think we should tell Clifton about the invitations?'

'No.' I felt a frisson of guilt at that but Clifton was implicated in this somehow.

An air of disuse hung over the room despite the fire glowing in the hearth and curtains drawn against the cold. We settled ourselves into the same seats as yesterday. Waiters arrived with pots of tea almost as we sat down, along with hot buttered toast and jars of marmalade, honey, and strawberry jam.

I'd eaten two rounds and was feeling more mellow when Billings was ushered in.

'So, you've had a bit of luck.' He strode over and sat down. 'I thought you'd cut and run.'

That put my hackles up. 'After your arbitrary dismissal of us yesterday.'

'I wasn't given a choice. That bloody lawyer, Wallace, went running to the chief and he ordered me to give you the elbow – the boss doesn't like using outsiders.' He plonked his hat on the table. 'I called Lord Clifton, he agreed to put in a word for you – it was the best I could do.' He sounded apologetic, or as near as the man was capable.

'Why did Wallace want to remove us?' I demanded.

'Doesn't like the competition, most likely.'

We shut up as a waiter brought in a fresh pot of tea and poured a cup for each of us. I was pleased to see it wasn't Browne, although I suspected he would be wary of us after Rossetti's revelations.

Swift waited until the waiter had gone, then placed the invitations one at a time on the table in front of Billings. 'Dr Moore, Rossetti, Browne.'

Billings grunted and opened the contents of each envelope. He read them without a word, then tucked them carefully into his jacket pocket. 'Fair enough,' he said, and reached for the sugar to spoon three heaps into his cup.

'The actress, Gloria Thornton, was De Ruyter's inamorata before Lillian Lamb,' Swift said.

'I know,' he replied while stirring his tea. 'What are they serving for breakfast?'

'The usual,' I replied.

That caused his brows to lower. 'Don't get clever with me, Major.'

I bit back a grin.

'Have the other diners been asked about their invitations?' Swift's focus was on the investigation.

'The Stanfords handed theirs over when I went and demanded it yesterday afternoon. I had to threaten them before they admitted they'd got it.' He sounded irritated. 'It had been addressed to Lady Stanford. Her instructions were to stay in her seat and watch the room while "a drama unfolded". She did as she was told, and said she didn't see anything odd, apart from Lady Clifton's antics – and De Ruyter dying, obviously.'

'Any information on who printed the cards?' Swift asked.

'Nope.' Billings shook his head. 'There are hundreds of small print shops in the city. It'll take time to track them all down.'

'Assuming they're a legal outfit,' Swift added.

'True,' Billings acknowledged. 'There are plenty of backstreet pamphleteers.'

'What about the artist chap, Richard Phillips?' I began.

'Better known as Dickie Phillips,' Billings replied.

'What's his connection to the Birdcage murders?' Swift asked.

Billings considered the question, then deigned to answer: 'He was once engaged to Daphne Clifton.'

'Daphne Clifton?' Swift exclaimed. 'But she was the heir's bride-to-be…'

'Yes, and she threw over Phillips for Xavier De Ruyter,' Billings said.

'I assume you investigated him for the Birdcage murders,' I stated.

'Of course we did. We investigated every last one of them, what the hell do you take us for,' Billings snapped.

I was inclined to tell him, but held my tongue.

The breakfast trolley was brought in on oiled wheels, only the rattle of china giving its presence away. We all looked around, and then straightened up as the heavenly scent of fried bacon, black pudding, pork sausages, eggs, and tomatoes filled the room.

Brundles' breakfasts were sumptuous and the meal improved our tempers; even Billings was mollified. We ate in silence as the waiters hovered, ready to replenish plates with more helpings at the twitch of a fork. Once finished, they cleared our table with choreographed efficiency, and left us alone with pots of fresh tea and a quiet room where we could speak freely.

'Diamond dust was used to kill off a pope and a duchess,' I announced to Billings. 'Apparently it's quite well known among historians.'

'Which pope?' Billings demanded. 'And which duchess?'

Typical policeman – always nitpicking over facts. I told him what details I could remember, and mentioned the London Library, which was virtually next door to Brundles. 'We could search their records to see if any of the suspects are members of the library.'

'Who the hell would go rummaging in a library to find outlandish ways of killing people?' Billings was unimpressed.

'And those sort of people would have Voltaire on their bookshelf,' Swift said in support.

'Yes, but would they have read it?' I replied, because I certainly hadn't.

Billings ignored that remark. 'Swift's right, the people we're dealing with have their own libraries. It doesn't matter where they found the idea, it only matters where they got the diamond dust.'

'And where was that?' I asked, a bit starchy after his arbitrary dismissal of my theory.

'I've had men looking into it the last three days. We haven't found any links to the suspects.' Billings' mood had improved with the meal, but he was still miserly with information.

Swift moved into full police mode and pulled out his notebook. 'What about Gloria Thornton?' he asked as he unscrewed his pen. 'Has she been interviewed?'

'We've interviewed all of them. She said she knew nothing about it, and had only gone because Dickie Phillips asked her,' Billings replied.

'Who is Ezra De Ruyter's heir?' Swift looked up from note taking.

'He's the last of the line. According to the trustees, the estate will go to the crown.'

'Nobody killed him for his money then,' I remarked.

'Perhaps he was more valuable alive,' Billings said dryly. He moved his chair back and stood up. 'Now, this meeting hasn't happened… but if you find anything useful, I'll thank you to pass it to me.' He patted the pocket where he'd tucked the invitations. 'I'm going to question Rossetti and Browne. And don't you forget – you're eyes and ears only – don't go trampling on police territory, no matter what any toff tells you.'

'No, sir, absolutely.' Swift was quick to assure him.

'And I appreciate the new leads. Well done, lads, keep it up.' He marched out with a steady tread.

'He said well done!' Swift was almost euphoric. 'And he wants us to carry on.'

'Fine.' I stood up. 'In that case, we'll go and track down some suspects.'

# CHAPTER 12

'Lennox, where are we going?' Swift followed in my tracks.

'To talk to Dickie Phillips.'

'We don't know where he lives.'

'We'll ask the oracle.' We'd walked to Brundles' front steps to find the sun sliding over the surrounding rooftops, sending rays of light to spark off cold grey slates.

'Morning, Major Lennox.' The doorman raised a gloved hand in informal salute. 'Inspector Swift.'

'George,' I acknowledged. 'We're looking for Dickie Phillips; apparently he's an artist.'

'Ah, yes, sir. The gentleman has a studio in Cork Street Mews.' George was a stocky chap with kindly brown eyes and wiry brows in a weathered face.

'Where would he be when not in his studio?' I prompted.

The doorman sucked his bottom lip. 'I believe Mr Phillips keeps an address in Piccadilly.' He thought for a moment. 'Corner of Old Bond Street. Number 5, if memory serves me right.'

'Excellent, thank you.' I turned to Swift. 'Old Bond Street isn't far.'

'I know where it is.' Swift fell into step next to me. 'Asking the doorman was a good idea, I should have thought of that.'

'Sending a man home is part of their job.'

'When they're too drunk to find their own way.'

'Something of the like,' I agreed.

We walked briskly through London streets slicked white with frost. Milkmen were still about, darting from horse-drawn carts to deliver milk bottles to doorsteps. Paperboys with weighty sacks plodded pavements. A youth peddling a delivery tricycle rushed by, his wicker basket piled with packages, and slow-moving roadmen swept away the night's detritus in readiness for the coming day.

There was a scattering of other denizens, workers hurrying to the warmth of shop or office, and a few city gents in sleek coats over tailored suits and neat bow ties. We strode along Duke of York Street to take a right into Jermyn and then a short distance to Piccadilly to reach Old Bond Street. An elegant archway below a cartouche proclaimed: *The CORNER, Old Bond Street*, and number five was right below it.

'It's hardly the average artist's garret,' Swift commented, gazing up at the handsome stone edifice. Old Bond Street was studded with pricey shops, and the flats above were the exclusive preserve of the very rich.

I'd expected a concierge but there didn't appear to be one. We studied the array of brass entry buttons.

'There aren't any names.' Swift was at my shoulder.

'I suspect it's one of those discreet places that doesn't exist,' I remarked, and pushed my finger onto each button, sending them all buzzing.

'What do you mean, "doesn't exist"?'

'These are private pieds-à-terre.'

'You mean where the wealthy can meet illicit lovers and dealers in vice?'

I would have debated the 'vice' part, but was interrupted by a shrill voice in a ripe East End accent.

'Oo's there? This is private, ye know.' A woman opened the door a crack.

'Good morning, ma'am.' Swift fixed his best smile. 'We're looking for Mr Phillips.'

'Why?' she demanded. A short lady with thin shoulders and a drab pinny over a shapeless navy frock. I guessed her to be the cleaner.

'We've commissioned a painting from him.' I improvised. 'He asked us to meet him here.'

'Oh, smutty pictures. Huh. I've met your sort before.' She tutted with distaste.

'We're not—' Swift began.

I stepped forward. 'May we come in, please?'

'Suppose I can't stop yer.' She stood aside. 'Ee's upstairs, snoring 'is head off, makin' a right ol' racket. You can 'ear 'im through the door.'

'Thank you, good lady.' I gave her a nod of the head.

'"Good lady" indeed...' She stomped off, muttering to herself.

The place was welcoming, apart from the char; a generous hall decorated in hues of blue, and an electric chandelier, brightly lit. The stairs were broad with a sweeping bannister rail and shallow treads. We trotted up two at a time and paused on the first floor.

'I can't hear anything.' Swift took off his hat to listen.

'Further up,' I decided. We carried on the routine until we reached the top floor.

'This one.' Swift pointed at a red painted door. The sound of snoring could be heard quite distinctly.

I tried the handle. It was unlocked, so I walked in. Swift muttered something about trespass, but followed me anyway.

We entered a drawing room made dark by heavy drapes pulled across the windows. Phillips' snores resonated from beyond a half-closed door set in the far wall. I stubbed my foot on a stool in the gloom, and cursed my way to the windows to yank back a curtain and let in the morning sunshine. Rays of light fell upon artwork propped against various pieces of fine furniture: a Rembrandt leaning against a handsome sideboard, a Stubbs on an armchair, a Rubens next to the empty fire grate, and Botticelli's Birth of Venus on the only easel in the centre of the room. They were replicas; quite good, but not quite right somehow.

'Smutty pictures?' I gazed at Venus; the paintwork had been applied in small dabs. 'He's a copyist.'

'You mean a forger.' Swift leaned in to frown at the brushwork.

'These are some of the most famous paintings in the world, Swift. No-one's going to get away with pretending they're genuine.'

'Perhaps he's going to exchange them for the real thing.'

'You think he's an international art thief?' My tone was ironic.

'It's possible,' he countered without conviction.

'This one is better.' I pointed to a lively picture of an attractive lady in modern dress, framed and hung on the wall.

Swift gazed at the nameplate. '"Gloria Thornton", so they know each other.'

'Obviously, Swift, they went to the dinner together.'

He ignored me. 'It's on a par with the portrait of Daphne Clifton hanging in their house.'

'Yes.' I glanced back at the replicas and wondered why he bothered with them.

A snuffling snore reverberated from the bedroom.

'Time to wake him up.' Swift moved toward the door.

'Wait,' I told him. A narrow archway led off in the corner. I went over to discover a small kitchen full of dirty dishes. I suspected the cleaner didn't come in here very often. There was a set of pans hanging on hooks next to a grill. I picked up two and returned to the drawing room to push open the bedroom door. Phillips was lying on his back, mouth open, eyes shut, oblivious to the day. I banged the pans together.

'Aaaaahhhh,' he screeched, his eyes flying open as he jerked up to a sitting position with his hands pawing his face. 'Whaaaatttt?'

Swift grinned. I put the pans on the bedside cabinet.

'Dickie Phillips, I presume?' I asked in a friendly tone.

'Who, who…what, what the…why did you do that?' His head swivelled to look at us on either side of the bed, shock and panic showing on his pudgy face.

'You were snoring,' I told him.

'What?' He stared in wide-eyed shock.

'Where's your invitation to De Ruyter's murder?' Swift cut to the crux.

'Oh, God, you're plod,' Phillips groaned, and dropped back onto the pillow, then pulled the blankets up to cover his face.

'Where is it?' Swift demanded.

'Don't know what you're talking about.' His reply was muffled by the covers.

'Yes, you do,' I replied.

'Clear off, why don't you.'

'I'll fill the pans with water,' I threatened.

'Oh for God's sake.' A hand came up from under the covers to point toward the blackened grate where coals still smouldered in the hearth. 'Mantelpiece.'

Swift went to start a search among the bills and papers piled at random across its length.

'Did you murder Ezra De Ruyter?' I decided to act the policeman.

Phillips threw back the covers to glare at me with red-rimmed eyes. 'He wasn't murdered. He died of a perforated ulcer. Dr Moore said so.' He sat up. 'And you're not the plod – not with that accent.'

'We're helping the Cliftons,' I told him.

'Ha, so you're sleuths for hire; but that doesn't explain who you are.'

'Major Lennox, and Inspector Swift.' I nodded in Swift's direction. 'Retired from Scotland Yard.'

'Oooh, retired from Scotland Yard,' Phillips mocked. He swung out of bed, crossed to the corner to pick up a rumpled dressing gown off the floor, and pulled it over his striped pyjamas. 'If it wasn't his ulcer, how was he killed?'

'That's classified information,' I told him.

Swift had found the invitation and held it up. 'This is evidence in a murder case. You should have handed it to the police.'

'I didn't think it was murder, and even if it was, I wouldn't help the police find their way across the road.' Phillips ruffled his hair, making it stand on end like a startled cat.

'You were questioned by Scotland Yard,' Swift stated. 'You know damn well it's a murder enquiry, stop playing stupid.'

'Oh, get off your high horse.' Phillips turned belligerent. 'De Ruyter would have been hanged years ago if the cops hadn't mucked up the enquiry.'

I sought to calm tempers. 'Those paintings in your drawing room can't be real.'

'Were you fooled?' He turned his bleary-eyed gaze up at me. 'I paint them to order. I'm considered to be rather good, actually.'

I can't say I agreed with his boast. I guessed him to be between forty and forty-five... He'd have been in his early thirties at the time of the Birdcage murders. 'Why aren't you doing portraits?'

'I used to, but people are so pettifogging. I haven't the patience to deal with bloody socialites, and they don't pay up when they should, either.'

Swift had been examining Phillips' invitation, and now brought it to where we were standing. 'The card is identical to the others.' He passed it to me. I glanced at the familiar image of the Birdcage, and unfolded the message: *Invite your muse, and await the wrath of Lady Justice.*

'Who's your muse?' I asked Philips.

'No-one in particular.'

'Gloria Thornton.' I indicated her portrait wryly. 'And you escorted her to Ladies' Night.'

'What of it?' Phillips snapped back.

'Did she receive an invitation?' Swift demanded.

'Why don't you ask her?' He stuck his hands in the pockets of his dressing gown; it was wine red velvet with gold braiding and threadbare cuffs.

I lost my temper. 'This isn't a bloody game. You took Gloria Thornton because the invitation demanded it. Now answer the question.'

His bluster deflated. 'Fine. I don't know if she received an invitation, but I had the devil of a job persuading her to come with me.'

'Why didn't you contact the police?' Swift sounded as irritated as I was.

'Why, so they could botch that up, too?' Phillips retaliated.

Swift flushed with anger.

'You knew the invitation was suspicious.' I maintained the attack.

'Suspicious?' Phillips gave a bark of laughter. 'The whole palaver was suspicious. I mean for heaven's sake, we were all invited to sit and watch that fat fiend stuff himself, waiting for justice or something. I don't know who got to him, but I say damn good luck to them.'

'How do you know everyone was invited?' Swift picked up the detail.

'It was obvious the moment they all trooped in.' Phillips turned abruptly and fled to the drawing room.

'What caused the breakup of your engagement to Daphne Clifton?' I followed him, seeking a way through his belligerence.

'Her high and mighty father didn't approve of a mere artist who had to earn his own crust.' There was bitterness in his voice. 'No-one was good enough for Daphne.'

'Not even Xavier De Ruyter?' I asked.

'Clifton hated him, and he wasn't alone in that.' Phillips was standing by the window, hands in pockets, bathed in wintery sunshine.

'Who else hated him?' Swift was quick to ask.

Phillips tried and failed to appear nonchalant. 'Everyone. He was a pretentious little nobody; spoiled, rich, and self-absorbed.'

'Did you love Daphne?' I asked quietly.

He hesitated. His jaw quavered. He must have been handsome once, but now his features were puffy from too many late nights and too much liquor. 'I thought so… But she'd been so sheltered from reality, her life was a gilded cage, trapped by riches – that's how they all lived. Ironic, isn't it, to be blown apart by the very symbol of one's own existence…' He sounded genuine, then returned to the bombast. 'Anyway, I'm still here, free from the burden of unimaginable wealth to while away my time in the fleshpots of London.'

Swift's brows snapped together. 'What's Gloria Thornton's address?'

'Not telling you, and you're not official, so you can't make me,' Phillips taunted. 'Unless you're offering an incentive?'

That really irritated me. 'We were told Gloria was Ezra De Ruyter's inamorata prior to Lillian Lamb.'

'Inamorata?' He smirked. 'Quite the gallant, aren't you. She was his lover, old boy, no need to mince words.'

'But not his mistress,' Swift replied coldly.

'What's the difference?' Phillips shrugged.

'A mistress is paid for,' Swift retorted.

Phillips grunted. 'De Ruyter would have paid, he enjoyed spending his money – not that it was his.'

'Was he wealthy before he inherited his uncle's fortune?' I asked.

'Not really, although I suppose wealth is relative,' Phillips replied. 'But once old Frederick was killed, Ezra was rolling in it like a hog in muck up to his eyeballs.'

'You know, we're just trying to help Lady Estelle: she's the primary suspect after her theatrics.' I tried reasoning with him.

It didn't work. 'Oh, save me the schmaltz. Clifton can buy anyone he wants, including you. Or do you think there will be a reward?'

'Don't push it, Phillips,' I growled.

'What did you see on Ladies' Night?' Swift demanded.

'Nothing. It was outlandish, then he died,' he snapped, then sighed in peeved exasperation. 'Look, just go away and leave me alone, will you, or I'll call the bloody police myself.'

# CHAPTER 13

'Phillips knows something.' I was convinced.

'He could have been playing with us,' Swift muttered, then gave a wry grin. 'His rude awakening probably didn't help.'

'Perhaps not,' I admitted, although I didn't regret it.

We were in a cafe, drinking coffee. The waiter had brought two cups of black brew topped with a layer of whipped cream and a sprinkle of cocoa powder. It was delicious, and rather a treat; we usually drank tea at home.

'Right gents, we got cakes an' dainties – whatta y' partial to? They're all made on the premises, fresh today with real butter an' cream – we don't use cheap shortenin', not like them other places.' The waiter was the chummy sort, a lanky young man in a starched apron over standard black and white garb. 'So, we got cinnamon roll with sultanas, Bakewell tart, slice o' Victoria sponge, marble cake, custard tart, or a plate o' lemon melts.'

Swift put a hand up. 'Bakewell tart, please.'

It was difficult to choose. 'Erm…I'll have the lemon melts.'

'Comin' up!' He scrawled on a small notepad and went to slap the order on top of a glass counter, where an elderly couple shuffled about with cakes and crockery.

I liked the cafe, a cozy place with walls painted two shades of green, and tinted prints of old London covering the damp spots. Doors and tables were dark oak, chairs upholstered in oxblood red, and the floor covered by well-trodden coir. It smelled of beeswax and coffee, and rang with the chatter of well-dressed clientele. We were seated in the bow window, opposite the entrance to Dickie Phillips' building.

'Every time we talked about what happened, he brought the subject back to money.' I sipped my coffee through whipped froth.

Swift drank slowly, his eyes glazed in thought. 'Did he? I should have taken notes; it would have focused my attention.'

'There was hardly the opportunity.' I wiped cream from my lips with a cotton napkin. 'Do you think he saw something and is planning to blackmail the culprit?'

'Or he's angling for a reward.' Swift put his cup down. 'He's the sort who's used to bargaining… he may have been trying to tempt us into offering money.'

I realised Swift had more experience of this. 'Should we go back and wave a five-pound note under his nose?'

'No, Lennox, we can't bribe witnesses.'

I'd read about detectives offering incentives for information. 'Nonsense. Even Sherlock Holmes had informers.'

'Phillips is hardly a snitch, Lennox, and we'd need him to testify on the witness stand if he had any real evidence.'

The waiter returned. ''Ere ye go. A plate apiece an' there's more where that come from.' He placed them in front of us, along with the reckoning on a dainty china dish.

'Thank you.' I picked up the bill and paid him, including a generous tip.

'Ooh, ta for that, guv.' The lad pushed the coins into a black leather purse and went off grinning.

'Whoever's behind the invitations knew that Phillips and Gloria Thornton were connected,' I said, then bit into a lemon melt. It was utterly delicious, light shortbread roundels stuck together with lemon butter icing.

'Yes…' Swift picked up a fork to cut into his Bakewell tart. 'But why did De Ruyter go to the dinner?'

'He probably received an invitation.'

He considered it. 'I suppose so, but he'd never been to Ladies Night before, it seemed out of character.'

'True.' I picked up another lemon melt.

'What about his mistress, Lillian Lamb?' he said and took another bite of tart.

'She may have had one, I suppose.'

'I meant as a suspect.' Swift sounded tetchy. He was on a mission, whereas I was trying to enjoy my coffee and cake.

'Hm.' I considered it. 'If she'd had any reason to kill him, there would have been plenty of opportunity in private; she wouldn't have had to put on a public show.' I turned to a question I'd been mulling. 'Swift, do you think De Ruyter could have been innocent of the Birdcage murders?'

He glanced up, then shook his head. 'No, Scotland Yard is thorough, they investigated the case for three years; they would have chased every fact, witness, and the smallest shred of evidence. I have absolute confidence in them.' He used a napkin to wipe crumbs from his lips, then pulled out his notebook and pen. 'To our knowledge, invitations were sent to Lady Clifton, Dr Moore, Rossetti, Browne, and Phillips.' He ticked them off a list he'd written. 'And Billings said the Stanfords had one.'

'We need to talk to Lillian Lamb.' I finished the lemon melts and my coffee.

'Not without permission,' Swift warned. 'She's a close associate of the victim. Billings won't thank us if we antagonise her.'

'I wasn't planning to antagonise her,' I objected.

'Did you intend antagonising Phillips?' he countered.

I ignored that. 'We need to stop and think about this for a moment. There are three routes to uncovering De Ruyter's murderer: one is to discover whatever triggered the plan to kill him; two is to track down the source of physical evidence; three is to narrow down the suspects.'

'We can only work on narrowing down the suspects, Lennox.' He sounded exasperated.

'Why?' I wasn't giving up.

'Right…' He raised fingers to count them off. 'One, we

don't know the trigger, but it must be related to the Birdcage murders, and we've been warned away from that. Two, Billings has men searching for whoever printed the invitations, and they're also looking into the source of diamond dust. Which leaves us with number three.'

'Fine,' I agreed. 'So, we find the person who put the dust into the dessert.'

'That won't necessarily be the same person who devised the plan,' he countered.

'Of course it must be.' I refuted. 'Would you commit murder based on somebody else's plan? The brains behind it must be the killer.'

He wrote this down, or something akin, then looked up. 'But the same person who uncovered the trigger may not be the actual murderer.'

'Erm, yes…' This was becoming confusing. I thought about it. 'Wallace may have uncovered the trigger. He's been investigating on Clifton's behalf for years and might have discovered something recently, and that set things off.'

'What?' Swift disagreed entirely. 'Clifton would go straight to the police, and so would Wallace…'

'Not if the evidence was dubious, or inadmissible.' Another idea occurred to me. 'Or, Lady Clifton found out what her husband and Wallace uncovered and decided to take revenge herself.'

'Clifton has just asked us to investigate; he wouldn't have done that if he thought his wife was behind it,' he reminded me tersely.

'He may not know.'

'Lennox, we have just agreed we're going to narrow down the suspects, will you stop tossing ideas about and focus—' he began a lecture, but was interrupted.

'Hello, are you the detectives?' A woman had come to a halt next to our table; she wore a cashmere coat with a colourful scarf about her shoulders. She was rather gorgeous; I recognised her.

'Gloria Thornton.'

'Ha,' she laughed. 'How remarkable…perhaps you truly are detectives. Dickie thought you were ambitious amateurs.' She sat down without being invited. 'Have we met? I'm sure I'd remember if we had.'

'No, Phillips had your portrait in his flat,' I explained. 'And you were described as his muse.'

'Oh, how awfully clever of you, bravo.' She gave a silent clap of her hands, long fingers adorned with clusters of colourful rings.

'How did you know we were here?' Swift cut in.

'I didn't. I've just called on Dickie and he told me all about you. He was quite livid, actually.' Her green eyes reminded me of a cat, watchful and alert. 'He said one was a fierce ex-policeman, and the other a towering toff in country tweeds. I saw the two of you through the window and immediately realised who you were.'

I introduced ourselves formally. She held her hand out to be kissed, obviously enjoying herself.

The waiter had returned. 'Mornin' Miss Thornton, what can I get you – the usual?'

'Yes, please, sweetie.' Gloria Thornton turned a beaming smile on him. He grinned and headed back to the counter, calling out to the elderly chap behind it, 'Strong black coffee for our favourite lady, Walter.'

'They make the best coffee in the district. I come here most days.' She raised a hand to push a strand of copper-coloured hair from her face; a striking looking woman in her late forties, with high cheekbones, an aquiline nose, and artful make-up over pale skin.

'What else did Phillips say to you?' Swift demanded.

'I cannot repeat private conversations,' she replied in haughty fashion, then laughed as he scowled.

'We're trying to find out what happened the evening of De Ruyter's death,' I said. 'We could do with some help.'

'Could you? Well, there's a humble admission.' Her coffee arrived and she picked up the steaming cup to blow with red painted lips. 'Are you expecting me to provide this "help"?'

'It would be appreciated.' I gave her my best grin.

She smiled back, causing fine wrinkles to gather around her green eyes. 'I may be open to persuasion…and you are awfully handsome.'

'I…ah…I wasn't, erm, it was just, just questions…' That caused an outbreak of babbling on my part. I shut up abruptly.

'Would you tell us what you saw on Ladies' Night, please?' Swift stepped in, his tone tactful.

'Oh, you're going to be tedious about this, aren't you.' She put her cup down onto the saucer. 'It was far below the drama the police have made it out to be. Dickie badgered me to go, I'd no idea why – I mean, who wants to eat in a dreary old club surrounded by dreary old men?' She formed a moue with her mouth, then carried on. 'Dickie made no mention of Ezra. If he had, I'd have refused entirely. So: we arrived, we sat down, we ate dinner – the food was better than expected – and then Estelle Clifton leapt up, throwing her arm about. The men dashed to the rescue. One of them put it out. We had dessert, and Ezra dropped dead.' She raised her hands in a theatrical pose. 'So, it ended rather well, didn't it!'

'No, it didn't,' Swift snapped, all tact gone. 'A man was murdered, and everyone there is now a suspect.'

'I am quite aware of that, Inspector,' she said, coolly. 'Why are you taking such an interest?'

'Scotland Yard brought us in.' There was a hint of pride in Swift's voice.

She laughed at that. 'Dickie said you were trying to dig Estelle Clifton out of a hole.'

Swift's frown returned. 'That, too.'

'Do you live near here?' I managed a coherent sentence.

'Are you going to come calling?' Her eyes were full of amusement.

'No…I…I…' I stammered.

She broke into a peal of laughter. 'My flat is the one below Dickie's; we've been friends and neighbours for years.'

Swift had been sitting with his pen in hand and now began writing. 'Which number?'

She sighed. 'Flat 10.'

He made a note, then shifted tack. 'Do you know how De Ruyter died?'

'Dr Moore said it was his ulcer, but I assume it wasn't, or there wouldn't be all this fuss.' She picked up her cup again. I rather liked the lady; she oozed confidence, and didn't appear to care a jot what we thought of her.

'Did you receive an invitation?' Swift continued.

'No,' she replied. 'I knew nothing about it until Dickie told me later.'

'You and De Ruyter were lovers.' Swift had a habit of throwing disconcerting accusations.

I saw her stiffen. 'A long time ago, before the Birdcage murders.'

'Do you think Ezra was behind that?' I managed to ask without stammering.

Her gaze became guarded. 'Ezra wasn't an intelligent man. I didn't think he could have done it at the beginning...but then everyone became convinced he had.' She sounded sincere. 'I knew how much he loved money, and all that it could buy. He certainly had motivation, but... it was evil. I had never thought him evil.'

'Was he close to the family – did he visit them often?' Swift began pedantic questioning.

'No, he only went to De Ruyter House for formal occasions.'

'Such as?' Swift continued.

'The New Year's Ball.' She watched him as he wrote. 'And another one in July, that was to celebrate the old

King's Day – the Belgian one – the De Ruyters were originally from Antwerp,' she added.

'Did you ever go to the balls?' I was watching her face, she was expressive and alluring.

'Yes, a few times at Ezra's insistence. He told the family we were engaged.' She laughed at my raised brows. 'It was just to satisfy their stuffy old propriety. We never were, and never would have been.'

'Had Ezra been invited to the Birdcage dinner, or Xavier and Daphne's wedding?' Swift looked up.

'No, they'd fallen out some time previously.' She became sombre. 'Ezra didn't like Xavier, he was terribly spoiled. At one time he demanded Ezra introduce him to some elite gambling club, but Ezra refused. Xavier had a tantrum, and it escalated into a horrible family row.'

Swift wrote this down.

'Dr Moore's son, Lionel, was a close friend of Xavier's…' I prompted her. 'He died in the explosion.'

'Oh, yes, poor dear Lionel.' Her lips dropped in sadness. 'He was such a silly boy, so easily led. He was dazzled by Xavier's wealth and put up with his ridiculous pretensions when nobody else would. Xavier's circle were all wealthy sons of the establishment and they weren't impressed by his peacocking ways, whereas Lionel was from quite an ordinary family, and as I said, he was in awe of Xavier's lifestyle.' She took another sip of coffee.

'What was Ezra like?' I returned to the subject.

She raised her head for a moment to gaze at the yellowed ceiling. 'He could be amusing, and was given to generosity when something caught his enthusiasm. He wanted to make me a star of the stage.' She smiled. '"Gloria in excelsis" he used to call me. He was terribly smitten. He would finance shows where I would play the lead – he adored the whole theatrical scene. He'd take a box, fill it with friends, cheer me to the rafters, and then afterwards we'd all go for dinner and party until the early hours…' Her smile trembled. 'They were good times…and I learned my craft through it. I was – I *still* am a very good actress. I have a feel for it…' She shrugged. 'But it's for the young and pretty. There aren't many roles for the mature woman.'

'You're beautiful,' I told her spontaneously.

She laughed and laid a hand over mine. 'Handsome *and* a darling, I suppose some lucky lady has claimed you?'

I nodded, annoyed at myself for having blurted like an idiot.

'When did your relationship with De Ruyter end?' Swift continued his questions.

'Shortly after the explosion.' Her answer was matter-of-fact. 'Ezra changed quite quickly after that happened. He'd been astounded initially, but then he became excited by the thought of the inheritance. That was delayed for years as the police investigation went on. Ezra vacillated between euphoria at the thought of the millions coming his way and desperation that it might not.'

'Wasn't he worried about the investigation?' I asked.

'Not from what I could see. He said he wasn't behind it and he was very convincing. I truly thought him innocent at the time, but as it became clear he was the only suspect…' She turned her cat's eyes to Swift. 'The joy went out of him, and I began to think perhaps there may be something in the accusations, so I distanced myself.' She shrugged eloquently. 'He didn't really notice; he'd already met Lillian Lamb by then.'

'How old was he at the time of the explosion?' Swift was still on his fact-finding mission.

She considered it. 'Thirty-eight, or thirty-nine, his birthday was in May.'

Swift made a note.

'What was his reaction when he saw you arrive in the Strangers Room?' I asked her.

'Nothing really; he nodded, I nodded back. The atmosphere was strained, quite intense actually, although he appeared not to notice… I saw him about town quite frequently – at the theatre, in restaurants, we still inhabited the same milieu, although we didn't talk. He'd grown horribly corpulent. Time and money had done him few favours.' She picked up her coffee and finished it.

'Did you see anything at all unusual about that evening?' Swift continued his questions.

'Everything about it was unusual…' She paused. 'But there was something…'

'What?' I leaned in, so did Swift.

She thought our reaction amusing, but held back the laughter. 'He kept looking at his watch, as though he had to be somewhere else. It was a wristwatch, a huge gold thing, and he pulled back his cuff to look at it a number of times.'

'But he didn't seem unduly concerned about the company or the atmosphere?' I asked, puzzled by the man's apparent attitude.

'I've already said that he wasn't.' She tapped the back of my hand in light reprimand. 'He seemed utterly uninterested, actually.'

A loud ringing came from the street. We paused as it approached. It was an ambulance, its brass bell clanging furiously; it pulled to a stop outside the entrance to the building opposite. Men in white coats leapt from the back and rushed through the door. A couple of bobbies ran from their positions in the street, hands holding their helmets on their heads, then a police car raced into view and slewed to a halt beside the ambulance.

Swift was on his feet. 'Lennox, come on.'

# CHAPTER 14

'Dead, or near enough.' The cleaning lady seemed to be relishing events. 'I found 'im lying on the floor, froth comin' out of 'is mouth. I didn't mess about – telephoned the ambulance straight off, though I could see it wouldn't do 'im no good.' She pursed her lips and nodded as though it was some sort of divine retribution.

We'd raced up the stairs to find the char on the landing and the door to Phillips' flat wide open. Medics and uniformed coppers were crowded around the convulsing form of Dickie Phillips, who was lying on the drawing room floor with his dressing gown twisted about his shuddering body. A Sergeant had ordered us to stay out of the flat. Swift had argued, of course, but without a badge, his protestations were in vain.

'You're certain it was the chocolates?' Gloria Thornton was rigidly calm, though she'd blanched white beneath her make-up.

'I said so, didn't I.' The char turned crotchety. 'The box was lying on the floor next to 'im. And I know exactly 'oo gave him them.' She aimed an accusatory finger at Gloria. 'And so I told them coppers.'

'Which I have freely admitted.' Gloria spoke through gritted teeth. 'You were the one who delivered them to me with the post.'

'Aye, it were in your pigeonhole with your name on it.' Colour rose in the char's thin cheeks.

'Admirers are always sending chocolates and flowers, you know that,' Gloria snapped back.

'You mean your fancy men,' the char retaliated.

'Madam,' I cut in. 'That's enough, thank you.'

'Don't you tell me…' She turned her fire on me.

'Downstairs,' I barked an order.

She opened her mouth, shut it again, then turned on the heel of her shoe and stomped down the steps.

The young constable guarding the threshold had become mesmerised by the terrible gasps emitted by Phillips, and didn't notice Swift slip into the room behind him. The medics knelt around the dying man, whose skin had flushed bright red. His jaw suddenly stretched wide open, the muscles contorting, forcing his back to arch upwards off the floor. A gargling rattle of air escaped his lungs and his body slumped flat to the floor. Swift remained for a few more minutes, watching the medics go through the procedure for ascertaining death, then he edged out again to join Gloria and me on the landing.

'Cyanide.'

Gloria's hand flew to her lips. 'No.'

I was quite shocked too. War had accustomed us all to sudden death, but those years were gone and we'd only been speaking to Phillips a short time ago.

'Are you sure?' I asked quietly.

'I heard the doctor say so.' He nodded toward the older of the three white-coated medics, one of whom was carefully closing Phillips' eyelids. Swift turned to Gloria. 'Do you have the packaging the chocolate box arrived in?'

'No, I threw it on the fire last night.' Her voice shook and she began trembling; tears ran down her face as she tried to stifle a sob. I gave her my handkerchief, it was freshly laundered, and Swift and I waited as she composed herself.

'I'm sorry,' I said to her.

'We were such friends…I can't believe it,' she gasped.

'It would help if you could explain what happened.' I tried a gentle tone.

She took a breath and straightened her shoulders, the handkerchief clutched tightly in her hand. 'The package was with a couple of circulars when I arrived home after rehearsals. I was cold, so I lit the fire and poured a glass of wine. Then I opened the post… I don't eat anything sweet, I never have. I tossed the packaging on the fire, then put the chocolates aside for Dickie. I gave the box to him when I came up this morning. He called me an angel, and told me about your visit…' Her voice broke and she swayed unsteadily on her feet.

I caught her arm under the elbow to offer support. 'Steady…'

'Thank you,' she whispered.

'Why didn't you come up earlier?' I asked her. 'You were in the flat below, you must have heard us talking.'

'I did, but I wasn't dressed, and I wouldn't intrude… oh dear God, those chocolates were meant for me…Why? Why would anyone want to poison me?'

Swift reached into his pocket to extract the invitation Phillips had given him. 'Did the writing on the package look like this?' He showed her the envelope.

She didn't seem to be focusing, but reached out her long fingers. 'I'm not…no, no it was a rounded hand.'

'Gloria Thornton?' Billings came tramping up the stairs and called out. There were two plain-clothes officers with him, they were the same men we'd encountered yesterday. 'We'd like to interview you.'

She slumped against the wall. 'I didn't… Somebody tried to kill me.' Tears began streaming down her face. She raised the handkerchief to her eyes, smearing her make-up.

'Go with these gentlemen, please,' Billings ordered. He nodded toward the men behind him. She stared, wide-eyed, then moved forward on stumbling feet. One of the officers offered his hand to lead her down the stairs.

'Where are you taking her?' I demanded.

'To her flat, initially.' Billings' expression was stony. 'The cleaner informed us about the chocolates. What are you doing here?'

Swift quickly explained about the doorman and our discussion with Phillips.

'You're supposed to be investigating at Brundles,' he growled.

'There's more to it than Brundles,' I replied.

He scowled then moved toward the open door. 'What's the situation?' he rapped out at the constable standing on the threshold.

'He's a goner.' The young constable's gaze was fixed on the body and medics, but suddenly he realised who he was talking to and snapped to attention. 'Passed away, sir. Doctor's with him now.'

'Where's the box of chocolates?' Billings demanded.

'Sergeant's got them, sir,' the constable replied briskly, turning to nod toward a dark-haired man in uniform who was questioning the doctor.

'Billings,' Swift said, causing the Detective to look round. 'Phillips had an invitation. He gave it to us when we questioned him this morning.' He held out the envelope.

'Right.' He took it with a large hand. 'I had a team lined up to interview him today…but good work. Come with me, Swift.' Billings beckoned, and they both entered the crowded drawing room. I paused, then turned on my heel and trotted down the stairs. The door to the flat below was closed, but I could hear the murmur of voices; Gloria's was higher pitched and louder than the two detectives.

I continued down into the foyer and threaded my way along the back passage to where I expected to find the cleaning cupboard. The char was leaning a brush next to a row of brooms and mops against a damp wall. I took a sidestep to avoid banging my head on a sagging shelf holding bottles of dark fluids and leaching bleach.

'Hello,' I began in friendlier fashion. 'I wanted to apologise for my tone, earlier.'

'Huh,' the char grunted. 'Just 'cause I'm the dogsbody don't mean I should be treated like muck.'

'It wasn't my intention, but Miss Thornton was becoming upset.'

'You think I weren't upset, then?' she retorted sharply. A few strands of grey hair had escaped her headscarf and stuck limply to her brow.

'Were you?' I asked. 'You don't seem the sort to let things upset you.'

'Nah, well, I've had it tough. A hard life, there ain't no-one to give me nothing.'

'You weren't tempted by the chocolates?'

'Didn't know they was chocolates, did I? It were just a brown paper parcel.'

'Would you have left them at Miss Thornton's door, had you known?' I used a pleasant tone, attempting tact.

'You sayin' I'd 'ave nicked 'em?' she retorted, folding her arms under her sparse bosom.

'No, no, not at all.' This wasn't going well. 'I…erm… Miss Thornton said she didn't like chocolates and always gave them away. I thought perhaps…erm. Did she ever give any to you?'

'Sometimes,' she conceded. 'If Mr Phillips weren't at 'ome. But she and 'im were close, always up and down in each other's flats. He even 'ad her picture on the wall.

They said they was friends…' She sniffed. 'Suppose that were true, 'cause I never saw no 'anky-panky.'

'Did either of them have any…erm…special visitors?' I swallowed a sigh. How did one phrase these things?

'Ye mean lovers?' she said, then cackled. 'Not that they brought back 'ere. This is supposed to a respectable place. Mr Phillips 'ad an artist's studio, or so I'm told. An' Miss Thornton was out a lot, goin' to parties and actin' on stage. I don't go to the theatre, I like the bingo me-self, an' the music hall.'

'Were the chocolates hand delivered, or…?'

'They 'ad stamps on.' She reached out and wrapped arthritic fingers around the handle of a mop. 'Came yesterday afternoon with the other stuff, like normal. I take the first post around to the flats after me mornin' cuppa, then do the same in the afternoon with the second post.' She stepped toward me, wanting to exit the cramped room. 'Now, I got floors to do, so ye'd best clear out from under me feet.'

'I think you may find the police would like to talk to you.' I stepped back as she shoved past me.

'Well they'll 'ave to talk to me while I'm moppin'.' She was already marching along the passage in the direction of the foyer.

I trailed behind and arrived in the hall at the same moment as the medical team came down the stairs. Two of them were bearing Dickie Phillips' body on a stretcher, covered with a sheet. The doctor followed behind, in close conversation with Billings; more policemen trooped along on his heels. They manoeuvred out of the front door and were met by 'oohs' and 'aahs' from a small crowd gathered on the pavement.

'Excuse me, madam.' One of Billings' officers spotted the cleaning lady. 'I want a word with you.'

She wasn't intimidated and put up a spirited riposte. They argued as another officer came downstairs with Gloria Thornton in handcuffs. She was tight-lipped, her head held high, her green eyes gleaming with fury at the indignity. Camera bulbs flashed as she was hustled outside; it seemed newspaper reporters had arrived to join the excited throng. Swift came down last of all.

'Come on, Lennox,' he called and strode out into the sunshine with a look of intent on his sharp face. More flash bulbs went off, which caused him to frown. I waited on the threshold until the last one had popped, then strolled out behind him.

'Did they really have to arrest Gloria?' I asked.

He sighed. 'I thought it heavy-handed, but this is a prominent case.'

'You mean they have to be seen to be taking action?'

'Something like that,' he admitted.

We looked over to where the medics were closing the rear of the ambulance. The group of onlookers craned on tiptoes to peer around the reporters, who had dashed forward to shout questions at Billings. He slid into the back seat of a waiting police car without a word. The doors slammed shut and the convoy edged into the traffic and drove away. The reporters and crowd peered after them, then broke into chattering groups before dispersing in different directions. In a matter of minutes the street had melted back to humdrum normality.

'What did Billings say?' I asked Swift.

'Not much. He questioned me about Phillips. I told him what we'd learned. I mentioned that we'd talked to Gloria Thornton in the cafe.'

'Does he seriously think she killed Phillips?'

He shrugged. 'Billings wouldn't speculate.'

'I spoke to the cleaning lady.'

'That was brave.' He grinned.

I smiled wryly, then told him what little she'd imparted.

'So, Gloria had given away chocolates in the past – that casts doubt on her guilt.'

'Exactly,' I agreed.

'But it also gave her the perfect means of poisoning him,' he countered.

'Right, yes...' I really didn't want to believe it. 'De Ruyter's death was revenge. This is different, this is wanton; it changes everything.'

'No, Lennox, it only changes our perception of things. Look, we don't have enough information to draw any conclusions yet, we have to keep an open mind.' Swift was speaking as the professional detective he'd once been. I knew he was right.

'Fine.' I turned to look up at the windows of the building. 'Should we search Phillips' flat?'

'The police are in there now, and they've just started on Gloria's place. They wouldn't let us through the door.'

'What about his studio?'

'Billings said they'd already been there too.'

'But we haven't,' I said. 'And Cork Street Mews isn't far from here.'

He considered it. 'If Billings didn't find anything, neither will we.'

'You mean he didn't find anything he was prepared to tell us about.'

He glanced at me. 'True.'

We set off at a smart pace. It took ten minutes to zigzag from Old Bond Street, along Burlington Gardens and into Cork Street. We entered the narrow entry to the Mews. It had once been a cobbled lane bordered by stables and coach houses, the domain of horses, ostlers, and grooms. Now it was a depressing back alley, of tradesmen's entrances and dustbins.

We didn't know the number but a helpful chap pushing a handcart pointed us toward the right door. It wasn't locked. We didn't knock, and Phillips' assistant jumped in surprise when he saw us.

'We're s-shut,' he stammered. 'You shouldn't have come in here like that.'

We were in a dimly lit corridor decorated in dull Victorian colours. 'Why?' I asked him.

'Cos we're not open yet.' He was a thin drip with lank hair, and spoke with an adenoidal whine. 'An' the proper door is round the front.'

'Police,' Swift announced.

'Oh, not again. What d'you want now?' The lad screwed

up his face as though in anguish; he was obviously the dramatic sort.

'To take a look around.' Swift stalked down the passage, not inclined to waste time on the lad. The building was an old tailor's workshop by the looks of it – there had been many in the district, it being close to Savile row.

'There were four of them searching 'ere three days ago, why d'you need to do it again?' The lad followed us as we entered a door into a ground-floor room. Shutters we closed across the only window, leaving the room in darkness.

'Lights,' I demanded.

'They're here.' The lad flicked on a light switch next to the doorjamb. The place was packed with art paraphernalia: canvases, paints, a couple of easels, smocks, and a small kitchen to the side.

'There ain't nothin' to find.' The lad watched us with a peeved expression.

'We'll be the judge of that.' Swift went to take a look at the kitchen for some reason. I returned to the passage and bounded up the stairs.

The attic room covered the whole top floor. It was spacious and airy and open to the rafters. Sunshine filtered through a row of grimy windows and reflected off whitewashed walls, spreading rays across dusty floorboards worn smooth with time. There was an overwhelming smell of linseed oil, paint, and turps. I rather liked it, it reminded me of the workshops in the aircraft hangers during the war.

One corner had been arranged with a chaise longue,

a velvet-upholstered armchair, a modesty screen, and various drapes. The rest of the area was dedicated to the serious business of creating art: more propped canvases, a spattered table arrayed with old jars of cleaning fluids, brushes, and tubes of colourful paints.

A single large easel stood in the centre of the room. It supported a portrait of a woman. I stopped to stare. Swift came up behind me, with the lad on his heels.

'Who's that?' I asked the lad.

'Lillian Lamb,' he replied. 'She's a looker, ain't she?'

We nodded agreement. She was utterly stunning; a face of perfect regularity with high cheekbones, a firm jawline and chin, pert nose, wide mouth with curling lips, and large eyes of intense violet. She wore a modern dress in layered chiffon, a cameo held by a black ribbon around her neck, and a sparkling tiara amid her pale blonde hair, almost as if it were an aura above her head.

'Phillips told me he didn't paint portraits any longer,' I said to the lad.

'He does if the price is right.' He smirked.

Swift had touched the paint. 'It's still wet, is it finished?'

'Near enough. Got to varnish it when it's dried off. That'll be a couple of weeks yet. Mr Phillips is teachin' me all about art and painting. He says I've got talent.'

'Does he pay you?' I asked.

'He pays in tuition.' The lad turned defensive. 'According to Mr Phillips I'll soon be good enough to earn my own bread, an' it'll be a pretty packet because he knows all the nobs and I can charge as much as I like.'

I decided against mentioning Phillips' unfortunate demise.

'Does Miss Lamb come to sit regularly?' Swift was gathering facts.

'She came twice a week for more than a month, but she don't need to no more. Normally, we don't have folk come in here. Mr Phillips prefers to work on his copies of the old masters – he says it's a lot less trouble than dealing with people.' He nodded. 'An' he's right. It took me ages to clean up before Miss Lamb came to make her sitting, and we had to mind our p's and q's round her. Right hoity-toity she was, puttin' on this posh voice, but she couldn't hide her real accent. I'd recognise it anywhere. She were an East Ender from the back streets of Whitechapel.'

Whitechapel had long been a notorious slum; its population a shifting mass of London-bred paupers, destitute immigrants, and hardened criminals.

'Were she and Phillips friendly?' Swift asked.

'I dunno, kind of I suppose. Not lovey-dovey, though…' the lad said, then began another whinge. 'She said I was a distraction when she were trying to sit still. She used to order me to clear off and Mr Phillips didn't do nothing to stop her.'

'She's beautiful.' I hadn't been able to take my eyes from her face.

'Yeah, on the outside,' the lad replied.

Swift had given up gazing and gone to take a look about the room. A contraption on another table had been shoved into a dark corner; he paused to examine it. 'What's this for?'

The lad grinned. 'That's what Mr Phillips calls his Canaletto camera, but its proper name is an Episcope Projector.' He pronounced the word carefully. 'It projects slides onto a canvas, and we paint the picture on it, just like Canaletto did.'

I went to join them next to the wood and leather apparatus.

'That's cheating,' I said, although it explained the reproductions in Phillips' drawing room, and the dabbed brush marks.

Swift wiped a finger to remove dust from the lens. 'Did Phillips ever bring chocolates to the premises?'

'Nah, he'd bring a bottle of wine sometimes, but he wouldn't share it.'

The doorbell rang downstairs. We all turned in the direction of the front door.

'Oh, Mr Phillips must have forgot his keys again.' The lad moved toward the stairs. 'I left them in the kitchen…' He called out more loudly, 'Hang on a sec, Mr Phillips, I'll be right there.'

I glanced at Swift. 'Police?'

'Yes, I think we'll let them break the bad news.'

'Agreed,' I said. We went down to slip out of the back door before they saw us, and headed back to whence we came.

# CHAPTER 15

'We can't interview Lillian Lamb without permission,' Swift insisted as we crossed back into Piccadilly, heading for Old Bond Street. 'The police have already searched Phillips' studio, they'll know about the connection.'

'Hm.' I didn't argue. 'The portrait was interesting though.'

'Yes,' he agreed. He was walking with his head down. 'It could be relevant, but I don't see…'

'Where do ladies purchase cosmetics?'

That flummoxed him. 'What?'

'Gloria Thornton was wearing shimmering eyeshadow, so was Estelle Clifton. Persi mentioned diamond dust was used in cosmetics by the Egyptians, and that ancient Egypt is becoming fashionable again.'

'Does Billings know about these cosmetics?'

'I've no idea.'

'Lillian Lamb's make-up was quite dark,' he commented.

'It was only a painting.'

'Florence wears a touch of lipstick when we go to the

mainland.' He stopped walking. 'I've never heard of shops that only sell make-up…'

'They must exist. We could try the Royal Arcade, there are dozens of shops in there,' I suggested. 'Come on.'

We set off along Old Bond Street and came to the richly decorated portal proclaiming itself to be *The Royal Arcade*, and slowed our pace. It was the sort of place to strike terror into the heart of the average husband. Huge bow windows formed a curved entrance, cleverly constructed to entice the unsuspecting browser to step inside. Glossy marbled pillars supported a galleried glass roof, which protected a broad parade of exquisitely designed shopfronts. We stopped to stare in a window glittering with gold and gems.

'We could ask a jeweller about diamond dust.' I nodded toward the glazed door where a smart doorman stood to attention.

'Lennox, wait, I thought we were supposed to be looking for cosmetics…' Swift began, but he was too late. The door had been swung open by the chap guarding it, and I crossed the threshold as though drawn by an irresistible force.

We were met with disdain.

'We do not create jewellery, sir, we provide unique objets d'art to discerning clientele.' A snooty chap in a sleek suit attempted to look down his nose at us – he might have succeeded if he'd been a foot taller.

We were standing in front of a polished counter of highly varnished rosewood. Around us were shelves displaying necklaces, tiaras, earrings, and bracelets sparkling with gold and precious gems. The very air felt thick with opulence, and I had a sudden longing for green fields and the soft Cotswolds countryside.

'Are you saying you don't know how diamonds are cut?' Swift goaded him.

'Of course not. I am perfectly familiar with the process, but as I have said, we do not cut stones ourselves—' The oily salesman's explanation was interrupted by the appearance of an elderly man in a dark suit.

'Rueben, Rueben…is this how we talk to our customers?' The old chap, bent and wizened by time, admonished the assistant. 'You must not say such talk to them. Now go do your work; leave this to me.'

'Uncle Moshe, I was merely trying to…' Rueben hissed.

'Go, go. I talk with them.' The old man waved a gnarled hand until Rueben slid off in retreat. 'My daughter's boy. He thinks I need to stay home. He thinks I frighten the customers.' Moshe put his head to one side, a beaming smile on his face. 'Maybe he's right.'

I grinned and offered my hand. 'Major Lennox, and Inspector Swift.'

'Moshe Cohen.' He shook hands with a vice-like grip belying his age. 'Now, you want to know diamond dust? This is an interesting question. Why for you want to know?'

'It's… erm…' Swift began, then stuttered to a halt.

'Robbery.' I came to the rescue. 'Traces of dust were found at the scene of the crime.'

Moshe's brown eyes widened in dismay. 'What they do? Smash the diamonds with hammers? Why for they do this?'

'A mistake, probably,' I reassured him. 'Or, they may have intended it for...erm... something...'

He gazed up at me. 'For what?'

Swift joined in. 'Could you tell us what diamond dust is used for?'

'Sure I can, I am working with gold and gems all my life. So too my father, and his father...but not here. This was in the old country.'

I assumed him to be one of the people expelled from Russia in the Pogroms at the end of the last century; there were many such in London. 'We know it's used in industry,' I said.

'Yes, yes it has many uses.' Moshe nodded. 'This dust can be for polishing, and we have diamond wires, they are very good for cutting gemstones. Diamonds is added to tools of all kinds. They put tiny little diamonds into steel by using *electricity*!' His voice rose as though in amazement. 'This is like magic. I cannot explain it.' He beamed. 'So did these robbers bring diamond dust to steal with? How for they use it? You must tell to me.'

'We think the dust may have rubbed off some tools... erm, during the robbery of a...a safe.' My story was beginning to unravel, I wasn't a terribly good liar.

'Is the dust graded according to use?' Swift took over.

'Ah.' Moshe nodded. 'You have secrets to keep. I understand. We must all keep our secrets. So...finest dust is like powdered sugar for icing the cakes, so fine it will float in the air. This is for polishing with a little oil. It is important not to breathe it, or will kill the lungs, so beware.' He held up an arthritic finger in warning. 'Next is smallest grains. This size is like caster sugar used in baking the cake. Then bigger grains is heavy, like sugar in tea. There are grades between. All is separated by machine before is sold. It is important not to mix up grains, or he will not do his job.'

So diamond granules were graded by size – that made sense – and the finest form would float, which put paid to Voltaire's critique.

'You suggested diamonds could be broken by a hammer. I thought diamonds were the hardest substance on earth.' I recalled this from a school book I'd once read.

'This is so,' Moshe agreed, his thick brows rising. 'Diamond is hardest and sharpest stone, the cutting edge cannot be affected by nothing! It is why he is used in tools. But a diamond gemstone is very brittle, can be smashed easy.' Moshe was evidently enjoying his lecture. 'Did your robbers smash their diamonds?'

'We cannot comment,' Swift sidestepped smoothly. 'Could diamond dust be purchased in shops?'

'No…Why for they buy it?'

'Cosmetics.' I gave the answer. 'It could be added to cosmetics for the eyes.'

'These robbers wore eye cosmetic?' Moshe looked astonished.

'No, no, it was something else entirely, not related to the robbery,' I assured him.

'Ah.' He shook his head. 'It would not be wise to add to the cosmetic. The dust will creep into the skin, and the eyes. I would not recommend this, no, I would not.' He looked up at us with a gentle expression, rather like my dog when he's hoping for a piece of steak. 'Now, I show you some of our most charming pieces. I am sure you want for to make happy your wives with beautiful gifts.'

He showed us one dazzling piece after another. We put up a determined resistance, until I settled on a pair of pearl drop earrings and Swift fell for a pretty brooch. We left the shop feeling we'd been ambushed by an expert.

'Florence will love the brooch,' Swift assured me as we returned to the arcade's main passage.

'And it's nearly Valentine's Day,' I added.

'Yes, we can't go home empty-handed.'

'No…where are we going, Swift?'

'Where we were supposed to go before your diversion. Look, there's a perfumery down there, they must know about cosmetics.' He pointed to a shop, its windows displaying glass shelves of small bottles in artful design.

'Fine.' I paused to tuck the small beribboned box into my jacket pocket. 'But we're not buying anything.'

'Absolutely,' Swift agreed. 'Because if we do, I'll be going home penniless.'

We received the same snooty reception as the jeweller's assistant had given us.

'We are a perfumery, not a cosmeticery,' the young lady in fashionable garb, and lashings of make-up, replied to my enquiry. I'd never heard of a 'cosmeticery' but she sounded sure of herself. She lifted a crystal atomiser and sprayed it in my direction. 'This is our latest perfume, Chanel Number 5. Your wife will adore it.'

Swift sneezed.

'Madam, would you...' Swift began, but was stopped by another squirt of the atomiser.

'Rose, ylang-ylang, jasmine, and lily of the valley.' The lady was undeterred. 'Vetiver, sandalwood—'

'Please stop doing that.' I held up my hand. She sprayed again. Swift sneezed again.

'Where's the nearest cosmetic shop?' I demanded.

'There aren't shops that just sell cosmetics.' She lowered the spray, her Cupid's bow lips forming a pout. 'One buys them at the chemist.'

'What about shimmery eye shadow?' I said. 'The expensive sort.'

'Oh, you mean "diamond eyes".' She changed her tone, and fluttered her lashes. 'Well you must have deep pockets. You can only find that at Gloria's Boutique. She's terribly exclusive; it's every girl's dream to go, but it's upper crust only...'

'Gloria who?' Swift had stopped blowing his nose to cut in.

'Gloria Thornton, the actress, of course,' the sales girl replied with an affected accent. 'She has her very own range, and it's just divine. Everything is personalised; she holds one-to-one sessions to match one's skin tone and eye colour. The ladies are accompanied by their personal maids so that they can be taught how to apply it properly.

It must be heavenly to be so pampered.' She sounded wistful.

'Where is Gloria's Boutique?' I demanded.

'Number 16, Arlington Street, just behind The Ritz,' she told us. 'But you can't go without an appointment.'

'We're police,' Swift said.

'Ooh,' the sales girl gasped, sprayed the atomiser at us again, then fled to the rear of the shop.

'There's a telephone box on Old Bond Street,' Swift told me once he'd finished blowing his nose again. 'I'm going to call Billings and tell him about Gloria's Boutique. He said we must inform him of any new leads…'

'Yes, Swift, I know,' I replied. 'Tell him we'll meet him there.'

'Right.' He dashed out. I hesitated. I'd already spent a small fortune on pearl earrings, but that perfume was rather alluring.

I crossed the confines of the shop to where the sales girl was standing, still armed with the atomiser. 'Chanel Number 5?'

Why is it that everything in London costs five times the price of everywhere else? I could have bought a new fishing rod for the price of a tiny bottle of perfume.

'Come on, Lennox. Billings is sending a team to Arlington Street.' Swift was waiting for me at the entrance to the Royal Arcade. 'It's only around the corner.'

'I know where it is.'

We crossed Piccadilly, and into Arlington Street, passing the side entrance to The Ritz where top-hatted doormen chatted quietly on the steps. Number 16 was at the tail of the dead-end road. There was little clue to the enterprise, other than the name 'Gloria's Boutique' listed on the row of doorbells.

I pushed the button; a porter opened the door. 'Yes?' He was chewing something, his lunch probably – he had a napkin tucked under his chin.

'Gloria's Boutique, please,' I requested.

'Police.' Swift wasn't interested in niceties. 'And there are more on the way.'

'Good Lord.' The porter took a step backwards.

Swift swept past him. 'Which room?'

'First floor. You'll see her nameplate on the door…' The porter pointed toward the stairs at the end of the hallway.

Swift raced ahead. I followed at a more leisurely pace.

'Stay where you are. Don't touch anything,' Swift announced, his face set stern in full police mode.

The young woman sitting at a marble topped table froze. 'What? Who are you?' She was in a small back room, situated beyond a stylish parlour, which I assumed to be Gloria's consulting room.

'Stand up slowly and move to the window,' Swift ordered as he closed in.

'What on earth for?' Her work table was scattered with small glass jars of colourful powders, lotions, and oils; she appeared to be in the process of mixing them.

'Police,' Swift announced, having forgotten to mention it. 'Gloria Thornton is in custody. We have reason to believe there is evidence on the premises linking her to a crime.'

'Oh, this is ridiculous.' She was a pretty girl with a classic English complexion and not a hint of make-up on her face. She rose to her feet. 'What possible crime could Gloria be involved in?'

'We're not at liberty to say,' Swift continued.

'Nonsense.' She was spirited and spoke with eloquently rounded vowels. 'You must tell me, or I won't answer your questions.'

I leaned against the doorjamb to watch Swift in action.

'It's part of a wider investigation…' he began.

The porter had followed us up the stairs. 'Gloria wouldn't break any laws, she's straight as they come,' he said.

'Go down and attend to the door,' Swift snapped. 'And show the police up when they arrive.'

The porter hesitated, muttered something under his breath, then puffed his way out again.

The young woman confronted Swift. 'Show me your identification.'

A flush rose to his cheeks. 'We're… erm…' he stammered.

I hid a grin and moved to join them. 'We believe you sell a cosmetic called "diamond eyes".'

She turned to me, puzzlement and exasperation on her pretty face. 'Yes, it's our specialty. Gloria devised it herself.'

'Where do you obtain the diamond dust?' Swift rallied.

She straightened her shoulders. 'Could you at least tell me your names?'

'Major Lennox, and Inspector Swift.' I introduced ourselves without mentioning anything about Swift being retired.

'I'm Gloria's assistant, Rebecca Hastings,' she told us.

'How long have you been working here?' Swift demanded.

'Just over eighteen months, and I'd rather you didn't bark questions at me.'

Swift coloured, and moderated his tone. 'I'm not barking, I'm merely trying to gain answers.'

'Major Lennox.' She turned to address me. 'I really must object. We aren't breaking any laws. We're very careful which ingredients we use; there's absolutely nothing harmful in any of our products.'

'We were informed diamond dust is abrasive and can damage the skin and eyes,' I told her.

'Is that what this is about?' She glanced back at the jars of vibrant powders on the worktable. 'It's not actually made from diamonds, it's a type of mineral. Gloria's spent years perfecting it. She simply used the term "Diamond Eyes" to describe it.'

That punctured Swift's bombast.

'And Gloria pretended it was made from real diamonds to charge a higher price,' I guessed.

Rebecca blushed. 'We didn't actually state that...' She faltered. 'But, yes, it was inferred, although it's hardly a major crime. Surely you haven't arrested Gloria for that?'

Swift ignored the question and asked, 'Could you show us the mineral, please?'

'Oh, very well.' She went to the table and picked up a jar filled with sparkling powder. 'It's mica – it's mined from underground seams, but you often see fragments in granite and marble. It glints when it catches the light.' She handed it to Swift. 'It's not in the least harmful.'

He raised the jar up to the sunlight coming through narrow windows; the powder sent tiny scintillas of light bouncing off the walls as he twisted it in his hand. 'This will have to go to the lab to be tested.'

'We're not doing anything wrong,' Rebecca protested.

The clanging of a bell sounded in the street outside, followed by car doors slamming, voices shouting, and then boots trampling up the stairs. The police had arrived. Swift sighed and went down to meet them.

# CHAPTER 16

'Lunch,' I insisted. 'It's past two o'clock and there's nothing more we can do here.'

Swift had wanted to stay and help the squad search Gloria's Boutique, but their fervour had cooled once we admitted 'Diamond Eyes' may not be the damning evidence against Gloria Thornton that we'd suspected.

'Fine, but we don't have to return to Brundles,' Swift said.

'Yes, we do.' I was already heading downstairs. 'You need to write notes, and I need to clear my mind.'

We walked out into Arlington Street, casually sidestepping police cars littering the road.

'Clear your mind of what?' he asked as he fell into step beside me.

'All the chatter, the noise…' I brushed hair back from my face. 'I live in the peaceful countryside, Swift. I'm used to cows and birdsong; London is frenetic, and we've spoken to dozens of people today. I can barely remember their names or what they said.'

'You must remember Dickie Phillips.'

'Obviously, Swift.' I was sarcastic. 'We just witnessed his terrible death.'

'You shouldn't lock yourself away in the sticks.' He became serious. 'The world's an interesting place, you need to be part of it.'

'Swift,' I objected. 'You live in a castle on a remote Scottish loch.'

'Yes, but I do things,' he retaliated as we turned onto Piccadilly. 'I'm part of the Braeburn clan; we manage the whisky distillery, and the upkeep of the village, and I'm happy doing it. You could do more in Ashton Steeple.' He warmed to the theme. 'Your parents must have opened The Manor for fetes and Christmas parties; you and Persi could do the same.'

'No, we couldn't.' The idea filled me with horror. My home had been my refuge after the war, and if it weren't for a strange turn of fate I'd still be there, spending my days quietly fishing and hunting.

'Is that fair on Persi?' he asked as we entered Duke Street.

'She knows I'm not sociable, and she seems quite happy with wallpaper, and now she has chickens. There are plenty of people for her to talk to, as well as me and Greggs.'

'Doesn't she miss digging up bodies?' He asked the question that haunted me.

'She said not.' I quashed the angst in my voice. 'I told her about the plague pit in the corner of the churchyard, and said she could dig that up.'

He grinned. 'You'd better ask the vicar first.'

'You're still hankering after Scotland Yard, Swift.' I switched tack.

He shoved his hands in his pockets. 'Not as much… but yes, I suppose I am. The ambition never abates, and I've always liked the challenge: chasing down criminals and murderers. I enjoy it, and being part of the team.' We were threading through crowds as we walked – the winter sunshine had enticed more people onto the streets.

I agreed with him about the challenge. It was like hunting, and hunting was part of my nature, even though I wasn't keen on killing. 'Would you come back, if Scotland Yard asked you?'

He thought about it before replying. 'No. I wouldn't ask Florence to live in London, she'd never adapt; she loves life in Braeburn…but I thought perhaps we could become consultants of some sort, if the Yard ever had use for us.'

'Like now.'

'Yes, like now.'

'Like Sherlock Holmes and Watson.'

'No, Lennox, not like Holmes and Watson. They were dedicated to detecting; we have lives to lead.'

'And they weren't real,' I reminded him.

He grinned, then reverted to earnestness. 'Would you consider being a consultant?'

'Swift, this really isn't my cup of tea…'

'Lennox, you're good at it: you're natural, you're

intuitive, and people open up to you. You don't realise how difficult it is to extract information from witnesses.'

We were almost at St James's Square.

'You'd have more success if you were less forceful,' I replied.

'Are you saying I'm a bully?'

'No, absolutely not, but you can be rather brusque, Swift.'

He was unrepentant. 'Which makes them turn to you – that's how it works. Nice copper, brusque copper.'

The gaggle of reporters had grown larger. They'd been huddled on the pavement opposite Brundles' entrance, but moved as one when they spotted us.

'Hey, you were at the flats when Dickie Phillips' body was brought out,' one shouted. 'Tell us what happened?'

There were more shouts, and flash bulbs popping off. Swift pulled his hat low. I ignored them. George moved deftly to open the door as we bounded up the steps to enter the cocooning confines of Brundles.

Rossetti must have been watching; he intercepted us as we were heading for the stairs.

'Major Lennox? Inspector?'

We swung around.

He walked over, self-composed and exuding an aura of command. 'Would you join me in the Strangers Room, please?'

'Now?' I replied.

'Yes, now, if you would...' Rossetti requested.

Swift glanced at me. I sighed. 'Very well.'

We trooped behind him. I had my hands in my pockets, irritated by the lack of lunch and keen for some quiet time to regroup my thoughts.

'Ah, there you are.' Clifton was waiting and rose to his feet as we entered. Lady Estelle was at his side, along with two people we hadn't encountered before. They'd been sitting in chairs around the fire, the tables having been pushed back into corners. Dr Moore was with them. Browne was standing just inside the door.

'Sir Humphrey Stanford and Lady Marina Stanford.' Rossetti introduced us to the couple. I recognised the names immediately; their daughter, Nancy, had died alongside Daphne Clifton.

We bowed and responded appropriately. Dr Moore lifted a hand in greeting. Lady Estelle smiled up at me.

'Mr Phillips is dead,' Rossetti stated. 'We believe you were present.'

I sat down, crossed my legs, and left it to Swift.

'Suspected cyanide,' Swift stated, and explained the circumstances, including Gloria Thornton's arrest. He was brief and kept details to a minimum. Dr Moore questioned him about the symptoms.

'So cyanide in chocolate, eh.' Moore nodded. He looked as though he'd been recently woken from a quiet snooze. 'Nasty. Where did the cyanide come from? Can't just walk into a shop and demand it.'

'The police are seeking to determine that now,' Swift replied in noncommittal terms.

'But why? I just do not understand.' Lady Marina spoke

in a drawling American accent. I'd been eyeing her: she wore a smart dress with matching jacket in pastel pink. A lady of middle age, slim, white-haired, and bore a close resemblance to Lady Estelle Clifton.

'You're related,' I guessed.

'Sisters,' Lady Estelle replied. 'I'm the stars, she's the sea, our mom was nuts.'

I smiled, and sympathised. 'I was blighted with Heathcliff. My mother's family was originally from the Southern States.'

The sisters instantly demanded where in the South, and who my connections were.

Rossetti quickly curtailed the flurry of questions. 'May we please proceed? Major Lennox, do the police believe Miss Thornton was responsible for the murder of Mr Phillips?'

'She was just arrested for it,' I stated dryly.

'The evidence suggests it was possible.' Swift was more diplomatic.

'Is she suspected of De Ruyter's murder?' Lord Clifton was stiffly formal.

'It's too soon to make a judgement…' Swift began.

'I really don't think she'd poison anyone,' Lady Marina declared.

'But who else could have done it?' Her husband, Sir Humphrey, asked.

Swift regarded them narrowly. 'Presumably the same person who murdered De Ruyter.'

'Why don't you believe Gloria Thornton poisoned Phillips?' I asked Lady Marina.

'She's…well, it's just so horrible.' Lady Marina stumbled over her words. 'Why would she do it?'

'That's what these young men are here to answer.' Estelle was quick to come to the rescue. She was sitting upright in a chair, sunlight shimmering on her ash blonde hair and the silk of her yellow frock coat.

All eyes turned to us.

'Our enquiries are still in the early stages.' Swift gave a policeman's answer.

'It would have helped if you'd given the police your invitations.' I was less formal. 'What else have you omitted?'

Lady Marina glanced at Estelle, then admitted, 'We talked about the invitations together before the night, and what it may mean.'

'And the murder?' I asked.

'Of course not.' Marina's cheeks flushed red. 'We didn't know he was going to be murdered.'

'Justice will be served,' I quoted. 'You were all invited to Ladies' Night dinner, you must have suspected he would be poisoned or harmed in some way.'

'We truly did not think he would be killed. We thought there would be proof of his evil deeds and he'd finally be exposed as the devil we know him to be.' Lady Estelle repeated her earlier assertion. Her sister fidgeted with the pretty handbag held in her lap. I noticed both sisters wore discreet touches of shimmering eye shadow.

'I did not know of the invitation,' Sir Humphrey Stanford said in a stentorian voice. 'My wife spoke of a desire to attend Ladies' Night here at the club, and I concurred.

I have absolutely no reason to believe her Ladyship anticipated a malicious act.' The chap had the look of the intellectual about him; sparse, hunched, and reproving – much like the old buzzards who'd aimed esoteric lectures at me in Oxford.

Clifton had previously declared himself ignorant of the invitations and said nothing.

'Well, I thought it dashed rum at the time.' Dr Moore spoke up. 'But I didn't imagine De Ruyter would be done away with. Jolly glad he was though!' He was in more cheerful form than the other men.

Swift turned to Browne. 'You were ordered to wheel the dessert in, what did you think was about to happen?'

Browne had remained near the door, but trod across the carpet to join us. 'I thought it quite possible De Ruyter's guilt could be exposed, but I did not envision his death, sir.' He spoke in his solemn Scottish accent, his long face without expression. 'If I were to offer an opinion, I would say the concept of a person devising an "execution" in so public a manner is absurd.'

'I agree,' Rossetti said. He had been standing stiffly, near the Cliftons. '"Justice will be served" is an ambiguous term, and your interpretation, Major Lennox, is only meaningful after the fact.'

'Precisely,' Clifton said in support. 'And this is not casting new light on the situation. We are most concerned about the death of Phillips. Is his murder connected with De Ruyter's? And does it present a danger to any of us here?'

'If anyone is hiding anything significant about De

Ruyter's death, then they may be a threat to his killer,' I replied. This caused their eyes to dart about the room, waiting for a reaction. It didn't come.

'DCI Billings will be able to give a clearer understanding of the situation,' Swift stated.

'We're not going to speak to him,' Lady Marina declared. 'My Nancy died and those policemen let the culprit get away with it. That Devil has been living like a king right under our noses all these years and nobody did a darn thing about it.'

'Now you just hush, Marina.' Estelle leaned toward her and tapped her on the knee. 'We want to let them explain themselves.'

'It's too soon to—' Swift tried to repeat the line.

'Do you know what information Phillips possessed, and if it may have given cause to his murder?' Sir Humphrey interrupted in irritation.

'No,' Swift answered concisely.

'It cannot be certain that Phillips was the target.' Rossetti joined in. 'From our understanding, the parcel containing the chocolates was addressed to Miss Thornton.'

'Where did you hear that information?' Swift was quick to ask.

'The reporters,' Rossetti replied. 'I questioned them myself.'

'Bravo,' Dr Moore said. 'Heroic act, old chap. I wouldn't go near 'em myself.'

'I would not generally do so, either.' Rossetti gave a sharp explanation. 'But it was a matter of expediency.'

Swift listened and answered with a standard line. 'We do not know the specifics, and cannot comment.'

'Well if you can't comment, what can you do?' Lady Marina asked.

Swift frowned.

'I really do not see how you have been helpful, gentlemen,' Sir Humphrey reproved. 'You cannot even tell us who the intended victim was.'

Swift's brows lowered further.

'Lillian Lamb could be behind it. Poison is often a woman's choice of dispatch.' Dr Moore threw in the suggestion.

'Oh, now that's a clever idea.' Lady Estelle beamed at him.

'But why would she?' Lady Marina contradicted.

That started a heated debate about imaginary motives, none of which were sensible. I cut into the babble. 'Is there anything you haven't told us about that night?'

They shut up again and shook their heads.

'Major Lennox, Inspector Swift.' Clifton stood. 'I have specifically requested your aid in this matter, and I must admit, I am disappointed…'

Swift was quick to react. 'We need more information and clear evidence,' he replied.

I broke in. 'Lord Clifton, your lawyer investigated the Birdcage Murders on your behalf. He promised to provide us with a copy of his report, but we have not received it.' This was a blatant lie, but I hoped it would goad him into action.

Clifton's pale cheeks flushed. 'Wallace hasn't mentioned it to me, but the police have the files and I doubt they will release them at this moment.'

That was a blow. 'Which leaves us fettered.' I was terse in reply.

'I have some handwritten notes that Wallace sent to me at the time of the investigation,' Clifton admitted.

'Then may we please see those?' Swift requested.

Clifton nodded stiffly. 'Very well, I will ensure they are delivered to you shortly, but I had expected more from you, Lennox.' He glared at me, then stood up. 'Ladies?' He put a hand out toward his wife and Lady Marina.

It signalled the end of the discussion and everyone rose to leave. I was keen to return upstairs, but hesitated, wanting to observe how the ladies exited the club. I knew they couldn't have entered through the front door.

Browne went to an area next to the bay window overlooking the garden, withdrew a key from his waistcoat pocket and carefully placed it in a hidden lock. The door had been papered in the same design as the walls; at first glance the opening was invisible. Browne swung it open on silent hinges and waited as the sisters were escorted out by their husbands, then closed and locked the secret door behind them.

Dr Moore had wandered over to me as I watched the process.

'Jolly good show, my boy.' He smiled amiably. 'You've got them rattled. You and your friend are a sharp pair. Which one of them do ye think did it?'

'Haven't a clue,' I said, then went off in search of lunch.

# CHAPTER 17

'We haven't eaten. Could you arrange for lunch trays to be sent up, please?' I asked Rossetti. I'd found him and Swift standing in the foyer.

'Of course.' Irritation flickered over Rossetti's smooth face. It was beneath his dignity to be given menial orders, but I hadn't forgotten my meeting with him last evening and I wasn't inclined to be friendly.

'Swift?' I turned to him.

He didn't move. 'I'm waiting for the notes from Clifton.'

'It'll be a while,' I said.

'Belgrave Square isn't far, he'll send a boy back as soon as he returns home.'

He really did take things seriously.

'Fine.' I left him to it and made my way up to my room.

I walked in to find Greggs prancing about with one arm around an imaginary lady's waist and the other holding a book. 'Greggs?'

'Oh, sir…ah, erm…' He stopped mid-prance, fumbled with the book, dropped it and flushed bright red. 'I am familiarising myself with the foxtrot.'

Foggy had been diligently watching him but dashed over as I walked in. I ruffled his fur then bent to pick Greggs' book up and hand it to him.

'I thought you were going to the theatre.'

'We were, sir, but Miss Fairchild expressed a desire to dance at the Ritz.' He took a handkerchief from his pocket and wiped his forehead. 'I fear it will be a heady affair, sir.'

'Heady?' I remarked

'It is quite the fashionable destination, sir,' he assured me. 'And I do not wish to disappoint Miss Fairchild with a less than proficient performance.'

'I'm sure you don't.'

'I think I should sit down, sir.' He tottered over to an armchair and sank into it.

I took the other chair and settled Foggy on my lap. 'Greggs, where would one buy cyanide?'

'Cyanide, sir?' He lowered the handkerchief.

'Dickie Phillips was poisoned with Gloria Thornton's chocolates.'

'Poisoned?' Both brows rose toward his scant hairline. 'That is appalling news, sir.' He recovered his equilibrium and spoke with a hint of eager anticipation. 'Potassium cyanide is an ingredient in silver cleaning powder. It is to be found at the iron mongers.'

'Really? So anyone can buy it?' That was shocking.

'Indeed sir, assuming one is aware of the contents of silver cleaning powder,' he straightened up. 'May I enquire how this tragedy occurred?'

I told him every detail I could remember – I knew he would regale it to Miss Fairchild later.

'That would explain the actions of the reporters, sir. They were stationed on the pavement this morning, and then they suddenly darted off like hornets from a nest. They have only recently returned.'

'I hadn't thought Gloria Thornton the type to murder anyone, and she said she and Phillips had been friends for years,' I mused. 'She'd have to be utterly evil to poison him in cold blood like that.'

'But if she did not poison the chocolates – and they were not intended for her – the poisoner would have to know her predilections very well, sir.' He considered the facts while folding his handkerchief. 'And they would also have to be familiar with the habits of Mr Phillips.'

'Hm...' I hadn't really had time to consider the permutations. 'If Dickie Phillips had been the generous sort, he could have offered the chocolates about, and any number of people might have been poisoned. It was reckless and indiscriminate.'

'As were the Birdcage murders, sir.'

'Yes. They were, weren't they.' I nodded. 'How much silver cleaning powder would be necessary to kill somebody?'

'I'm afraid I do not have that information, sir. Are you considering an experiment?'

'Hardly,' I said wryly, and glanced at the telephone. 'Lady Persi might know…' I sighed. 'But she's probably in the garden, tending chickens.'

'Have you eaten, sir? I could ring for Pinner…' He shifted to raise himself from his chair.

I waved him to remain seated. 'I've asked Rossetti to arrange it, it's the least he can do.'

'Very well, sir. As I will be escorting Miss Fairchild this evening, I will not be present for Mr Fogg.'

'Right o, I'll keep him with me.' I put my little dog on the floor. 'Where's Tubbs?'

'Mr Tubbs followed Mr Pinner downstairs after he had served my lunch, sir. I suspect he is in the dining room.'

I grinned. 'Causing chaos for his own amusement.'

'Quite probably, sir.'

Swift entered without knocking, excitement in his eyes. 'Clifton's delivery boy just arrived. I've got Wallace's notes.' He waved a brown envelope.

'What about lunch?'

'Pinner's putting it in my room, come on.' He went off.

I followed with Fogg gambolling alongside me.

Pinner was just leaving and gave a cheery greeting. 'It's only sandwiches and cold cuts, sir, but Chef said he'd cook something special if youse be wanting it.'

'I'm sure it will be fine, thank you,' I told him as I entered Swift's chamber.

He'd already opened the package and begun pulling out yellow sheets of paper to place on the table between the fireside chairs.

A tray of sandwiches, fruit, sliced beef and ham, various cheeses, and two glasses of white wine stood on the desk. I went over and picked up a sandwich; it was ham and egg. I bit into it and strolled over to gaze at Swift's event board.

'The notes are in date order from 1911 to 1914, which was when the investigation was halted,' Swift said, and held up a letter on fine white paper. 'And this is from Clifton asking for a report on our findings.'

'We're not telling him anything,' I replied.

'Fine.' He slipped it back in the envelope.

I gave a chunk of my sandwich to Foggy, picked up a red crayon, and wrote 'Ezra De Ruyter' at the top of the middle section, then drew a box around his name in black. 'He's the crux of it all,' I remarked. Swift merely grunted.

I drew another black box around Dickie Phillips' name. 'And he's dead.'

'Wallace was thorough.' Swift was engrossed in sorting papers into piles. 'I've put them in order of the date and year they were written.'

'Greggs said potassium cyanide is used to clean silver...' I went back to the desk for another sandwich.

'And plating metals, and fixing photographs after they've been developed.' He didn't look up. 'Deadly chemicals were part of our training.'

'Is cyanide easy to buy?'

'If you were buying it in pure form, you'd have to sign the poison register, but if it's merely in a cleaning product, or for use in photography, then it could be purchased as easily as anything else.'

I picked up a glass of wine. 'Did Billings mention where the chocolates were purchased?'

'Any one of a dozen shops. They weren't the uncommon kind. He's sent a couple of officers to make enquiries.'

'What do you make of it all, Swift?' I asked.

He sighed, put the papers down and came to stand beside the desk where he could reach the tray. 'If the target was Dickie Phillips, he must have known something.'

'Perhaps he'd tried blackmailing the killer… if he did, it would only have happened in the last day or two. Billings should trace his movements.'

'Yes, Lennox, and that's what they're doing. They're very thorough.'

'At least one of each couple received an invitation,' I stated. 'As did Browne and Rossetti. And either De Ruyter or Lillian Lamb must have received one.' I shook my head. 'We need to talk to her, Swift.'

'I told you, we can't. Billings said she's a key witness, we need permission.' He reached for a sandwich. Foggy's eyes had been following our every movement. I gave him another piece of ham.

'What did you make of the assembled?'

'You mean the suspects,' Swift corrected me. 'They were shaken by Phillips' death.'

'Probably with good reason,' I remarked. 'I can't see Gloria Thornton being behind it, she doesn't have a motive.'

'She doesn't have a motive that we know of,' Swift corrected me.

I sipped my wine, a nice Sauvignon Blanc, perfect for a light lunch. 'It was completely indiscriminate, Swift. I thought the culprit was a grief-stricken relative seeking revenge, but poisoning chocolates is unprincipled.'

'Yes.' Swift studied the sandwiches and picked out a beef and tomato.

'You were right.'

'About what?'

'Perception. The murderer hasn't changed, our perception has.'

'Yours may have done, Lennox – mine didn't. You need to learn to deal with facts and not fill in the gaps from your imagination.'

'Which explains why most policemen don't have imaginations.' I taunted him.

He didn't rise to the bait. 'Exactly.' He grinned and bit into the sandwich.

I grinned too. 'The American sisters, Estelle and Marina, both received invitations, and they admitted discussing it between them.'

'Yes, I know.'

I waited for him to say more, but he just ate another sandwich. 'Their husbands both said they knew nothing about it.'

'Yes.' He reached for another sandwich.

'I think Rossetti and Browne collaborated together on the night.'

'Agreed.' He tossed Foggy a crust.

'Swift, I'm trying to review what we've learned,' I said in exasperation.

'I was there, Lennox. I saw and heard precisely the same as you, and if you kept notes, you would have all the facts written down, rather than buzzing around in your head.' He went back to the fireplace and picked up a stack of papers from the low table. 'We need to study these carefully.'

'Fine.' I knew he was about to turn tedious. I followed him and sat in a chair, glass in hand. He handed a few dozen pages to me. 'I'll start with 1911, you can read the following year.'

Wallace had signed and dated the papers, but the writing was made by a different hand, presumably by some underling. I flicked through the short notes of explanation, which stated EDR – Ezra De Ruyter – had been shadowed by various members of Wallace's team. The name, date, and location was neatly underlined above the suspect's movements and who he'd accompanied, or encountered.

In 1912 De Ruyter spent his time between shops, restaurants, theatres, and home. He escorted Gloria Thornton on a few occasions, mostly to rehearsals and once to dinner. As I scanned each page, it became clear he saw less and less of her, which tallied with the account she'd given us earlier today at the cafe. Lillian Lamb's name cropped up more and more frequently, evidence that he'd switched his affections to the younger woman.

I placed the notes referring to Gloria and Lillian into one pile and everything else into another, and reached for another stack of yellow papers. These were for the year 1913. His time was spent in similar fashion to 1912, except Lillian Lamb's name was on almost every page. I shuffled through the papers to the last set. On 19th September 1914, Ezra de Ruyter purchased a house in Lillian Lamb's name. The address was number twenty-one, Chester Square.

'Swift, where did De Ruyter live?'

'De Ruyter House.'

'Isn't that where the Birdcage murders were?'

'Yes, he inherited it, remember.'

'They all died there.' The thought made my skin crawl.

'I expect he had it decorated first,' he said dryly.

'Hm.' I didn't share policemen's black humour. 'Where is it?'

'Chester Square.'

I glanced at the window; the sun was lower in the sky. 'We should go and take a look before dark.'

'Why?'

'To be thorough, like proper detectives.' I didn't give him chance to argue. I gathered up the papers, including the ones in front of him and stuffed them into the envelope. 'I'll take these to Greggs for safekeeping.'

'Lennox,' he protested, but he was too late. I walked out with Foggy at my heels and went to my room.

'We're off out, old chap,' I told my trusted retainer, and held out the envelope. 'Hold onto this would you?'

'Certainly sir.' He was in the chair by the fire. I think he'd been asleep – his face looked crumpled. 'I will be leaving for the Ritz shortly before dinner,' he warned.

'We'll be back by then.' I looked at my little dog, his eyes bright with expectation. 'Keep Foggy with you.'

'Certainly, sir.'

I found my greatcoat in the wardrobe, pulled it out and shrugged it on. 'And tell Pinner we'll be dining in.'

'Yes, sir.'

I found Swift coming along the corridor. He was wearing his overcoat and hat, a look of irritation of his face. 'Lennox, is there really any need…'

'Yes,' I replied and headed for the stairs.

Chester Square was some little way from Belgrave Square, where the Cliftons lived. We took the same route across Green Park, and crossed busy roads to find the genteel glory of Chester Square.

The usual rows of white Georgian mansions with black painted ironwork formed a frame around the communal garden. It ran the length of the square, which was actually a rectangle, and had been laid out in similar style to most London parks: trees, grass, shrubs, and pathways peppered with benches, fountains, or the occasional statue. The leitmotif, it would appear, for gracious living.

'De Ruyter House.' Swift stopped outside a very large mansion, even larger than Clifton's manse, and gazed up at it. 'What do you want to do now?'

The interior shutters were closed, the chimneys were void of trailing smoke: the place had a deserted look about it. I went up and rapped the brass door knocker. Nothing happened.

'Nobody lives there no more.' A paperboy was passing, delivering copies of the *Evening Standard*. 'It's haunted y'know, by all of them what died in it. If ye give me a penny I'll tell ye all about it.'

'We already—' Swift began, but I was delving in my pocket for a coin.

'Here.' I gave him thruppence. 'Who was living here recently?'

The scruffy urchin grinned with delight. 'Cor, thanks, guv!' He put it carefully inside his woollen glove. 'It were that Lord what killed 'is family. He 'ad a butler, two maids, an' a bloke what helped 'im get dressed. Then he died last week – in all the papers it was – and there's even more written about it tonight.' He dug into his large sack and pulled one out. 'Here, see, another of them was poisoned with chocolates, and it were that actress, Gloria Thornton, what did it! Just amazin' it is, like the moving pictures, only real.'

'What happened to the staff?' Swift asked.

'Scarpered.' The lad wore a school cap over bushy brown hair, a thick duffel coat that was too large for him, trousers too short, and a cheery expression. He reminded me of an older version of my bootboy, Tommy. 'The cops came in three motors. There were loads of them, an' they searched all through the 'ouse. Took them two days, an' they took the servants away to the Yard to interrogate them. Then afterwards they came back to get their stuff and then they cleared off. House 'as been shut up since.'

'Is there any way into it?' I asked, jangling coins in my pocket.

He was quick to catch on. 'Me big brother used to go in there, after that explosion what killed all them toffs. It were empty for years before the war. They wouldn't let no-one live there, 'cause they didn't know who did it. My brother said there was a coal chute round the back what weren't locked, and some of the kids used to go in there for a lark. I never been in though, I was only a nipper then.'

'Thank you.' I took out a silver sixpence and gave it to him.

'A tanner! Cor, that's great.' He grinned and skipped off, whistling gaily.

'You wasted your money,' Swift remarked as we walked toward the end of the road, looking for a passage to the rear of the houses. 'The police would never leave a coal chute unbarred – every burglar in the city would be in there.'

'It's worth the chance,' I told him. There was a narrow alley almost hidden behind a jutting wall and a cluster of battered dustbins. We skirted around them and into the dark passage; it smelled of rats and dogs. I lit my torch and we trod carefully to emerge into a muddy lane bordered by high wooden fences. The sun was slipping below the houses, long slanting rays and black shadows giving the place a foreboding air. We walked along the track and stopped at the rear of De Ruyter House.

'There aren't any lights on in the windows.'

'Of course there aren't,' Swift replied.

There was a narrow gate amid the fencing. I tried it; it was locked.

'Told you.' Swift sounded smug. 'And even if we could get over the fence, I guarantee the chute will be locked too.'

'Fine.' I stood back to peer above the top of the wooden panelling. There were a few leafless trees to be seen between us and the house, but little else. 'This is number eleven.'

'Yes…' Swift sounded suspicious.

I walked on, counting the houses, then stopped. 'And this is number twenty-one.'

'What of it?' Swift demanded.

I tried the gate. It opened at a push. 'Lillian Lamb lives here.'

'Lennox, you did this deliberately,' he accused.

The house was as dark as De Ruyter's, except for a faint glow of light in a room downstairs – it looked like a kitchen, and its door was standing wide open.

# CHAPTER 18

'You planned this, Lennox,' Swift hissed as we approached the house.

I could confess, or I could remain silent. I chose the latter. I hesitated at the door, and decided I'd best knock first. I tapped on the panelling. We waited; our breath streamed white in the air.

'Come on,' Swift said when nothing happened, and stepped over the threshold. He didn't call out, he merely walked into the kitchen. It was as cold as the small garden we'd just crossed – the door must have been open for a while. Coals were still smouldering in the stove; a dim light bulb hung over a plain pine table, illuminating the room. The rest of the house looked to be in near darkness. I ran my torch beam round then went over to a door facing the one we'd just entered.

There was something wrong. We could both sense it; the hairs on the back of my neck prickled with tension.

'Hello?' I shouted out, making Swift jump.

'Lennox,' he hissed under his breath, then called up the stairs, 'Miss Lamb?'

We were in a spacious hallway, expensively decorated in the modern monochromatic style. A chrome framed mirror hung above an umbrella-stand placed near the front porch, two doors led off, and the staircase ran up against one wall.

'Perfume,' I said. The scent was strong.

'Yes.' Swift nodded. 'Come on.'

We raced up the stairs, our steps muffled by a thick carpet running along its centre. I shone my torch about: there were wall switches, but we didn't pause to turn them on. I swept my beam across a silk scarf strewn on the floor, its peacock hues brightly coloured and dappled with blood. A door gaped open – we ran through it.

A young woman lay prone in front of the fire, curled on her side, one hand resting palm up, the other tucked around her waist. A blood-soaked cap covered her face. More red spots had spattered onto her black and white uniform.

'Hell,' Swift swore and reached the light switch to flick it on.

I knelt next to her, moving the cap aside to feel her neck for a pulse. 'She's alive.'

'Alive?' He strode over.

'Just barely.' There was blood under her head, congealing on the thick wool rug. 'She must be Lillian Lamb's maid.'

'I'll call an ambulance, and then Billings.' He looked

about, realised there wasn't a telephone in the room, and sped off in search of one.

I remained with the maid, gazing down at her...a plain girl, dark hair, clear skin as pale as death, which was unnerving. I wasn't sure what was the best course of action; she was unconscious, and barely breathing. Should I put a towel or something under her head? I turned my torch off, dropped it into my pocket, then placed my hand on hers – it was cold and clammy. I gave it a gentle squeeze. She didn't respond, so I went to the pretty French bed and pulled the top cover off, then carefully placed it over the length of her body. Her head wound appeared to have stopped bleeding. I remained by her side, then realised there was nothing more I could do for her.

I decided to take a look about. The room had been ripped apart as though by a madman: hairbrushes and perfume bottles dashed from the dressing table, shattering the glass and leaving the room engulfed in scent. Expensive dresses had been dragged from opened wardrobes and thrown across the room, some ripped apart at the seams.

The glitter of spilled contents attracted me to a large jewellery box, lying smashed at the base of the far wall. It had been expensive, inlaid with mother of pearl on an ebony base.

Ruby and emerald earrings, gold bracelets, a jumble of chains and pendants, a heavy necklace set with amethysts, and a leather covered half-moon case were amid the splintered remains. I recognised the type – my mother had one, it was locked in a trunk in the attic of my home; I was going to give it to Persi for her next birthday, or sell it and pay off the mortgage, if needs must.

The case was new. I picked it up and flipped the brass catch to lift the lid; sparks of light flashed off an arc of glittering diamonds. It was a tiara, exquisite in the way of finely wrought riches. I assumed it to be the same one as in Lillian Lamb's portrait, although that had been a mere blaze of white dots on canvas, whereas this was a very solid reality.

The jeweller's name was printed in gold on the lid's silk lining: *Cadogan Bros, Bruton Street, Mayfair*, with a crest below, signifying the Royal Warrant. I picked up the tiara, turning it over in my hands, observing the expert craftsmanship and stunning stones dazzling with light. It was beautiful, but of unusual design. I returned it to its case and flipped the clasp down to close it firmly. I noticed an imprint stamped into the brass: Bronski'. That was strange – there couldn't be many with the name – the only Bronski I knew of was a chap who reloaded rifle cartridges.

I rooted through the rest of the jewellery. It was an expensive collection, but nothing out of the ordinary for the wealthy classes. Lillian Lamb had only been a mistress but she'd been showered with riches, including this house… Perhaps she'd been dearly loved – I thought back to the portrait of the lady in the painting; somehow that didn't ring true, what was it that had bothered me? I'd been dazzled by her beauty, but there was something…I suppose it was the sense of display, as though she were a trophy––

Swift walked in. 'They're on their way. Don't touch anything.' He went straight to the maid. 'You should have stayed with her, Lennox.'

'She's comatose, Swift, there's nothing I could do.' I picked up the leather case and carried it over to him. 'Look.'

'We're not supposed to touch…' he repeated in exasperation.

'Tiaras are usually set with stones of varying sizes, it's part of the style.' I opened the box and handed the bauble to him. 'These diamonds are all the same size.'

He turned it over with precise movements. 'Billings said the diamonds attached to the Birdcage were one carat each.'

'Precisely, and these are the right size.'

He gazed at it and swore quietly.

Jangling bells in the road outside signalled the arrival of police cars. Seconds later voices were heard, followed by boots on flagstones.

'I'll go and let them in,' Swift said and strode out. I heard the front door open, felt the draught, then heard the sound of men in the hallway.

'And there weren't any other servants in the house?' Billings' voice was the loudest coming up the stairs.

'Only the maid,' Swift answered, his voice muted.

'Are you sure, have you searched the place?' Billings snapped a question.

'She only had one maid living in, sir,' another voice answered. 'A cook and cleaner came in every morning before breakfast and left at five.'

'Find them and take them to the Yard for questioning,' Billings ordered. 'And find Lillian Lamb.'

'Yes, sir.' I heard the rattling steps of someone going back down the stairs.

'Lennox, this is becoming a habit.' Billings entered ahead of the rest.

I didn't answer, merely gave him a nod of the head.

'She was attacked?' Billings crossed directly to the maid. Two medics in white coats came in behind him, carrying a stretcher.

'There's blood beneath the head,' Swift told him.

Billings stood by as the medics stooped over the unconscious maid; they worked with methodical efficiency.

'Search the place. Start from the top, make it thorough,' Billings barked. Four more men had arrived and instantly turned around to take the next flight of stairs up.

'It must have happened in the last two hours,' Swift said. 'The fire is still burning.'

One of the medics sat back on his haunches. 'The blood is from a head wound. It looks as though she hit the edge of the fireplace. We will move her to the hospital, and the doctor can put her under the X-ray machine.'

'What's her chances?' Billings was coldly professional.

'Oh, I'm always the optimist,' the chap replied as the other manoeuvred the stretcher closer to the girl. 'It'll depend if there's a crack in the skull, or a brain bleed, but she's a young lass and strong by the looks of her.' His gaze switched to his colleague. 'Let's get her loaded, Bert.'

They lifted her onto the heavy canvas stretcher, wrapped her in a large grey blanket, then firmly tucked it into place around her.

I recognised the procedure. 'Medical Corps?'

'RAMC, yeah, both of us.' He referred to the Royal Army Medical Corps. 'Right, Bert, she's ready to go.'

They carried her out of the room, skilfully steering through the doorway and down the stairs.

'What the hell's all this about,' Billings muttered through his teeth.

Neither Swift nor I had an answer to that.

Swift knelt to examine the blood-stained rug where the maid had been lying. He used a magnifying glass, which he'd had in his pocket, along with his usual detecting paraphernalia. He took his time over it, then stood up again. 'Nothing apparent.'

'Do you think the attacker had expected Lillian Lamb to be here?' I asked.

'Her, or something she had hidden here.' Billings scanned the room, a deep furrow between his brows.

'Swift said you'd interviewed the lady,' I asked.

'Twice.' He nodded. 'The day after De Ruyter died. At the time, we'd pegged it as an unexplained death, but once we knew it was murder I came back here and interviewed her myself. That was three days ago.'

'Before you knew about the invitations?' I said.

His frown became a scowl. 'Yes.'

'Presumably there wasn't one found in De Ruyter's possession?' Swift's tone was respectful.

'No, nor in his house.' Billings' answer was curt, then he sighed and made an effort to be civil. 'Lamb or De Ruyter must have had one; he was the star of the show – something lured him to Brundles.'

'Someone said he ate there on occasion,' Swift stated.

'Yes, but never on Ladies' Night,' Billings replied.

'Perhaps the attacker was looking for the invitation.' I suggested.

My gaze ran across the mantelpiece. It was undisturbed. An ormolu clock ticked with mechanical precision; a pair of gilded cherubs sat either side of it, and two fancy porcelain candlesticks took position at each end. They'd all escaped the destruction, and none showed signs of supporting papers or envelopes.

'They could have found whatever they were looking for before they got this far.' Swift had followed my line of sight.

'Or they were interrupted by the maid, and attacked her,' Billings replied.

'And then fled,' I added.

'Obviously,' Billings said sharply.

Two of the officers came in. 'All clear upstairs, guv,' one of them said.

'You men, carry on here – scour the room down to the floorboards. You two...' He nodded at me and Swift. 'Come with me.' He turned abruptly and left the room.

We followed as he barrelled downstairs; a big man, his coat open and flapping against the bannisters.

He led us into the small kitchen. Someone had shut the door but it was still freezing cold. We sat at the pine table, the single bulb throwing a feeble pool of light above us.

'We know about your meeting with the suspects this afternoon,' Billings began in a pugnacious manner.

'What of it?' I challenged.

'Eyes and ears at Brundles, is what I said,' he rapped. 'Now I find you at every turn.'

'Actually we're ahead of you,' I needled him.

'You just listen, mister…' He jabbed a finger at me.

'Cut the bluster, Billings,' I snapped. He'd been bellicose since he arrived. 'You brought us in and you've blown hot and cold since we started. Clifton wants us to look out for his wife, you want information you can't access, and we've delivered on both points.'

I thought he was going to demand I tell him exactly what we'd delivered, fortunately he banged his trilby down on the tabletop, instead. 'Damn it to hell, another body is the last thing I need.'

'The maid would probably agree with you,' I said wryly.

'It sounds as though there's a good chance she'll survive,' Swift reminded us.

Billings brooded, his dark brows drawn together, then he shifted in his seat. 'We questioned Gloria Thornton this afternoon…I don't think she poisoned the chocolates.'

Neither did I, but refrained from saying so.

'Do you have leads on who did?' Swift asked, his angular face sharply defined in the pool of light.

'No.' Billings looked down at his hands. His fingernails were bitten short.

'Then why don't you believe it was Gloria?' I asked.

'Copper's instinct, if you like,' he admitted. 'We see plenty of criminals, liars the bloody lot of them, but I thought she was telling the truth.'

'She's an actress,' Swift reminded him.

'I know, and probably a good one, but there's a difference between parroting lines written by somebody else and answering questions in a police station.'

'Are you letting her go?' I watched him, the deep creases around his eyes betraying the pressure he was under.

'No, of course not. We might have instincts but we don't rely on them,' he replied tersely. 'We'll keep her in custody as long as the law allows, but we can't charge her unless we find something substantial to charge her with.'

'But she can't have attacked Lillian Lamb's maid if she was in a cell,' I reasoned.

'That's blindingly obvious,' he retorted. 'But it doesn't mean she's innocent of poisoning Phillips.'

'Have you received the test results from the chocolates?' Swift tried to calm the tension.

'They'd been sliced open at the bottom, the insides removed and mixed with powder containing potassium cyanide, then put back together again. The bases had been melted together, probably over a candle flame,' Billings explained. 'It's early days, but the wonks think it was silver polish. Phillips had eaten three chocolates before he started vomiting.'

'My butler said silver polish contains potassium cyanide,' I mentioned.

'Your butler?' Billings was sardonic.

'Greggs is remarkably knowledgable about such things,' I replied, and added, 'We went through the war together.'

Billings frowned at the obtuse remark. Swift pulled out his notebook and pen and wrote the date, place, and who was present.

'You'd better make sure you keep those notes safe,' Billings warned.

'Yes, sir.' Swift nodded.

'Surely the chocolates tasted off?' I said.

'He had them with his morning brandy,' Billings replied.

Swift's gaze shot up. 'He drank brandy for breakfast?'

Billings shrugged. 'Gloria Thornton said it was his standard start to the day, and it was found in the stomach contents, which confirmed it.'

'Did you find anything significant in his flat?' Swift asked as he wrote.

'No, nor in Gloria Thornton's,' Billings replied briskly. 'But there was a register at her boutique which listed all her clients. Lady Estelle Clifton was one, so was her sister, Lady Marina Stanford.'

'We thought there was a connection – they all wore the same make-up.' Swift stated the obvious.

Billings nodded. 'Gloria's assistant wasn't particularly helpful, but she said that the ladies were on amicable terms and sometimes had tea together. Apparently Gloria was also an advisor on diets and concocted special menus for her clients – she's got a good business head on her.' There was admiration in his voice.

'Then her aversion to eating chocolate must be well known.' Swift made a note.

'Was Lillian Lamb on her client list?' I asked.

'No, and according to people we've interviewed, there was animosity between them,' Billings replied.

'I suppose they were rivals of sorts,' I said.

'Hm,' Billings grunted, then stated, 'De Ruyter had a portrait of Lillian Lamb made recently.'

'We know, we saw it,' I replied. He frowned at that.

'Did De Ruyter actually commission it?' Swift quickly stepped in.

'He did.' Billings nodded. 'And paid for it. We found the receipt in his house.'

Swift wrote this snippet down.

'Phillips told us he'd stopped doing portraits, and he hated De Ruyter,' I said.

'Well, he didn't hate his money.' Billings was acerbic.

'The diamond dust that had been fed to De Ruyter.' I switched tack. 'Were the grains all the same size?'

A grim smile creased Billings' lips. 'You've been doing a lot of sniffing around.'

'Yes,' I replied.

I thought he was trying to sidestep the question, but then he admitted, 'They were of random sizes; the dust didn't come from an industrial source.'

'We were told diamonds could be shattered with a hammer,' Swift remarked.

'And that's probably how the dust was prepared,' Billings acknowledged. 'Someone smashed a diamond into tiny fragments, and kept on hitting it until it was ground to dust.'

'Very few people could afford such a means of murder,' I said.

'Precisely, Major Lennox. There's a toff behind this.' Billings picked up his hat from the table, pushed the creases firmly into place, then put it on his head. 'Right, I'd better go and see what the lads have found.'

'There's a tiara among her jewellery,' I told him. 'It's from Cadogan's. The diamonds are all the same size – could they have come from the Birdcage victims?'

A tic suddenly pulsed in Billings' temple. 'I'll take a look,' he said, then shook his head. 'Who the hell would decorate jewellery with diamonds cut out of corpses?'

'A devil,' I replied.

# CHAPTER 19

'He confided in us.' Swift was overjoyed as we walked back toward Green Park in the dark. Reporters had descended outside Lillian Lamb's before we'd even exited the house. We left by the kitchen door and skirted the back alley to avoid them. I wondered how they communicated the news between them, as they seemed to know everything that happened within minutes of the event.

We entered Chester Square and strode along to the other side of the gardens. Apart from the reporters outside Lillian Lamb's house, the streets were devoid of life. Lights shone through gaps in curtains, smoke from a million coal fires seeped into the cold night air, and London suddenly felt a lonely place as our footsteps echoed on the pavement. I raised my collar as we extended our stride.

'What did he confide?' I demanded.

'His thoughts about the case, the diamond dust, and Gloria Thornton's innocence.' He listed the nuggets of information Billings had tossed our way.

I was more interested in dinner, and the connections

between the suspects. 'Gloria knows Estelle and Marina through her boutique, and they take tea together. They're more closely connected than they'd led us to believe.'

He turned serious. 'Yes, we've already agreed they're all in it together…but which one is the actual killer.'

We crossed the road to gain Green Park. A row of glowing lamps each side of the path lit our way.

'Do you think Lillian Lamb knew where the diamonds had come from?'

'Yes,' he said without hesitation.

'Really?' I almost stopped walking.

'Of course she would know, and I doubt she had any scruples about it all, or she wouldn't have been De Ruyter's mistress in the first place.'

'It's hard to believe a woman could be so…iniquitous.'

He turned tetchy. 'Lennox you really must give up these romantic delusions about women.'

He was a fine one to talk; he was always ready to rescue any damsel in distress. I shoved my hands in my pockets. 'Do you think the attacker was looking for the invitation?'

'Possibly, but we need to focus on facts now, Lennox.'

I was pleased to reach Brundles; George swung the door open for us. 'Evening, Major Lennox, sir. Inspector Swift. Them reporters have run off again.'

'They're in Chester Square,' I informed him.

'Are they now?' His brows rose.

I grinned and continued into the foyer. Rossetti emerged from his office. I'd been expecting it.

'A tragedy...' he began.

'They think she will recover,' Swift was quick to cut him off.

'Ah, that is indeed a blessing.' His smooth face lost some tension. 'After Mr Phillips' misfortune, we were concerned that events were spiralling out of control.'

'Whose control?' I asked sharply, which caused a frown to crease between his eyes.

He recovered quickly. 'The madman behind these atrocities, of course. I wish you good evening.' He gave a sharp nod of the head and retreated back to his office.

We took the stairs with quick steps and parted outside my room.

'Eight o'clock,' Swift said. 'I'll come and find you.'

'Righto,' I replied, and entered my room to be greeted with yips of delight from Foggy. Greggs looked up in disconcerted surprise.

'Erm... sir.'

'What are you doing, Greggs?'

He was sitting in the armchair, and was in the process of snipping the newspaper into pieces. Actually, it was more than one newspaper judging by the cuttings all over the floor.

He reasserted his dignity and puffed himself up. 'I am gathering articles about the case, sir.' He waved a large pair of scissors in the direction of his handiwork.

'Why?'

'For my scrapbook, sir. It is a hobby.'

I peered at one of the cuttings; a photograph was included – Swift emerging from the entrance of Number 5, Old Bond Street. There was another of me on the steps of Brundles. I read some of the report. It was journalistic hyperbole and ridiculously overdramatised. 'Was this in the *Standard*?'

'It was sir, and in the morning newspapers. There will be more tomorrow.'

'How do you know?'

'Because the reporters ran off earlier, sir. So I imagined something must have happened.' He said this with a gleam of expectation in his eye.

I sighed and sat down on the armchair opposite. 'Brandy first, Greggs.'

'Certainly, sir.' He removed strips of newspaper from his lap and went in search of the decanter. It had found its way into his room. He returned with a sheepish grin and poured a generous snifter.

'Have one yourself, if there's any left,' I told him.

'There is more than sufficient, sir,' he assured me and poured a modest tipple into a glass.

'It was Lillian Lamb's maid.' I announced the news he'd been waiting for.

'Oh.' His eyes rounded. 'Why?'

'No idea.' I sipped my brandy, then told him the events of the afternoon, ending with the tiara and the diamonds.

'The diamonds from the bodies?' His chins wobbled in genuine dismay.

'Well, it's not confirmed, but we think it likely.' I finished my drink and put the glass down on the low table. 'I should dress for dinner, old chap.'

'Indeed, sir.' He got up and shuffled toward the wardrobe. 'M'lady called on the telephone while you were out.'

'I'll ring her later,' I replied.

'I'm afraid there has been a calamity, sir.' He brought over my evening togs.

'Not Tommy's chicken?'

'I am afraid so, sir.' He looked suitably hangdog.

I handed him my tweed jacket. 'Dead?'

'No, sir, but the attempt to fix the creature's leg was singularly unsuccessful.'

'What happened?'

'The leg fell off, sir.'

'What!' I'd been trying to step into my dress trousers and nearly toppled over.

'The tourniquet had been tied too tightly, sir.'

'Ha, we're having it for Sunday dinner, are we?' I tucked in my shirt, then adjusted my braces.

'I very much doubt it, sir,' he said dryly, and passed the bow tie over.

I hated tying bow ties; it was always such a fiddle. I went to the mirror. 'What did her ladyship say?'

'She suggested Tommy be allowed to keep the bird in his room on a perch above a sandbox.'

'He'll catch something from it,' I disagreed.

'Or possibly next to the kitchen stove, sir.'

'Then we'll all catch something from it.' I finished the bow tie and turned about. 'Shoes?'

'Certainly, sir.' He'd polished them to a perfect sheen.

'By the way, you were right about the silver polish in the chocolates.'

He grinned in delight. 'Really, sir? Miss Fairchild will be most interested to hear it.'

I grinned. 'What time does the dancing start?'

'It is a dinner dance, sir. I am about to commence dressing,' he said as though it were a major announcement.

'You can exchange theories about who did what, over your meal.'

'Possibly, sir.'

Swift walked in. 'Lennox…oh Greggs, where are those papers I gave you earlier?'

'The yellow ones, sir? They are safely hidden inside the pillowcase in my room.'

'Good, well done.' He clapped his hands together. 'Dinner, Lennox?'

'Right behind you old chap,' I told him.

'I telephoned Billings, they found Lillian Lamb,' he said as we walked downstairs.

'In one piece?'

'Yes, she was at some dress shop.'

'Buying mourning clothes?' I suggested.

'I didn't ask,' he replied dryly. 'But I doubt it.'

I'd hoped for a quiet meal with little need to engage the brain for a while, but Dr Moore called out a greeting as soon as we walked into the dining room.

'There you are,' he hailed us. 'Well, well, you've stirred up a hornet's nest, haven't you?' He came toward us. 'Oh, and you've brought your doggie.' He bent to pat Fogg's head; the dog wagged his tail in response.

'Would you care to join us?' Swift was polite.

'I would, yes, indeed I would.' Moore was in jovial mood. 'Coppers want more statements from us, y'know.'

'Why?' I asked.

'After Phillips was killed. They want to hear where we all were. That'll rile Clifton. Doesn't rank himself with the hoi polloi; doesn't expect to be treated like 'em either.'

Browne arrived to guide us to a quiet table. He was his usual dour self, but made attempts to be solicitous, even offering to spread napkins on our laps – which we declined.

'Would you prefer white or red, gentlemen?' he asked.

'The same white we had last evening, please,' Moore was quick to reply. 'It's a jolly good refresher to start with.'

I wasn't in the mood to chat, so sipped my wine and let my eyes wander about the room. It was busy, mostly with city types; they were becoming more prevalent nowadays. The world had begun to rebuild itself after the war, and trade was picking up. One of the eccentrics was seated alone at a table near the magnificent fireplace, a spot reserved for the favoured few. He wore a boater and flamboyant bow tie with a striped jacket. It wasn't the customary evening rig, but he'd obviously been granted dispensation. I wondered who he was, a poet probably, or a highbrow scribbler of some sort.

The entrée arrived. It was another delicate offering; thin slices of seared venison, chopped apples, sprouts, and quince jelly. It was really very tasty. I ate quietly, sharing a few morsels with Fogg.

'What?'

'I just asked Dr Moore if any of the ladies had visited the club before.' Swift was tetchy at having to repeat himself. 'He mentioned New Year's Eve.'

'It's the only other time they come,' Dr Moore said. He'd already cleared his plate. 'They're allowed into the garden to watch the fireworks with the rest of us. It's quite a treat.' He smiled benignly.

'The fireworks or the ladies?' I said.

'Oh, haha! Both, of course.' He laughed then drained his glass. Browne was quick to step forward and refill it. 'We chaps go and stand outside, the ladies are shown in from the garden gate, the staff serve the booze, we all watch the whizzbangs, then go home. Or rather they do, I live here.'

'Has Lillian Lamb ever attended?' I asked him.

Moore grasped his glass. 'I think she was in the garden this New Year just gone.' He turned to Browne. 'Do you recall, old fellow?'

Browne had remained in close vicinity. 'I believe she attended with Lord De Ruyter, sir.'

'But only in the garden,' Moore insisted.

'There is a ladies' powder room just beyond the Strangers Room, sir. She may have entered the club to take advantage of the facility.' Browne supplied the answer.

'Ah yes.' Moore nodded. 'Forgotten about that. They had to put one in when they started inviting ladies.'

'How many couples usually attend Ladies' Night?' I asked Browne.

'It varies, sir.' He became circumspect.

'Were all the members given the chance to attend the dinner this year?' Swift added, although he knew they couldn't have been.

Browne looked uncomfortable and began backing away. 'If you will excuse me, sir,' he replied and cleared off before we could ask him anything more.

'Ladies' Night was restricted, wasn't it, Dr Moore?' Swift turned to him. 'To De Ruyter and the bereaved only.'

'Nothing to do with me.' Dr Moore tried to look clueless, and failed. He shifted the topic. 'I heard Lillian Lamb's maid was injured.'

'Where did you hear that?' Swift asked.

'Oh, just chat, you know.' Moore drained his glass and looked about for a refill.

Dinner arrived. I thought we'd upset the old fellow enough and turned the subject to cricket. That started him off on a rambling conversation and we ate as he talked. Dessert was apple crumble; I had cream rather than custard. We called it a night after that and bade a polite good evening to the doctor. He ambled off to the smoking room. We left for our chambers with Foggy at our heels.

'I'll fetch the papers from Greggs' room,' Swift offered.

'I'll fetch the decanter,' I offered. I found Tubbs in front of the fire and picked him up. I could swear he was heavier than when we'd arrived. We all repaired to Swift's chamber. He had the papers, I had the decanter and cat. Neither were standard tools of investigation, but both quite useful in their way.

'Moore's involved,' Swift said as he closed the door behind us.

'I know, we've already agreed on this, Swift.' I put Tubbs on the hearthrug. Fogg went to join him and they began one of their patting games.

Swift was engrossed in his papers, placing them studiously on the low table. 'Only the relatives of the Birdcage victims were at Ladies' Night, Rossetti must have excluded everyone else.'

'Yes.' I don't know why he kept stating the obvious. I poured a snifter each of brandy from the decanter.

'It's important, Lennox. It's building the picture.' He was still separating the papers into piles.

'We'll need coffee, too,' I decided and put the decanter on the table. 'I'll ring for some.'

He tapped the yellow papers. 'I think we should make a careful analysis of De Ruyter's movements and the people he knew, and look for any aberration.'

'Coffee for two please,' I told the switchboard. 'And biscuits of some sort…and some treats for my dog and cat.'

'Certainly, sir. Is there anything else we could provide?' the operator asked with polite professionalism.

'No, thank you.' I replaced the receiver on the hook.

'And we should write a synopsis of each—'

'Swift, just read the damn things.' I handed him his snifter.

'But I really—'

'Note anything suspicious,' I told him as I sat down next to the papers, picked up a pile, and began reading the damn things for the second time.

The arrival of coffee broke the silence. I took the tray from the waiter and did the honours myself. It took two cups and three snifters to reach the end of all the notes.

'De Ruyter purchased Lillian Lamb's house and signed the deeds over to her in 1914,' Swift said.

'I know, that's where I saw her address.'

'They visited numerous jewellery shops the same year, but it doesn't list what they bought.'

'Jewellery, I'd imagine.'

'Very helpful, Lennox,' he said with sarcasm.

I grinned, then decided I should apply myself. 'Billings said the investigation was brought to a halt when the war began in July 1914. De Ruyter was granted his inheritance just after that.'

'Including the diamonds retrieved from the bodies,' Swift reminded me.

'Yes.' I sighed. 'Lillian Lamb is barely mentioned in the year of the explosion, but her name appears more and more frequently afterwards. By 1914 she's on almost every page... How old was she at the time of the explosion?'

'There's mention of a dinner to celebrate her twenty-first

birthday in June 1914,' Swift said. 'The Birdcage murders were…' He looked up at the date on the event board. 'May 24$^{th}$ 1911. Just short of her eighteenth birthday.'

'Hm…' I picked up my brandy. 'They went to a pub before Christmas in 1914.'

'Yes, I thought that peculiar.' Swift shuffled the papers in his hand.

'It was the Chequers Tavern in Duke Street. Do you know it?'

'Lennox, St James's is toff territory. I rarely had reason to come here.'

'Well, it's a tradesmen's pub, and not everyone here is a toff.' I was heartily sick of hearing that term. 'It backs onto Masons Yard, and I can't think of a less likely place for someone like De Ruyter to go; he'd have stood out like a sore thumb.'

'It was the first Christmas after the war started, it would probably have been packed with soldiers back on their first home leave.'

I nodded at that. 'Good point.' I finished my brandy and put the glass down. 'Did you notice the brass catch on the tiara case? It was made by Bronski – he used to have a workshop in Masons Yard. He was a good chap, ran a small business reloading rifle cartridges. Everyone took their used brass cartridge cases to Bronski; it was a tradition.'

He digested the information. 'It could be relevant… De Ruyter may have gone there to have his cartridges reloaded.'

'Why would he take his mistress?'

'Hm,' Swift grunted agreement.

I poured another brandy and leaned back in my chair. 'What do you make of it all, Swift?'

He pondered that. 'The suspects were linked by the explosion and are apparently still acquainted. Phillips and Gloria Thornton were close friends and neighbours, Estelle and Marina are sisters – and clients of Gloria's boutique. Lord Clifton and Stanford are brothers-in-law and they both belong to Brundles. Dr Moore lives at Brundles. Rossetti is master, and Browne is steward.'

'And Phillips was commissioned to paint Lillian Lamb's portrait,' I said, and added, 'maybe they were having an affair and wanted to bump off De Ruyter.'

'Why not just poison him then? Or rig up an accident? And would Phillips really have wanted Lillian cut off from De Ruyter's funds?'

'True,' I agreed. 'I can't imagine either of them would.'

'He didn't leave a will...' Swift mused. 'I'm surprised by that.'

'Why? He had no family, he only cared about himself.'

'What about Lillian Lamb?'

'Perhaps he was ready to trade her in?'

'There wasn't any sign of that,' he remarked wryly. 'She has the least motive of any of them.'

'Maybe that's why he didn't write a will.' I grinned.

He laughed. Foggy had been asleep but suddenly sat up, his ears cocked. Tubbs woke up too, and yawned, then looked about to see what was happening.

'I should phone Florence.' Swift looked at his watch.

'And I need some fresh air,' I said, thinking I'd take my little duo out for a breather. 'Good night, Swift.'

# CHAPTER 20

I wandered downstairs, cat under my arm, dog running about my feet and my skeleton keys jangling in my pocket. The keys were a treasured prize I'd taken from a petty thief a couple of years before and I'd grown quite proficient in their use.

The walled garden behind the Strangers Room intrigued me; I'd never been in it before. I looked about – there were very few members around, and those that were, were in their cups.

The Strangers Room lay in darkness, lit only by the faint glow of moonlight through the open curtains. I crossed to the area next to the bay window, which I'd seen Browne open. I ran my fingers over the wallpaper and felt a small hand hole and lock recessed in the wall. I pushed. It resisted. I bent to stare at the lock, then deftly picked it.

Fogg dashed out as soon as I swung the door open. I followed, stepping out onto a stone-flagged terrace, and continued onto frozen grass, then put Tubbs down. The garden mostly consisted of lawn skirted by shrubs and surrounded by a high brick wall. I strolled to the end of the path to where a gate was set in an arch; I tried it, it was locked. There wasn't much else to see, so I called the little duo. They ignored me. Tubbs went skittering across the grass, then jumped up at Foggy, who was snuffling under a bush. I grabbed the little cat firmly, called Foggy to heel, and returned indoors. I locked the door, and returned to my chamber.

Two bowls of cold chicken had been left on the windowsill. I put them on the floor and let the duo eat their supper, while I went to the desk and picked up the telephone.

'Persi?'

'Oh, there you are. I was about to go to bed.' There was warmth in her voice.

'I've been out all day...' I made my excuses.

'Did you unravel the mystery?'

'Not yet. Some of it is clearer, but there was another murder, and a maid was injured.'

'How unpleasant. What was it about?'

I told her the events; it made me realise how long the day had been.

'And the grains in the diamond dust had been ground down very finely, but were of irregular size, so someone had smashed up a diamond.'

'That must narrow down the suspects,' she replied.

'Yes, and that's what we've been trying to do, but they're maintaining a united front.'

'Even after one of them was poisoned today?'

'Perhaps that's why Lillian Lamb's house was targeted...'

'What do you mean?'

'Well, she's the only outsider. They may be trying to point us towards her to relieve the pressure on them.'

'By injuring her maid?' She sounded tired. I realised how late it was.

'That was probably an accident, but...I don't know, perhaps they wanted to plant something incriminating?'

'I'd have expected them to be searching for something.'

'We did, too, but...' I wasn't sure what I thought. 'It's all a bit of a puzzle. Swift and I keep agreeing on a course of action, then something happens, and we go off on a tangent.'

'That must upset Jonathan.' Her voice warmed with laughter.

She was right. Swift had a methodical mind, whereas I tended to chase the scent on the wind.

I switched tack. 'What happened to Tommy's chicken?'

She laughed again. 'It's now called Hoppy. You should have seen their faces when its leg fell off, it was quite awful. Brendan had used cotton to tie the splint on yesterday, but the bird would insist on pecking at it and of course it came loose. The other chickens took the cotton for a worm and chased her around the garden until she was exhausted. That was when the boys decided to use copper wire...' She paused to yawn. 'And tied it too tightly. Now she can only perch, but the boys hope she will be able to shuffle about.'

'Tommy can't keep it in his bedroom.' I was quite stern.

'No, but if she recovers, I think we will need a cockerel to keep order, or the others will bully her to death.'

'How have you been?' I asked, not wanting to waste our conversation discussing chickens.

'Oh, terribly busy. Have you any idea how dense the bramble bushes have grown in the walled garden? We had to use an axe apiece to cut them back, and now we're all covered in scratches.'

'So, it hasn't all been tea and cakes with the Women's Institute,' I teased her.

'That's next week. I've invited them for afternoon tea; we're going to discuss a garden fete.'

'What? Persi, we can't…'

She laughed again. 'Sleep well, my love. I miss you.'

'I miss you, too, Persi,' I said and meant it. 'Goodnight.'

I'd intended to go to bed, but there was something urgent I had to do. I raced downstairs and out through the front door.

'George.'

'Sir?' He straightened up.

'I need a cockerel.'

He paused at that. 'Now, sir?'

'No, not now, but soon…before I leave, anyway. It's for my wife, and bootboy.'

He leaned forward to peer at me from under the top hat. 'Should this cockerel be alive or dead, sir?'

'Alive. Someone must sell them.'

'I'm sure they do, sir, probably at one of the markets.

I will put a word out.' What little I could see of him between scarf and topper looked bemused.

'Excellent, thank you.' I gave him a ten-shilling note, which should easily cover a cockerel and a generous tip.

'Good night, sir,' he said with an informal salute.

I wished him the same and returned to the warmth of my room. I slept deeply, squeezed between dog and cat, and woke early next morning to the sound of Greggs' snoring in the adjacent room.

Swift arrived on the doorstep, I'd barely finished dressing and Fogg and Tubbs hadn't emerged from among the bedcovers.

'I've been thinking – you're right, we should interview Lillian Lamb.' He was neatly dressed, hair combed, shoes shined, ready for the day.

'It's too early, Swift.'

'I don't mean at this moment.'

'Good, then we have time for breakfast.' I moved toward the door.

Swift followed. 'The maid is recovering, but she's not able to speak, yet.'

'How do you know?' I enquired.

'It was in this morning's newspaper.'

'And you're taking this as fact?' I was sardonic.

'Hardly, but at least she isn't dead. I could call Billings…'

'No.' I closed the door firmly behind me. 'Come on.'

A number of waiters were present in the Morning Room, but there was a complete absence of members, which was the way I liked things. I'd rarely eaten in the place before, preferring my own company at breakfast.

The decor was pale blue and white, and rather restful. We settled at the best table by the window overlooking the square, where the sun was just rising to shimmer between bare-branched trees in St James's garden.

'There aren't any reporters today,' Swift commented as tea was poured by an attentive waiter.

I wasn't interested in reporters. 'I had a look around the club's garden last night.'

'Oh?' His ears pricked up.

'There was nothing there, but it was because of Lillian Lamb.'

'Lennox, what are you talking about?'

'At first I thought she couldn't be involved in the invitations or the murder, because she'd have to know the layout of the Strangers Room, but if she attended the New Year fireworks, then she may have used the opportunity to come inside.'

He was quick to challenge. 'Even if she had known the layout of the Strangers Room, she'd need the cooperation of Rossetti at the very least, to ensure no other members attended the dinner.'

'Not necessarily; the invitation he received would have caused him to exclude other members,' I countered. 'The message suggested proof of De Ruyter's guilt would be revealed. Rossetti wouldn't have allowed anyone else to attend on that principle alone.'

He mused upon that as the breakfast trolley was wheeled

in. We ordered everything. I asked for dishes to be sent up to Fogg and Tubbs, and Greggs, because he was on holiday.

'We should focus on Dickie Phillips' murder,' Swift said between mouthfuls. 'It's an aberration; it's frightened them all and obviously wasn't part of the plan.'

'It may have been part of somebody's plan.' I cut a sausage in two.

'We need to systematically gather facts, Lennox, not go running off on tangents.'

Actually, there was a tangent I had in mind, but I thought I'd better wait until we were outside before springing it on him.

Half an hour later, after we'd donned coats, gloves, and hats, because it really was freezing outside, I set my scheme into motion.

'Billings is bound to go and interview Lillian Lamb this morning,' I said. We nodded a greeting to George, who was holding the door open for us.

'Yes, I thought he might let us join him.'

'We risk him refusing, and forbidding us from talking to her,' I warned.

He bit his lip in indecision.

'Actually, there's a chap I wanted to see.' I set off purposefully. 'It's not far.'

'No, Lennox...' He was too late – I was already heading in the direction of Masons Yard.

He argued as we strode along King Street. He was still arguing when we reached Masons Yard's gates, which were closed and locked.

'There's a narrow passage by The Chequers Tavern,' I recalled.

'Look, it's not that I mind interviewing this man.' Swift was still simmering. 'But we have to be systematic…'

We were walking in single file through the passage. It was a typical London yard where the true cogs and wheels of the city ground: grimy with soot-rimmed walls, uneven cobbles and the familiar aroma of coal tar, festering damp, and woodsmoke.

The sound of a clanking hammer drew us to an open doorway; it looked as though it had been a blacksmiths at some time in its past.

'Greetings,' I called to the chap bashing a bent bicycle frame back into shape.

'Yeah?' the swarthy man replied. He was dressed in dark dungarees, a thick checkered shirt and a heavy leather jerkin.

'We're looking for Bronski,' I told him. Swift said nothing; he just stood with his arms folded.

'He's cleared out.' He paused to wipe sweat from his brow. 'If ye want yer cartridges loadin', there's a gunsmith back out and up the street.'

'I know, but Bronski was the best. I still have a box of empty cartridges to reload.'

'Ain't you the lucky one,' he replied, then returned to his hammering.

'Hey, Ted.' A short chap emerged from the rear door of the tavern. 'What are you griping about?'

'Couple'a toffs askin' about Bronksi,' the man with the hammer grunted.

The short chap turned to us. 'Ted's not given to chit-chat, he prefers hitting things with hammers.'

'You begger off, Joe Spriggs,' Ted growled.

Spriggs laughed and nodded to me. 'I remember Bronski… Look, I'm just getting going for the day, come and have a drink.' He indicated the pub. I assumed him to be the landlord. He had curly brown hair, a shrewd look in his dark eyes, and a persuasive manner.

'Lead the way,' I said and followed Joe Spriggs into the welcoming arms of The Chequers Tavern. Swift came with us, his sharp face watchful.

'Bitter?' Spriggs picked up a pint glass and held it under a beer tap.

'Please,' I agreed readily.

He waited until the head settled, filled it to the rim and placed in on the brass topped counter in front of me.

'And for yourself?' Spriggs glanced at Swift.

'It's too early.'

Spriggs was undeterred. 'Have a nip of whisky, it's on the house.'

'No, thank you.' Swift was adamant.

I took a sip of bitter; it was excellent stuff. I extracted some coins from my pocket and placed a half-crown on the counter. 'Keep the change.'

Spriggs' grin broadened. He pulled himself a pint and turned to Swift. 'You're a copper.'

Swift pursed his lips, then nodded.

'Anythin' to do with all that stuff in the newspapers?' Spriggs continued.

'No,' Swift lied.

I leaned on the bar to enjoy my pint. The pub was a long narrow room with a counter taking up most of one wall. The remainder was furnished with a scattering of stools and pews, and smelled in the usual way of pubs of spilled beer and stale tobacco.

'What do you recall of Bronski?' I asked Spriggs.

His genial expression didn't alter. 'He was a good bloke – had half a dozen men working for him over in the corner of the yard. His ammo was top quality, if you could afford it.' Spriggs perched on a stool behind the bar. 'Is there a reward for information?'

'Possibly,' I replied. 'What else can you tell us?'

'About Bronski?'

'Yes.'

Spriggs took his time. He sipped his beer, making us wait. 'The war finished his business off. The government requisitioned all the brass, powder and shot. I think he held some stock back, Bronski wasn't stupid.' Spriggs took another sip of beer and wiped his mouth. 'He bought some brass stamping machines and used them to press out fancy little bits and pieces for the jewellers – hinges and clasps for handbags and jewel boxes mostly. He'd have done bigger stuff, but there were factories doin' that, so he had to make do with what he could. Then after the war finished, just when things were picking up, one of his workers came back and set up in competition. The bloke must have done well for himself, because he ended up squeezing Bronski out, along with a few others in the district. The bloke's got a big factory now, down on the docks and lives on Queen Anne's Gate with the nobs. God knows what for, they aren't going to speak to an uncouth foreigner like him.'

'What's his name?' Swift suddenly took an interest.

'You wantin' another drink?' Spriggs asked me, his brows raised in meaningful fashion.

I drew out a crisp pound note from my wallet. 'Just the name, please.'

'Markov. He's Russian.' Spriggs deftly pocketed the money.

'When did he emigrate from Russia?' Swift stood by the bar, next to me, his expression intense.

'I dunno, must be years ago,' Spriggs answered amiably. 'According to gossip, he started off in the East End; there's people from all over the world down there – it's a regular melting pot. Dangerous place though, wouldn't go near it myself.' Spriggs put his empty glass on the counter.

'What did Markov do when he worked for Bronski?' I brought him back to the subject.

'And when?' Swift added.

'He mixed the gunpowder – he'd been a conscript in the Russian Army – we all reckoned he was a deserter. Anyways, he knew his way around gunpowder and shot.' He stopped to cough into a handkerchief, then turned back to us. 'Sorry, I was gassed in the war… Markov left here about the same time I joined up, right at the end of 1914.'

'Where did he go?' I asked.

'No idea.' Spriggs shrugged. 'Someone said back to Russia, but I wouldn't have thought so, not if he was a deserter, and he was too keen on the good life to go back to that kind of poverty.'

'What number in Queen Anne's Gate?' Swift asked the question.

'Haven't the foggiest, but someone down there will tell you – there aren't many Russians in that part of London.' Spriggs grinned.

Swift was already striding toward the front door. 'Come on, Lennox.'

'Right.' I drained my beer, and made to follow. 'And thank you, Spriggs.'

# CHAPTER 21

'We're only going because we need to be thorough.' Swift was pacing along the street. 'This Russian is unlikely to be related to the murders. Queen Anne's Gate is just behind Birdcage Walk. The man would have to be an idiot to choose to live there if he'd been involved in the explosion.'

'It's not actually on Birdcage Walk,' I remarked as we zigzagged through the streets towards Pall Mall. It was quite a distance and I'd have hailed a taxi if it hadn't been such a nice day.

'The connection between De Ruyter and Markov is barely even tenuous, Lennox.' He was clearly beginning to have doubts.

'There are too many coincidences, Swift.' I countered. 'The clasp was stamped with Bronski's name, his workshop was in Masons Yard behind the Chequers Tavern, which is where De Ruyter and Lillian Lamb went at the end of 1914. That's the year the investigation ended, and De Ruyter inherited his money, and the diamonds, and the same time Markov moved away. Then he returned a few years later, rich enough to set up a factory on the docks and buy a house in Queen Anne's Gate. How could a penniless Russian earn enough money in such a short period of time to move into that sort of address?'

'It's possible…' he didn't sounded convinced.

'Let's go and find out, shall we.'

We waited for an omnibus to chug past us on the broad thoroughfare of The Mall, then crossed to enter the expanse of St James's Park. We took the path leading to the lake.

Geese honked on the banks of the water, swans ruffled their feathers, children threw bread to congregating ducks; it was a pretty spot in winter. We strode across the old iron bridge, only pausing for a moment to gaze out over the lake to Buckingham Palace in the distance.

'We need to ask a policeman,' Swift announced as we took a narrow road leading from Birdcage Walk into Queen Anne's Gate.

There weren't any, or not in evidence, anyway. I stopped a middle-aged lady with a basket.

'I don't live 'ere, I'm just bringin' some mendin' to me daughter. She's a maid at Lady Brickhouse's.'

'Ah, excellent.' I gave her my best grin. 'But you must have heard of this Russian chap, Markov.'

'I'm not one to gossip, and me daughter ain't neither… but it's caused a bit of a stir. He's a rough 'un. Not like the usual sort what lives 'ere.'

'I'm a detective.' Swift was formal. 'Scotland Yard.'

'Well if you're a copper, you should know where he lives, then,' she replied.

'We should.' I kept the grin in place. 'But would you mind…?'

'Aye, I suppose.' She softened. 'Go along to Cockpit Steps, he lives next to 'em, it's called Wolf House. Got two great stone wolves each side of his door. Ridiculous it is, I dunno why they 'aven't been stolen, can't leave nothin' around…' She left, muttering to herself.

We set off along the road to the narrow entrance of Cockpit Steps and walked down the worn stone treads. The lady was quite right, the house was at the bottom: three storeys high, built of dark brick with white mortar joints, and looking very spruce. The stone wolves were as large as Labradors, with snarling jaws and baleful eyes; they looked incongruous in the genteel setting.

Swift rapped the brass knocker.

'What?' A grumpy housekeeper in a shapeless black frock opened the door.

'Could we speak to Mr Markov, please?' Swift asked.

'Why?' she demanded.

'Police,' I announced. Swift frowned at me.

'Ha, we'll see what he has to say to that.' She opened the door. 'Come on in, you can surprise him.'

I gained the impression she wasn't keen on her employer. We followed closely behind as she stomped off down the narrow hall and entered a room opposite the staircase. 'It's the coppers. They wanna talk with you, and I 'ope they put you away.'

'Get out, woman,' a voice growled. 'Why you still here?'

'Don't you worry, I'm goin' home after I finish my work. An' I wouldn't be comin' at all if I could find another job,' she retorted and stalked toward the rear of the building.

It didn't sound the happiest of households.

We walked into the drawing room, bizarrely decorated in modern style, with shiny chrome, gold inlays and black leather.

'Police,' I repeated.

Swift frowned again, but didn't contradict me.

'I don't talk with police.' Markov rose from a leather chair to face us. He was a big man, heavily built with thick dark hair, expensively tailored but unshaven.

'In May 1911, Ezra De Ruyter paid you to place explosives in a jewelled Birdcage, resulting in the deaths of eight people,' I accused him with harsh words.

His eyes widened in shock and his mouth fell open; the moment of involuntary reaction gave him away. He recovered quickly, his jaw tightening as he advanced on us, fists clenched. 'You do not come in my house and say this to me,' he growled.

'You can answer our questions or—' Swift began.

Markov swung a fist at him. Swift ducked, swerved, and stumbled over a stool.

I moved forward. Markov twisted around, nimble on his feet; he charged me like a prop forward on the rugby pitch. I sidestepped, he bounced off the wall. I hammered my fist between his eyes, his nose erupted in a spurt of blood. He let out a howl of rage as he fell backwards.

'I get my gun and shoot you,' Markov bellowed from the carpet, his hand over his nose, trying to quell the bleeding.

'You're coming with us. You're under arrest for attacking a policeman.' Swift was determined. Markov started scrambling to rise to his feet.

I grabbed Swift. 'We're leaving.'

'No—'

'Yes, come on.' I dragged him into the corridor. Markov was crashing through furniture, presumably looking for his gun.

I shoved Swift, still arguing, out of the front door, slammed it shut behind us, and forced him into Cockpit Steps.

'We'll go back to the club and call Scotland Yard,' I told him.

'We can find a local Bobby,' he countered. He was breathless beside me; we were racing up the winding passageway.

'And tell him we entered a private house under false pretences, attacked the owner, and left?'

'We had good reason——'

'Swift, we had no authority, no evidence, and no handcuffs. How the hell do you think we could have arrested him?' We reached the top of the steps.

'But he can't be allowed to escape.'

'Escape where?' I spotted a taxi and threw up my arm to hail it. It puttered over to us.

'Anywhere, Russia, or…' he continued arguing.

'Brundles,' I ordered and made Swift climb in. Ten minutes later we walked through the doors and straight upstairs.

'I'm calling Billings,' Swift announced.

'Fine, I'll be with you shortly,' I said and entered my room.

'Sir, your hand?' Greggs was pootling about.

'It's only a scratch, just needs some cold water on it.' My knuckles had swollen and were bleeding from the force of my fist hitting the bridge of Markov's nose.

'I have some tincture of iodine, sir.'

'No, it will stain.'

'Very well, sir.' He took the hand towel from the washstand and dipped it into the bowl of water, then brought it to me.

'Fisticuffs, was it?' He wound the damp towel around my hand.

'Not really. I hit him, he went down, we formed an orderly retreat.'

'You and Inspector Swift, sir?' His brows rose. 'I would not have thought the Inspector was the type to engage in a fight.'

'He's not, but we think we've uncovered the savage who supplied the Birdcage explosives.'

'Good Heavens, really, sir!' His eyes almost goggled.

'Not a word to a soul, Greggs, not even Miss Fairchild,' I warned him.

'Absolutely, sir. But who is this person, and how did you discover him?'

I recounted our visit to Masons Yard and the links, tenuous as they were, and the look on Markov's face when we confronted him. I have to admit, it was less convincing in the telling.

I sighed. 'It could be him, Greggs, but…well, I've no idea how to prove it.'

'I believe it is the job of the police to uncover proof, sir,' he reminded me.

I didn't reply. After this morning's fracas they might be more inclined to dismiss us first and prosecute us later. I looked around. 'Where's Fogg?'

'In the Morning Room, sir. I had taken him to the park and on our return Dr Moore spotted us. Mr Fogg greeted him warmly and the doctor kindly invited him to breakfast.'

'And Tubbs?'

'He had already made his way downstairs, sir, and was last seen eating a sausage on the Earl of Albemarle's table.'

That caused me to grin. Brundles was at least giving good cheer to my little duo – and my butler. 'I'll be with Swift,' I told him and made for the door.

'Very good, sir.' He gave a discreet cough. 'Sir, I have something of which to inform you.'

'Yes?' I turned about.

'I…erm, ahem…Miss Fairchild and I had an excellent evening at the Ritz, sir. We dined in splendour, we danced until the early hours, and…and…well I said something rash, sir.'

'What did you say?'

'I suggested that Miss Fairchild and I should wed, sir.'

I didn't know how to reply. I must have stood in stunned silence for moments, then realised I should do something. 'Congratulations, old chap.' I went to shake his hand, which hurt, and made the damp towel fall off. I gave it to him. 'Sorry, but, erm…marvellous news. I know she'll make you very happy.' My heart plummeted as I forced out the words.

'Thank you, sir.' He held the damp towel, looking rather forlorn. 'I'm sure it will be just the thing…a new life in London, with all the attractions on the doorstep…'

'Yes, and a wonderful wife to care for you, and…and all the things wives are good at.' I was running out of jocular phrases and felt as though slow paralysis were creeping up my back.

Greggs' face wobbled, then his cheeks fell. 'It was the romance of it, sir. The music, the dance, the Ritz…'

'Erm, do you mean, you got carried away?'

He nodded dumbly. I felt suddenly cock-a-hoop.

'Well, you can explain, she's bound to be quite upset, but…'

He sniffed, I thought he was close to tears. 'I don't think I am cut out for marriage, sir.'

I thought I'd better try some encouraging words in the hope it wouldn't work. 'I hadn't thought I was either, Greggs, but it's not so bad.' Then I had another idea. 'Did she actually accept your proposal?'

'She did, sir, and we drank champagne, and the orchestra played a romantic tune for us while we danced cheek to cheek…' His voice quivered to a shuddering halt.

My heart took another plummet. 'Right. I suppose there's no easy way out, then.'

'I fear not, sir.' He gave a loud sniff. 'We are to spend the day at the Crystal Palace, and grounds. I expect things will appear in a more positive light after such an excursion.'

'Crystal Palace is quite a distance, Greggs.' Especially if things went amiss, I thought, but didn't say.

'George's brother has a taxi service; he is willing to take us.'

'Oh.' I sighed 'You'd better tell me how things go on your return.'

'I will, sir.' He sniffed again, as though he were heading for Tower Hill, rather than the glories of Sydenham.

I traipsed into the corridor, and was poised to enter Swift's chamber, when Pinner called me.

'Major Lennox, sir. Message came through on the telephone while you were out. It's from Lady Stanford. She's askin' if you and the Inspector would go and talk to her at Stanford Court.' He stood looking up at me, an unaccustomed expression of solemnity on his creased face.

'Thank you… Is everything all right, Pinner?'

'Aye, sir, it is.' He tried a grin. 'Strange times, ain't they?'

'Indeed they are, Pinner.' I commiserated, then entered Swift's room.

'I haven't written anything significant on the event board,' he blurted. 'Just the names of the Birdcage victims and the people in the dining room when De Ruyter died, and the connections.'

I could see he was agitated. 'What are you talking about, Swift?'

'Someone's been in here. I think the room's been searched.'

'Ah.' That explained the strange outburst. 'Brundles would not stoop so low. Pinner must have been in to tidy up.'

'It was already tidy, I did it myself. I think the papers from Clifton have been found.'

'How?' I was incredulous.

He reddened. 'I put them on top of the wardrobe… I thought Pinner would see them in my pillowcase, so… I couldn't think of anywhere else.'

'You either hang them out of a window in a sack, or roll them in a sock and tie it to the curtain pole behind the curtains – that's what we did in boarding school, anyway.'

'Well, I didn't have that privilege.' He turned tetchy. 'And they're bound to know about toffs' tactics anyway.'

I took a breath. 'Swift, Brundles would never rifle through your room, and anyway, Markov is the real news, and nobody knows about that.'

'No…and I haven't called Billings yet. I was checking if anything was missing…' He looked about the room again.

'You'd better call him,' I said tetchily.

'I'm going to, but the operator may be listening in.'

'Then be careful what you say.'

'Of course I will, Lennox.' He crossed to the telephone

and asked for Scotland Yard. I could hear the exasperation in Billings' voice at Swift's oblique wording, but he agreed to come and see us.

'Do you think we should have suggested meeting him elsewhere? We might be overheard,' Swift fretted.

'Nonsense, you're becoming paranoid.'

He remained at the desk, plainly upset. 'I should write my notes from this morning's... erm...incident.'

'Swift.'

'What?'

'Greggs is getting married.'

'What! Good God, really?' He looked as shocked as I felt. 'Oh, hell, I'm sorry Lennox. I mean, I know it's a wonderful occasion for him, but...but you'll miss him.'

I nodded dumbly and picked up the morning newspaper and sat down to pretend to read it while he wrote yet more notes.

'What Russian?' Billings demanded when he marched in.

We waited until he sat down, then confessed all, including the fracas.

'You hit him!' He was furious. 'You hit a prime suspect, a man who might be behind the Birdcage explosion. You bloody idiot. That's it, you're sacked, both of you. You've destroyed my case—'

'We found the begger,' I cut off the tirade. 'All you have to do is go and question him.'

'And you think he's going to answer our questions?' he barked. 'He's probably with his lawyer. If they find out I brought you in, they'll throw the bloody book at me, and then I'll throw the bloody book at you.'

'He won't be with a lawyer,' I retorted. 'If he supplied the explosives, he's more than likely to be hunting us down with a pistol.'

'Then you should go home,' he carried on. 'I don't need you blundering about my case like this.'

'Billings,' Swift suddenly snapped. 'We found him, he attacked us. You should be thanking us, not dressing us down.'

Billings stopped, took a breath, then stalked to the telephone on the desk. 'I'm calling the boys. What's Markov's address?'

Swift told him.

'Scotland Yard,' Billings barked at the switchboard operator. 'And you'd better not be listening in on this conversation, or I'll have you in front of the beak.' He then went on to rap orders at his team, directing them to Queen Anne's Gate. 'And don't go near the house until I get there,' he ordered, then clunked the receiver down and marched toward the door. 'And I'll deal with you two when I get back,' he growled and slammed the door behind him.

Swift's shoulders slumped.

'Right,' I said. 'Ready?'

# CHAPTER 22

'Ready for what?' Swift asked.

'Lady Marina Stanford would like to talk to us,' I said.

'Lennox,' he protested. 'We're supposed to stay here.'

I was in no mood for any opposition; my hand hurt, I'd been dressed down by Billings again, and I was in danger of losing my butler.

'I don't give a damn what we're supposed to do, Swift. Come on.'

He complained all the way downstairs, then pointed out that we didn't know where she lived, which was true, but George did.

'Ah, now, Stanford Court is round the corner, and then a bit.' George was stationed in his usual position on the doorstep. 'It's at the end of Park Place, a great big house. You can't miss it.'

He was right, and we discovered it only five minutes' brisk walk away. The place was huge; it even had its own private gateway, which was standing wide open. We entered the spacious courtyard – I expected to be challenged but nobody took any notice of us. A gardener was trimming a sculpted bush with what looked like nail scissors. He didn't even look up as we passed.

A uniformed flunky spotted us and suddenly leapt forward from a shaded doorway and rushed to ring the doorbell.

'You are expected, sirs,' he said and stood aside to allow us to wait under the shade of the tall stone portico.

'How do you know who we are?' I asked.

He gave me a sideways look, but refrained from replying.

'The newspapers,' Swift answered the mystery.

'Ah,' I muttered, then frowned at the thought.

An elderly butler, amiable in the way of old family servants, arrived to bow us indoors.

'This way, please, gentlemen.' He led us through a vast entrance hall, grand and yet somehow homely, with tapestries and rugs in a quaint floral style. We continued upstairs to my lady's parlour.

'Oh, you came!' Lady Marina smiled in apparent delight as she stood to greet us.

'Lady Marina.' I pecked her proffered hand.

Swift followed suit.

'You must think I'm such a nuisance.' There was a tremor of nervousness in her voice. 'But there's been so much in the newspapers and I decided I just had to talk to you.'

Sunshine filled the parlour, a cozy spot adorned with crocheted blankets, knitted doilies, and a line of stuffed toys on the windowsill.

'What would you like to talk to us about?' Swift asked her in a friendly tone.

'I'll get onto that.' She settled back in a cushioned armchair. 'You boys sit right down. Can I offer you some tea or coffee?'

'Coffee,' we agreed and perched on pretty bergère chairs opposite her.

Lady Marina glanced at the butler.

He bowed and uttered, 'M'lady,' then slipped out to instruct the staff.

'It's Dickie Phillips.' Lady Marina's smile dimmed. 'I can't get him out of my head, and I read that woman's maid was attacked last night.'

'You mean Lillian Lamb's maid,' Swift was pedantically correct.

'Well, yes, I do, but I can't bear to speak her name. Now, I have to ask you what you're doing about getting Gloria out of jail – she wouldn't have harmed Dickie and she certainly couldn't have attacked that poor maid.'

'We think she was injured rather than attacked, but there's nothing we can do,' I stated. 'Because we don't have all the facts.'

'Is there anything you would like to tell us?' Swift continued in encouraging fashion.

'No, I can't tell you anything, but…but why did Dickie die? It's so confusing…it's all getting out of hand…'

We held our breath in the hope of a revelation, but a discreet tap on the door broke the moment. The butler returned armed with a laden tray.

I turned the conversation while he poured coffee.

'Is that your daughter?' I nodded toward a painting on the wall opposite; it was one of three, mounted in identical Italianate frames.

'Yes, that's Nancy.' Lady Marina gazed at the portrait. 'She was eighteen when Dickie Phillips painted that picture. She and Daphne were to be presented at court.'

Nancy had been portrayed in a similar debutante's white frock and pearls as her cousin, Daphne. Both girls shared the same fresh-faced look and happy smiles. I felt a pang of sorrow, and fury, to think of their terrible deaths.

'I'm sorry,' Swift said.

Lady Marina sighed. 'Those girls were pure sunshine, and a whole heap of mischief.'

'Whose are the other two portraits?' Swift held up a hand to refuse sugar.

'They're our boys. Aren't they handsome – just like you two young men. That's Bobby.' She smiled as she raised a finger. 'He's the oldest. He's working on Wall Street and he says it's a doozy. And that,' she pointed to the third picture, 'is Joey, although he prefers Joseph. He takes after his father. He's an academic; he teaches history at Yale.'

'Are either of them in England at the moment, or have recently left?' Swift asked the policeman's question.

She wagged a finger at him. 'I see your game, Inspector. You want to know if they could be involved in all this. Well, I can assure you that they are not. Their papa sent a telegram to them in the States just yesterday – they haven't been back here since Christmas.'

The butler picked up a pair of silver tongs and held it over the tiered cake dish. 'May I serve, m'lady?'

'Please do.' She smiled at him.

They were petits fours – miniature macaroons, eclairs, chocolate squares, and meringues. I had one of each, they were barely a mouthful apiece.

'Do Lord and Lady Clifton have other children?' Swift asked.

'No, Estelle lost three before Daphne, none went full term…' Her lip quivered. 'You grow up thinking you've been blessed with everything in life, and then you find out it doesn't add up to a hill of beans.'

The butler left us to it and I switched back to the crux of the matter.

'What did you mean when you said it's all getting out of hand?' I asked.

She glanced up, seeming more in command of herself. 'I mean that there's a crazy person out there doing terrible things, and it's not Gloria. We have to do something – she shouldn't be in jail.'

Swift finished his coffee and leaned back in his chair. 'You know Gloria from her boutique…'

'Me and Estelle both. She supplies make-up and advice.' Lady Marina hadn't touched her dainty cakes. 'And she's a good friend and a good person.'

'Wasn't she connected to De Ruyter when the explosion took place?' Swift asked between sips of coffee.

'I think you know she was. We were acquainted back then, but after the…the explosion happened, Gloria left that devil quick as could be.' She looked down at her hands, where she was winding her wedding ring round and round her finger. 'Estelle and me kept away from her, because...well because we didn't know what to make of it, but a few years went by and we met her here and there, and she was real nice, you know. We figured we were being mean, so we started up with her again.'

I wiped my hands on my napkin. 'Lady Marina, you're withholding information. You're placing Gloria Thornton at risk of prosecution and no-one can do anything to help her unless you tell us the truth.'

She looked away. Her lips trembled, then she spoke quietly. 'It was the tiara. That woman had it. She wore it for her painting.'

'You mean Lillian Lamb?' Swift asked, surprise on his sharp face.

'Yes.' Lady Marina suddenly sat up. She spoke defiantly, as though someone had forbidden mention of the words. 'The diamonds were all one carat. Dickie saw it and confronted her at once. That's when she told him her tale. She said that devil gave it to her as a Christmas gift. Can you imagine a more disgusting thing?' Her voice shook. 'She insisted to Dickie that she hadn't given a thought about where those diamonds came from. When Dickie told her, she turned pale, or that's what he said, and she threw it across the room. Then she declared it was the last straw and she was going to leave him – the Devil, I mean – De Ruyter,' she whispered his name. 'Dickie asked her if… if De Ruyter had ever admitted what he'd done, and she said he'd always denied it, and she'd believed him until that moment.'

'When was this?' Swift asked.

'The first week of January,' she replied, all her effervescence gone.

'Did you and Lady Estelle plan his murder?' Swift asked her directly.

'No, no, we'd never do that.' She attempted to sound affronted.

I didn't believe her, and I could see Swift didn't either.

'You had the invitations printed, you arranged for the victims' relatives to be present at Ladies' Night,' I accused her coldly.

'I did not, Estelle...' Her eyes flew to mine, she jumped to her feet. 'I need to find Humphrey, I—' She fled the room, almost at a run, with her hand clasped over her mouth.

We'd stood as she left; the butler entered, puce with outrage at the upset we'd caused. There was nothing to be gained by trying to explain and we exited at his terse behest.

'They organised the whole bloody show,' I said as soon as we left the mansion.

'Yes,' Swift agreed, his face animated, he spoke quickly. 'Phillips was in on it. He was in direct contact with Lillian Lamb. He probably persuaded her to attend Ladies' Night with De Ruyter.'

'Exactly,' I agreed. 'Let's go and talk to her.'

'Should we speak to Billings first?'

'No.'

Clouds had rolled across the sun as we left Park Place, and the first drops of sleet touched my face in Green Park. It was turning to snow by the time we reached Chester Square and were admitted through Lillian Lamb's front door.

'She's in the drawing room, sirs.' A maid had answered, and now trudged ahead of us, a colourless soul in an ill-fitting uniform. She didn't announce us at the threshold, merely gave a perfunctory wave to indicate we should enter, then turned and trudged off. To my observation, it wasn't difficult to spot an unhappy servant.

Lillian Lamb was seated in a lounge chair in front of the fire, her long legs outstretched onto a footstool. She looked up as we entered, but didn't rise.

'Well, well, the great detectives.' She leaned her head back as though to better appraise us. 'And you really are as handsome as they say.' It was an act of brazen bravado. If it was intended to discomfit us, it failed. Swift and I remained stony-faced.

'How is your maid?' Swift asked coldly.

Her lips twisted at his harsh tone. 'You mean the one in hospital?' Her voice was laced with sarcasm. 'According to the doctor, she should be back at her duties tomorrow.' She wore a dress in baby blue, sewn with geometric lines of sequins and sparkling diamanté. It was a strange choice for daytime wear, although it set off her blonde hair and lucent skin to perfection.

Dr Moore was right, she was beautiful, and Dickie

Phillips had perfectly portrayed her flawless beauty, but entirely failed to capture her bewitching allure.

'Have the police completed their interviews with your staff?' Swift spoke in formal manner.

She'd been filing her nails, and turned back to the task. 'Yes, but none of us saw anything, and nothing was taken, as far as I know. There's an insurance man coming round later.'

My terrible habit of babbling when confronted with alluring women threatened to render me speechless, but I took a deep breath. 'May we sit down?'

She threw a smile at me; my heart skipped a beat. 'I wish you would,' she said with lips curved in a beguiling smile.

We sat opposite on a modernist sofa in black. A low table in sleek ebony stood between us and her, and a zebra skin lay splayed in front of the fire. The room was decked in black, white, and chrome. I didn't like it, although I recognised the skill and expense in its design.

'Ezra De Ruyter's death must have left you in a difficult situation,' I said without stammering.

She glanced up, a glint of amusement in her violet eyes. 'Perhaps, but I own this house. I'll manage.'

I'd expected her to plead poverty, so was surprised at her reply. 'Did you know he was to be murdered?' I asked blankly.

She laughed. 'Oh, please. I've had the coppers here almost every day demanding I give them an answer. Of course I didn't know… God it was awful,' she muttered, her face suddenly solemn.

'Dickie Phillips asked you to go to Ladies' Night,' Swift stated.

'Oh, for cryin' out loud, give it a rest.' She returned to her nail filing and blasé attitude.

'Why did De Ruyter keep checking his watch?' I asked, recalling Gloria Thornton telling us.

'He was bored. He wanted to go home,' she replied, sounding bored herself, which annoyed me.

'Then why did he stay?' I asked. 'Was it because you made him?'

Her gaze snapped toward me, then returned to her nails.

'Your tiara triggered the murder.' Swift reached for his notebook and tugged it from his pocket.

'You put that away.' She pointed with long fingers. 'No-one's writing anything without my lawyer here.'

'When did De Ruyter give you the tiara?' Swift was unruffled by Lillian's rising hostility.

'Christmas,' she snapped. 'I've told the coppers that already.'

'And now you can tell us,' Swift returned.

'Who chose the case the tiara came in?' I asked.

'Ezra, of course.' Irritation in her voice.

'The police will verify that with the jewellers,' I warned her.

'What of it? He took me to the jewellers, I had to have a fitting so the tiara sat properly on my head. They showed us a bunch of cases and we chose one.' She slid her gaze through thickly mascaraed lashes to watch me.

'You said Ezra chose it, and now you state both of you did.' I picked her up on the contradiction.

'So, it was just a case.' She shrugged.

'What does Bronski mean to you?' I asked.

'Never heard of it,' she responded casually.

'Ezra De Ruyter's murder was planned, and you led him to his place of execution,' I accused her.

Even Swift looked shocked.

'What are you saying? That I'm responsible?' Her eyes flashed in sudden rage. She stood up to confront me. 'If anyone did it, it's that stuck-up bunch of toffee-nosed women.' Her voice rose an octave, and her East End accent rose with it. 'You've got nothin' on me. We got an invite and Ezra decided we'd go, and that was all there was to it – and you can take your bloody accusations and stuff them where the sun don't shine.'

'You had an invitation?' Swift focused on that piece of news.

'Yeah, I burned it after Ezra died, not that it's any business of yours. You aren't even proper police.' She was standing upright, her chin held high, her fingers tightly curled.

'You knew about the diamonds in the tiara,' I accused her. 'You wore it in the portrait Dickie Phillips was painting of you.'

'He was the one that spotted the diamonds an' told me what they were.' She was almost spitting the words. 'I never had a bleeding tiara before, how the hell would I know what it meant.'

We were all standing near the fireplace. She'd had a cup of coffee on the stool next to her, it had overturned when she'd leapt up; the contents dripped onto the zebra skin rug.

'Nobody knows what was said between you and Phillips because he's dead,' I retorted sharply.

She gasped, her rose-painted lips parted. 'So you're accusing me of killin' Dickie now?' she shrieked. 'I'm sick of this. You get out, both of you, go on, get out, or I'll call them coppers back meself.'

We didn't have much choice but to retire with what grace we could muster. Moments later we were back on the front doorstep overlooking Chester Square.

I clapped my hands together against the cold. 'That went well,' I remarked.

Swift looked furious, then he glanced up at me, and broke into a wry grin. 'You really do have a way with women, Lennox.'

# CHAPTER 23

'Lunch,' I declared.

'Fine, but I need to sit somewhere quiet to consider all this, Lennox, and write it down.'

We'd been discussing Lady Marina's disclosure and Lillian Lamb's motives as we'd crossed Green Park with snowflakes swirling about us.

'We'll eat in your room.'

'Good idea, yes…' He was distracted. 'Do you think I spoke too harshly to Billings? It wasn't intended, but he can be abrasive, and I couldn't …' His words petered out and he bit his lower lip.

'Swift, you don't work for Billings, and he has no right to abrade either one of us.'

'I do know that.' He shoved his hands in his pockets.

'Look, punching a witness may have earned us – or rather me – a dressing down, but we found Markov, which is more than Billings and his team achieved.'

'They lost control of the Birdcage case because of the

assault on Reynolds,' he reminded me. 'It's hardly surprising Billings reacted the way he did.'

'These are entirely different circumstances,' I said firmly. We'd turned into St James's Square, expecting to find more reporters, but the pavement was vacant.

George swung the door open; we walked in and upstairs without interruption. Pinner was in the passageway outside my room, a stack of freshly laundered sheets in his arms.

'Two trays to Swift's chamber,' I told him.

'Right you are, sir.' He gave a lopsided grin. 'An' your little dog's in there waitin' on you. Mr Greggs has just left. He said no doubt you'd be back for lunch shortly.'

'He said that?' I raised a brow.

'It wasn't exactly in them words, sir, but that were the gist of it,' he replied brightly, then continued on to a cupboard just beyond Swift's room.

Foggy yipped with delight as we entered, then ran in frenzied circles before jumping up around our legs. You'd think we'd been gone for half an eternity. I picked him up and went to sit next to the fire, extending my snow-damp boots toward its warmth.

'We'll start our assessment with what we learned at Masons Yard.' Swift sat down at the desk and opened his notebook.

I groaned; he was in full pedantic mood.

*'Discussion at Chequers Tavern led to information regarding Markov,'* he began briskly. *'Markov is a Russian immigrant who had worked for Bronski reloading rifle cartridges*

*with primer, powder, and bullet. Markov had lived in the East End (where?), and disappeared at the end of 1914. Ezra De Ruyter and Lillian Lamb visited Chequers Tavern on December 23rd 1914. Lillian Lamb grew up in Whitechapel in the East End, according to…?'* He broke off to ask, 'Who supplied that information?'

'Dickie Phillips' assistant; he said her accent was from Whitechapel, which isn't actually proof she came from there,' I replied while stroking my dog's long ears as he lay on my lap.

'No,' he agreed, then sighed. 'We should have asked her.'

'Swift, just get on with it, will you,' I told him.

'Fine… *Markov's address is Wolf House, Queen Anne's Gate, south of Birdcage Walk. When calling at the address, Markov became aggressive under questioning, resulting in violence…*' He paused to look up. 'It's so tenuous, Lennox. These events are nothing but the sort of coincidences that happen in all big cities.'

'Bronski's name wasn't a coincidence,' I replied. 'The leather case was chosen by the same malicious mind who commissioned the tiara. It's a memento of the explosion.'

'A trophy, chosen by De Ruyter to remind him of his triumph.' He spoke slowly, then looked up. 'Both of which he gave to Lillian Lamb.'

'Or she demanded from him?'

His eyes flicked to meet mine. 'She barely knew him at the time of the Birdcage murders.'

'Are we sure of that?'

'She was only seventeen, Lennox.'

'Some people are born evil,' I said.

He turned back to his notebook. 'She's the only one who doesn't have a motive. Her life of luxury ended with De Ruyter.'

'She didn't seem concerned about that,' I replied.

A rap on the door interrupted us and Billings walked in. 'Thought I'd find you here,' he announced by way of greeting. 'I ordered another tray from the Scouser.'

'You mean Pinner?' I said.

'How many Scousers work here?' Billings came to rub his hand together in front of the fire. 'Markov isn't going to press charges.'

That was good news at least. 'What did he say?'

Billings told us; it was another episode of vile cursing and threats of violence. 'He's sworn he'll get even with you.'

'Not a confession then,' I stated.

Billings grunted in agreement, then grinned. 'It was a good lead, lads. The boys are chasing down his history now, and if we can link him to the Birdcage or De Ruyter, then we might just crack the case.'

I guessed that was as close as he'd ever get to apologising for the bawling out he'd given us earlier. 'Where did Lillian Lamb grow up?' I asked.

'East End. Whitechapel primarily, but then around the docks. She's a child of the slums. No parents that we know of; she was passed around until she was old enough to run away.'

'A hard life,' I remarked.

'There's thousands like her,' Billings replied.

'I hope not,' I muttered.

Lunch arrived, borne by three men, one of whom was Browne. He was close-mouthed, his long face more doleful than ever. He directed the waiters to remove the covers from the trays, then ordered them out. He hesitated, as though to speak.

'Something you want to say, Browne?' Billings confronted him.

'Only that I hope you enjoy your lunch, sirs,' he said, then left quietly, pulling the door closed behind him.

'Not very talkative,' Billings commented of the dour steward.

'Lady Marina virtually confessed to the invitations,' Swift said as he came to inspect the food. 'We think Browne and Rossetti cooperated with her and Estelle.'

'You've taken your time to come to that conclusion.' Billings picked up a pork pie. 'We're convinced they did. We haven't found out who printed the cards yet, but when we do, we'll have them.' He took a bite from his pie. 'What else did she tell you?'

Swift repeated the conversation regarding the tiara, he was basking under Billings' good humour and unconcerned about admitting that we'd acted against orders. I poured a glass of wine each, and we ate as we discussed all that we'd learned, including the spat with Lillian Lamb.

'Who sent the poisoned chocolates?' Billings threw up the question.

'There's nothing to actually pinpoint anybody,' I surmised.

'Or why,' Swift added.

'Phillips was in cahoots with the actual killer, but knew too much and had to die.' Billings lifted a finger to list possible motives.

'That suggests Clifton could have had him killed to stop him implicating Lady Estelle,' Swift said.

'How?' Billings was scathing. 'Clifton isn't the sort to dirty his hands with murder, and his lawyer might run a private spying agency, but he doesn't hire out assassins.'

'We should consider the Stanfords,' Swift said.

Billings grunted, but didn't reply.

'Phillips' death must be related to the tiara,' I stated.

'How?' Swift asked, which led to a long discussion on how it could, or could not have been.

'And the target may have actually been Gloria Thornton,' I reminded them, which led us back into the same cycle of arguments.

'What happened to Bronski?' I asked.

'He's retired and moved to Essex. I've told the local police to go and interview him,' Billings answered.

'Have Cadogan's been interviewed?' Swift asked.

'Yes,' Billings admitted. 'De Ruyter commissioned the tiara. The jewellers were dubious about the design, but De Ruyter was willing to pay more for their cooperation and they eventually agreed.'

'What about the case? Who chose that?' I asked.

'De Ruyter and Lamb,' Billings replied.

I sighed; that tallied with Lillian Lamb's account, or rather her revised account.

We passed another hour in debate, but didn't make any real progress.

I decided we'd speculated enough. 'Tell me what happened to Reynolds?'

'He hanged himself in his cell.' Billings was defensive.

'We know, but why were you so convinced he was the link to De Ruyter?' I asked.

We were sitting around the fire. I'd thrown more coal on it. Foggy was lying full stretch on his back snuffling in his sleep; snow was piling against the windowpanes.

We heard a mew at the door. I went to let Tubbs in.

He sauntered across the room, eying us all. Billings raised a wry brow, and Tubbs made straight for him. He hopped onto his lap, made himself comfortable and proceeded to knead his paws into the policeman's knees, purring loudly. To Billings' credit, he barely flinched when Tubbs dug his claws too deep.

'Reynolds was a strange one,' Billings began. 'He'd been in the army before joining Aaron Goldstein's workshop. He was a meticulous worker, technically brilliant with mechanical devices, and the more intricate the better.' He stroked Tubbs between the ears as he spoke. 'The army discovered his talent fairly quickly and put him to work making explosives to fit in small devices; they were mainly for assassinations as far as we could discover. Most of the workings were based on watches and automatons. Reynolds was one of those peculiar sorts, couldn't look anyone in the eye, barely able to string a sentence together unless it were about a specific subject and then he'd talk for hours and wouldn't shut up. He couldn't integrate or take orders; he'd become so agitated if instructed to do something to which he objected, he'd shut himself in a storeroom and wouldn't come out until everyone had left the workshop.'

'We had a couple like that in army intelligence.' Swift was leaning back in his chair. He was probably the most relaxed I'd seen him. 'They were locked in on themselves, often quite brilliant in specific areas, but impossible to work with.'

'That was Reynolds' problem: he couldn't function in a team. In the end they kicked him out of the army,' Billings explained. 'Aaron Goldstein heard about him, and offered him a job as a watch-mender. He gave him his own work area and left him to it. When the Birdcage came in, Goldstein designated it to Reynolds, he became obsessed with it. He wouldn't let anyone else touch it. Finally the cage was reassembled with all the gems in place, and this excited Reynolds even further. He was fascinated by the diamonds – he'd shine lights through the facets and turn the cage round and round on its base. When it came time to return it to Frederick De Ruyter, Goldstein had to wait until Reynolds went home before he could deliver it. It was well after midnight before it arrived at De Ruyter House.' Billings' gaze remained on the flames as he rubbed Tubbs' ears.

'What happened when Reynolds returned to work and

the Birdcage was gone?' I sipped my wine; we'd made the bottle last most of the afternoon.

'Nothing. No fireworks, no histrionics, he just got on with the next job. Goldstein said he was astounded, he'd thought Reynolds would walk out.' Billings sighed. 'The day after that the Birdcage exploded. It took the force less than twenty-four hours to point the finger at Ezra De Ruyter, and Reynolds as his inside man. We couldn't break De Ruyter, he slithered around our questions like the snake he was – we had absolutely nothing on him. Reynolds was another matter. When we brought him in for questioning, he refused to talk, just sat looking at his hands with a smirk on his face. We let him go, followed him everywhere, hoping to witness a meeting between the two of them. When that didn't happen, we took him in again and this time we kept him.'

'Were any of the real diamonds replaced with paste ones?' Swift asked the policeman's question.

'Yes, and we think he did exactly that. It took days to pick bits of the Birdcage out of walls and ceilings. We had surgeons extract the gems and fragments from the bodies...' He paused for a second, then continued, 'There should have been fifty diamonds in total. Those taken from the dead were intact, those that had smashed into walls or furniture were mostly broken into splinters. But that only accounted for twenty-five. Diamonds may break but they don't disappear. The wonks concluded the missing stones must have been paste and had melted in the explosion.' Billings' expression soured. 'We confronted Reynolds, he wouldn't admit it, but he was charged with theft and detained in a cell. We were convinced he was working under De Ruyter's orders and had been paid with one or more real diamonds to plant the explosives and exchange the diamonds. We began a routine with Reynolds: he'd be interrogated for two or three hours, then taken back to the cells for a cooling-off period, usually twenty-four hours. After a week of this he was beginning to crack, but still wouldn't admit anything. Then one night he went berserk, smashing the bunk in his cell and anything he could get his hands on. One of the officers went in, thinking he'd be exhausted and admit the truth, but Reynolds cowered in the corner of his cell talking gibberish. They had to move him, they couldn't leave him in the mess he'd made, so they took him to the interview room. He began crying. The officer in charge questioned him. Reynolds still wouldn't admit what he'd done, and then lost his head again; he threw a chair at the DCI, injuring him. The DCI lost his temper and hit Reynolds, and you know the rest.'

'The case died with him,' Swift stated, ever pedantic.

'Effectively, yes,' Billings grunted.

'So Reynolds swapped the diamonds,' I concluded. 'But it was Markov who supplied and fitted the explosives.'

'He probably had easier access to gelignite,' Swift added.

'If Markov fitted the explosives, how do you think he did it?' Billings glanced up.

I replied, 'You said the Birdcage was transported at night. It would have been by horse and carriage back in

1911. It would have moved slowly enough for Markov to climb in the back and fit them.'

Billings nodded. 'And if De Ruyter had instructed him, he'd have known its route.'

'How long was the route?' I asked.

'They had to cross Westminster Bridge. It would have taken forty minutes or more,' Billings replied.

Swift turned back to his notebook. 'De Ruyter could have met Markov at Masons Yard.'

Billings agreed. 'The toffs went to Bronski's to have their cartridges reloaded – according to you, Lennox.' He looked at me.

I nodded without speaking.

'All we have to do is track Markov's financial dealings. He's a rich man now, we could demand proof of where this originated…' Enthusiasm rose in Swift's voice.

'Not so quick.' Billings picked Tubbs from his lap and placed him gently on the hearthrug. 'You two have done better than any of us thought possible.' He stood up. 'I'm glad I brought you in, you've vindicated my decision, but your race is run, lads. I'm standing you down.'

# CHAPTER 24

Swift argued. Billings was unmoved. I let my mind wander over the last few days, and the fate of Dickie Phillips. Was he the intended victim of the poisoned chocolates? And why?

'Billings,' I cut in on his intransigence. 'We're going to see this through, and we have Clifton's support.' Actually Clifton may not be so supportive, but Billings probably wouldn't know that.

'Don't be so damned stupid, Lennox. Your photographs were taken in the doorway of this club and printed in the newspapers,' Billings warned. 'Markov will come here and try to carry out his threat.'

'Then your men can catch him when he does.' I was dismissive. 'This case is void of firm evidence, we need to shake the truth out of the suspects.'

'What the hell do you think we've been trying to do?' Billings declared.

'Lennox is right,' Swift said in my defence. 'They need to be brought together so they can witness each other's reactions—'

Billings interrupted, 'Do you think I haven't already considered this? I'm telling you now, it's a waste of time – if we put them together in the same room they'll just start singing the same song.'

'Lillian Lamb won't,' I stated. 'She'll be facing blanket hostility. It could be enough to trip her up.'

'Why the focus on Lillian Lamb?' Billings demanded.

'We're convinced she's the key to the case.' I was determined. 'She knows everything De Ruyter has done.'

'Ha,' Billings let out a snort of derision. 'Of course she does, but there isn't a scrap of evidence against her, and without it, no-one will get her to crack. She's as tough as nails.'

'Lennox has broken cases like this before,' Swift said. 'Gathering them in one place and pitting them against each other is sometimes the only way to squeeze out the truth, and he's good at it.'

Billings eyed me appraisingly. 'I've seen you, Lennox, but striking lucky a couple of times doesn't mean it's an effective method.'

'It wasn't just a couple of times, Billings.' Swift was adamant. 'And what do you have to lose?'

I glanced at him. He was fierce in resistance, even forgetting his usual deference towards his old boss.

Billings glared, his wiry brows drawn together. 'It's my neck on the line, and my job, and my pension.'

We said nothing.

He let out an exasperated sigh. 'Right, damn it, we'll do it. My officers will instruct the suspects, Rossetti can organise the room. I'll bring Gloria Thornton with me. Nine o'clock sharp tomorrow morning, gentlemen.' He flung out the order, then stalked out of the door and slammed it behind him.

'Was he always so trenchant?' I asked as I leaned back in my chair.

'Yes,' Swift replied, then corrected himself. 'No, not all the time. We'd relax over a pint sometimes, then he could be quite human.' He shook his head. 'It's the pressure of the case, Lennox, and the frustration.'

I understood the weight of responsibility. I'd ended as a Major in the war, leading a squadron, deciding which man should go where and when, sometimes knowing the chance of them surviving was slim. I'd sworn to avoid such responsibilities once the war was over. I sighed. 'I'm not convinced this is going to work, Swift.'

He looked abashed. 'You can do it, and it's all we have.'

I stood up and went to the event board pinned to the wall. 'Could we use a fresh sheet, and summarise the information we have on each suspect?'

'Of course we can.' A grin spread across Swift's face and he leapt to his feet. 'This is proper policing, Lennox!'

He spent a happy half hour replacing the event board with another section of wallpaper, then drew up the list of suspects and their motives. We both took notes from the finished article, then he burned it, because security was important. Then we did it all over again with locations, time frames, evidence – of which there was very little – and made more notes in our notebooks. The afternoon slipped into evening; snowflakes continued to drift against the window. I closed the curtains. We sipped wine, followed by coffee – because the details were becoming fuzzy with all the imbibing.

Fogg sat up to remind me that a trip to the garden was required. Tubbs decided he wanted to come too, but I knew he wouldn't like the snow; I handed him to Swift, explaining he should divert him. I put Foggy under my arm and headed for a quick outing to St James's Garden.

'Evening, sir.' George raised gloved fingers to the rim of his top hat. 'The Master mentioned we must all be wary of potential miscreants in the area.'

'Did he now.'

'Indeed yes, sir. The police inspector was quite blunt about it.'

'Ah.' That explained where the information came from. 'Have any miscreants been spotted?'

'They have not, sir, and if any such villain were loitering in the vicinity they'd have doubtless perished from the cold by now,' George assured me.

'But you're out here.' I put Foggy down onto the snow covered step as he was squirming to escape.

'I retreat indoors when no-one is about, sir.' He grinned behind the muffler.

'Very wise, old chap,' I commended him, and followed Foggy across the white smothered road. The snow was crisp and frozen, it crunched as I trod the undisturbed surface. There was nobody about, not even a solitary reporter. The gas lamps' amber flames flickered behind glass glazed by ice. I shoved my hands in my pockets and took a brisk turn about the statue of William of Orange, who was now more white than bronze, then called Fogg to return to the club.

He stood stock-still with one paw raised above the layer of snow, his nose pointing in an alert stance. There was rustling from a bush and the brief flap of a bird's wings, then silence fell once more across the square. I realised the hairs on the back of my neck had risen, and decided we'd braved the world enough for one night. I scooped Foggy up, made a quick march back to the club, and carried him straight upstairs to Swift's chamber.

I requested dinner to be delivered on trays. We ate quickly and quietly, then discussed our plan for the next morning's gathering. I admit my confidence waned as we talked; it was true I had forced the truth from suspects in the past by setting them against each other, or confronting them with the truth, and it had worked. But there were some who would always be impossible to break, and I feared I faced that now.

Greggs had returned – I heard him snoring in his room when I entered mine. I wondered how his day had gone and if his plans to wed would lead him away. I went to bed with an unquiet mind and was just drifting to sleep when I realised I hadn't called Persi. I fumbled for my pocket watch on the bedside cabinet and saw it was too late. I muttered a curse, then sank back into the pillows and slept fitfully until a knock on the door woke me.

'What? Who is it?' I sat up abruptly. Foggy let out a

sleepy growl, then fell back to snoozing. He never was much of a guard dog.

'It's me, Pinner, sir,' came the reply. 'The police are here.'

'Why?' I pulled the switch on the bedside lamp and tried to focus on my watch. It appeared to be five thirty. 'They're not due for hours.'

'May I come in, sir?' Pinner's voice sounded plaintive.

'Yes, of course.'

He held a lantern, its wick turned low. 'They're questioning everyone about where they were last night, and they're asking about you and the Inspector, sir. There's been a murder.' He was whispering, which was ridiculous, but I understood the reaction.

I threw the bedcovers aside, trying not to disturb Tubbs and Foggy. 'Who was murdered?'

'A foreigner, sir. Russian, by the sounds of it. "Markov" they said his name was. Someone found him in Queen Anne's Gate. Crawled into his garden and died of his wounds.' He lowered his voice further and hissed, 'He was tortured.'

'Good Lord.' I grabbed my dressing gown. 'Have you woken Swift?'

'Not yet, sir…' He hesitated. 'They'll be up here soon, thought I'd best let you decide what to do.'

That gave me pause. 'You don't think we did it, do you?'

'No.' He was quick to deny it. 'You never would, sir. But…well, if you wanted to scarper, now would be a good time to do it.'

I almost laughed. 'Go and wake Swift. Tell him to come here.'

He went off, almost running in his strange lopsided gait.

Greggs entered from the adjoining room, attired in a voluminous dressing gown with an old-fashioned nightcap on his head. 'Sir? Is there something amiss?'

'Things are turning nasty, old chap. Someone's killed Markov, tortured him first, apparently.' I gave him a wry glance. 'Pinner thought Swift and I may have done it.'

'No!' Greggs was aghast, and fascinated. 'Where was the wicked deed done, sir?'

I told him the little I knew.

'Greggs, how are your plans for erm…' I began

Swift burst in. He too wore a dressing gown, but his was new and neatly pressed. 'Pinner said Markov's been killed and the police are downstairs questioning the staff.'

'We know,' I replied. 'Where's Pinner?'

Swift looked blank. 'He went back downstairs.'

'Markov was tortured first,' I told him.

'Yes, Pinner said. Probably to find out the truth about the Birdcage explosion.' Swift was focused and on the case.

'But how did they find out where he lived?' I persisted.

He paused, then frowned. 'The switchboard operator may have listened in on Billings yesterday.'

'I doubt it, given the threat Billings made to him…I think someone's been listening to us, Swift.'

'How?' Swift demanded.

'The cupboard next to your chamber,' I said. 'I saw Pinner carrying sheets to it.'

'Let's have a look.' Swift marched out.

I grabbed my skeleton keys and followed.

'It's locked.' Swift stated the obvious.

It took only minutes to open. It was indeed a linen store, but amongst the sheets, blankets, and towels, we found a glass tumbler resting on a shelf at head height. It was perfectly placed for holding against the wall and listening to the conversation in Swift's room.

Greggs had followed us, enjoying the minor drama.

'Would you fetch the iodine from your first aid kit, old chap?' I asked him.

'Certainly sir.' Greggs went off, his nightcap skew-whiff upon his head. He was back in moments with the bottle firmly clutched in his hand. 'What is the intention, sir?'

'To leave a stain and catch a sneak.' I took it from him and carefully rubbed the rim with iodine using my finger. 'We'll soon find out who's been eavesdropping.'

Swift had watched the process, his face sharp with anger. 'We should get dressed, the police will be here any moment.'

He was correct, they appeared ten minutes later with Billings leading the way. We'd scrambled into our clothes and were waiting in Swift's chamber. We stood up when the door swung open.

'Did you do it?' Billings demanded, his face set hard.

'No.' Swift's response was instant. 'We didn't leave the club after you saw us yesterday.'

'I took my dog to the garden,' I confessed.

We'd been drinking tea. Greggs had called the switchboard to request a pot for us, then toddled off to begin his ablutions, ready for the day. His demeanour had been chirpy, almost radiant actually, and I hadn't had the heart to ask him again of his marriage plans.

'Nobody else knew who Markov was, or where he lived,' Billings barked at us.

'Oh, come off it Billings.' I put my empty teacup down with a bang. 'We didn't kill him, and you know it.'

He stared at us in silence. He was accompanied by two plain-clothes officers; they were equally granite-faced.

'What did the staff say?' Swift asked.

Billings let out an exasperated sigh. 'They said that no-one saw you leave, but there are ways and means if you know your way around the club's kitchens and rear garden.'

'It snowed last night,' I reminded him. 'You'd see our footsteps if we'd sneaked out the back.'

'There was nothing there,' Billings admitted. 'But there had been activity through the cellars.'

'Anything specific?' Swift asked.

'No. They take the rubbish to the bins through there – the area was thoroughly trampled,' Billings explained.

'Just a minute.' I raised my hand to stop the conversation, then strode across to open the door and shout down the corridor, 'Pinner?'

A moment later he emerged from the cupboard looking flustered, with a pile of towels in his arms. 'Yes, sir?'

'Come in here will you?' I stood by the door, waiting.

'Righto, sir. I'll just leave these on the shelf.' He darted back into the cupboard, locked it, and carefully placed the key in his waistcoat pocket before hurrying to join us.

Swift glared at him. 'You've been listening in on our conversations, Pinner.'

'N-no, I'd never do that, sir,' he stuttered.

'Look in the mirror,' I told him.

He glanced over to it: a perfect round mark in bright purple was circled about his ear.

'Iodine,' I said and held up my finger for him to see the stain. 'We put it on the glass.'

His shoulders sagged along with his expression. 'It wasn't nothing personal, but the Master said I had to do it…' He was almost in tears. 'We…we're all scared and Master's just lookin' after us, but he can't do that unless he knows what's goin' on.'

'You told him about Markov?' Billings stalked over to him, intimidating in both height and manner.

Pinner cowered before him. 'It wasn't through badness, honest, sir, we…they wouldn't kill no-one.'

'Who do you mean by "they"?' Billings demanded.

'The Master and Mr Browne. They've always worked together.' Pinner cuffed a tear from his eye.

'Go and sit with Greggs in my chamber,' I told him.

'I haven't finished,' Billings growled.

'Yes, you have,' I snapped. 'Pinner, go.'

He went as quickly as he could, ducking past the detectives scowling down at him.

'Damn it, they'll know everything,' Billings swore. 'They must have had Pinner listening in from the beginning.'

I wondered if that was the reason Rossetti had placed us in these rooms. I knew he was clever; I should have been more careful. 'It's too late to do anything about it now,' I replied sharply.

Swift sought to calm the spat and turned to Billings. 'Could you tell us what happened to Markov, sir?'

Billings looked as though he might stalk out, but then raised a hand to take off his hat. 'It's a mess,' he muttered, then went to sit in one of the armchairs by the fire.

We went to join him; the two officers remained, near the door.

'We were told he was tortured…' I prompted him.

Billings responded with a nod. 'Yes, and left for dead. The perpetrator entered the house through the back door. It was late into the night, the housekeeper had gone home. Markov was in night gear, he'd either come downstairs having heard a noise or he was woken at gunpoint.' Billings bent to pick Tubbs up, who'd woken and followed us to Swift's room. 'Markov was hit in the knee with an iron bar – it smashed the kneecap and incapacitated him. His right forearm was also broken – we assume it was done as part of an interrogation. Despite his injuries, Markov had retaliated; furniture was broken and a knife was found under a settee – it was of Russian manufacture.' Billings was rubbing Tubbs' ears. 'Markov was hit again, this time across the temple. It must have knocked him senseless, but he recovered at some point and crawled into his garden. A milkman found him at four thirty-eight this morning.'

Nobody said anything while we digested this; the only noise came from Tubbs, who was purring loudly as he lay curled in Billings' arms with his eyes closed.

'The attacker may not have intended killing him,' I said, and was duly ignored.

'Were there fingerprints?' Swift asked the policeman's question.

Billings shook his head. 'Nor any identifiable footprints. The milkman had walked all over the place.'

'Who do you think was responsible?' Swift continued.

'We thought it could have been Browne or Rossetti, but there isn't a mark on either of them,' Billings explained. 'It doesn't exclude them, but it leaves us without any proof against them. Or it could be one of Wallace's men acting under orders from Lord Clifton.'

'Have you questioned Wallace?' I asked.

'A couple of my lads gave him a rude awakening this morning.' Billings raised a grim smile. 'They took him down to the Yard. He's being interviewed now.'

'Are you bringing him to the nine o'clock meeting?' Swift asked.

I glanced at Billings, wondering if he'd call it off.

Billings frowned, then nodded. 'Yes, but if this goes wrong, and Clifton's lawyer is a witness to it, they'll have all the ammunition they need to well and truly scuttle us.'

A frisson of fear slid down my back.

Swift was more sanguine. 'Lennox won't let you down, there's nothing to worry about.'

Which was easy for him to say.

# CHAPTER 25

'Ah, Dr Moore, please be seated.' Greggs had been placed in charge. We were in the Strangers Room, having eaten a hearty breakfast with Billings and his men, and were now waiting for the suspects to arrive.

Rossetti had attempted to obstruct the meeting but Billings had told him it was the club or the Yard, and we mentioned Clifton would certainly support us – this was an entire fiction on my part, but Rossetti didn't risk calling his Lordship to find out. I felt a twinge of guilt for not having reported anything back to Clifton, but as he was on our suspects list, I absolved myself.

Swift had the bit between his teeth and had given clear instructions that each participant must be seated in the same places as on the night of De Ruyter's murder, apart from Lillian Lamb, and those who were now deceased.

'Well, what a turn-up, eh!' Dr Moore shuffled to the chair indicated by Greggs. 'What are we going to do, poison another blighter?' He chortled. 'Not serving custard, are you Rossetti?' he called to the Master, who was speaking in quiet undertones to Browne. Both men ignored Dr Moore's jolly quip; the doctor didn't appear to mind in the slightest.

Rossetti's smooth face reflected barely suppressed fury. He'd been told firmly by Swift that he was to remain silent until otherwise instructed, and to allow us, or rather Greggs, to direct the seating.

'This is completely irregular,' Wallace came in, complaining loudly. None of us took any notice, which caused his scowl to deepen. Greggs showed him to a chair placed in the corner – we thought he'd feel at home there.

I was standing near the spot where De Ruyter had died. We'd moved the table to one side, against the wall, and Swift sat at it, pen in hand and notebook open. Billings was near the garden door, which was unlocked and standing open, waiting for his men to wave the suspects in. He'd decreed that everyone be brought through the garden, apart from those already present in the club. The snow had been swept from the path in preparation, a nicety insisted upon by Rossetti, who, despite his anger, was punctiliously correct.

Lord Clifton stalked in with Lady Estelle on his arm. Browne took coats while Greggs fussed over her Ladyship, settling her comfortably. Her husband crossed the room to confront me.

'Lennox, this is not in accord with my expectations,' Clifton berated me. 'The police insisted my wife and I be present, despite my objections. I warn you now, if you proffer any unsupported accusations against my family, I will instruct Wallace to begin a prosecution against you, personally.'

'Clifton, if there were any other route to resolve this, we would have taken it.' I squared up to him. 'And Lady Estelle is involved, as you are well aware.'

A flush rose in his pallid cheeks. 'You stand on perilously thin ice, Major,' he snapped, then turned on his heel and stalked to join his wife. Lady Estelle's usual effervescence was stifled, her expression steely, her eyes watchful. She had omitted the shimmering make-up, but was exquisitely attired in a primrose yellow ensemble heavily embroidered with ivory-coloured flowers.

Gloria Thornton was escorted in by a police officer. My glance met hers; she forced a smile, then turned to follow Greggs as he showed her to her chair. She sat down, stiffly upright, her face pale after her brief incarceration. Her make-up was minimal, but she'd dressed in her usual classy style: a tailored velvet jacket in dark green, a bright scarf about her neck, her copper-coloured hair neatly coiffed, and suede gloves on her hands, which she tugged off. She caught Billings' glance and smiled. He returned the smile then straightened his face as he saw me watching. I wondered if there was a burgeoning romance between the two, then dismissed the thought as nonsense.

Sir Humphrey and Lady Marina arrived; Greggs moved deftly to seat them before they could divert toward the Cliftons. I noticed the two sisters avoided each other's gaze. Sir Humphrey appeared to be as furious as Clifton, and glared at all and sundry from under bushy brows.

One of Billings' officers ushered Lillian Lamb into the room. She strolled in with her head held high, wearing a white fox fur coat over a pink chiffon dress – she looked as though she could have just stepped down from a movie poster.

A hush fell over the room as Greggs bowed ponderously and led her to the chair opposite Gloria Thornton; it was the seat Dickie Phillips would have taken had he not been lying in the morgue. The two women shot icy glares at each other, then at me, then sat in cold fury.

The clock on the mantelpiece struck nine. Billings nodded to his officers. The doors were closed and locked, and a man designated to stand guard in front of each. Two other men positioned themselves against the walls where they could leap into action, should the need arise.

Murmuring broke out as the tension rose. Dr Moore sat beaming, as though a stage show were about to begin. Foggy leaned against his legs, waiting for treats to be passed to him, which they duly were.

Billings walked into the centre of the room. 'Quiet,' he barked. Silence fell as he turned to me. 'Lennox, get on with it.'

It was a curt introduction. I stepped forward and stood quietly for a moment.

'You're all guilty of murder,' I announced to gasps of indignation and outrage.

'Nonsense, my boy.' Dr Moore was unperturbed. 'Never harmed a hair on a single soul's head, and never would.'

'You knew about the plot to murder Ezra De Ruyter.' I turned to face the doctor, then I slowly pivoted on my heel to gaze at each of the others. 'You all knew about it, and that makes you all guilty.'

'Prove it,' Wallace demanded.

'Shut up,' Billings growled.

I ignored the interruption. I wanted to shake them and I had to turn the screw.

'Ezra De Ruyter's murder must have been on your minds since he masterminded the Birdcage murders.' I took a couple of paces. 'I'm surprised it's taken so long… De Ruyter's rapacity, his venal greed, led him to destroy not only members of his own family, but yours too. And he didn't care; he murdered without compunction – he knew there would be multiple deaths and he didn't give a damn.'

I turned and retraced my steps. 'Why now? Why after so many years has this revenge been enacted?' Nobody answered. They all gazed at me with expressions of guarded hostility. 'And it was an act, played out with as much theatre as a Greek tragedy, starting and ending in grief.

'But if De Ruyter's murder was a matter of revenge, what was behind Dickie Phillips' death?' I gazed across the room once more, noting that some of the expressions had changed from hostility to distress. 'Why kill Dickie Phillips?' I swung on my heel. 'Or was it meant for you, Miss Thornton?' I faced her. 'Were you a threat to someone? Are you hiding secrets?'

'Absolutely not,' she railed, two spots of high colour in her cheeks.

'Yes, you are.' I cut across her protestations. 'You all are, every one of you is guilty of murder.' I repeated the accusation. 'Something triggered the decision to kill, and whatever that was, one of you sought to convince the others to act. You gathered together and planned how, and when, and where the murder would take place.' I turned to face Clifton. 'Lord Clifton, you know who made that decision.'

With his haughty patrician cast, he could have been Caesar in the Senate facing his accusers. He glowered at me. I waited.

'De Ruyter deserved to die.' He spoke slowly. 'He murdered my daughter, and all those poor innocent souls. I will not condemn his murder… nor will I hide the truth.'

Wallace looked astounded as I breathed a silent sigh of relief.

'Arthur…' Lady Estelle turned in horror to him. 'You mustn't say anything…'

Clifton held a hand out to her and spoke quietly. 'I can't lie any longer, my love, and I won't. I am as guilty as any.'

'Neither will I.' Lady Marina's voice trembled as she spoke. 'We have to confess to what we've done, Estelle. You know there's no point in lying any longer.'

'Oh dear Lord, Marina, they'll hang us for it.' Estelle stared at her sister.

'I don't care. Nobody in this dang country punished that man for killing our babies.' Marina's eyes gleamed with anger; she had risen to her feet, and faced her sister. 'He lived like a king after mutilating our girls.' Her voice rose higher as grief and fury shook her. 'Then he takes the diamonds dug out of their poor bodies and sticks them in a stupid bauble for his strumpet to wear. Now if anyone thinks we're goin' to stand by and just let that lie, then they haven't dealt with Texas gals before.' She sat down abruptly and burst into tears. Her husband put his arms around her. I felt an utter heel.

Wallace stood up. 'M'lady, you will not hang, I'm certain of it, and I promise I will do everything in my power to mitigate any sentence imposed.'

'Thank you,' Clifton said quietly.

I gave Wallace a nod of appreciation. I may not like lawyers very much, but they had their place in the system.

'Please explain how you arranged the invitations.' I asked Lady Marina directly. She opened her mouth, but uttered no words. I turned to Estelle and waited. There was no real proof against them, neither Clifton nor Marina had actually confessed; this was the moment the case pivoted on a knife edge.

Estelle straightened her shoulders and rose to her feet. 'I did it,' she announced loudly. *'Justice will be served*, that's what I told them to print because that's what we were going to do. We designed them, me and Marina, then I asked Dickie Phillips to find a discreet printing man, and he did.'

I looked at Swift – he looked as relieved as I felt. I gave a light nod to indicate he take over.

He glanced at this notebook, then at Lady Estelle. 'Seven cards were printed, – were there any more?'

'No, seven was all that was needed,' Estelle declared, her eyes now gleaming with determination. 'I wrote the messages with Marina, and Mr Rossetti gave us the addresses. We delivered them ourselves.'

Rossetti's eyes widened at this; there was no way out for him now. Browne had turned to look at him, but he didn't react further.

'Could you confirm the recipients, please?' Swift was in full police mode.

'One each to me and Marina, to make it look right. One to Dickie Phillips, another to Dr Moore, one each to Mr Rossetti and Browne, and one to that woman.' She pointed at Lillian Lamb, who shrugged in reply, apparently indifferent to the proceedings.

Estelle sat down as Rossetti stepped forward. The anger hadn't left his face; he appeared icily resolved.

'My father was murdered. The police failed to secure justice.' He glared at Billings and his men. 'When I was approached with a proposal to punish that devil, I willingly agreed.'

I moved to face Rossetti. 'The tiara triggered the plan?'

Rossetti nodded stiffly. 'It was the final insult,' he said, his smooth face twisting in fury. 'He was a member of Brundles, he murdered his family and inherited the club through his vile deeds. He owned the very premises where I lived and worked. I was expected to serve him, the very devil who murdered my own flesh and blood. That was an insult every day.' He raised his voice, 'And the tiara was the last straw. I should have strangled him with my own hands.'

'Did you know De Ruyter would be murdered that night?' I asked the question which could condemn them all.

'Yes,' he hissed.

That resulted in a few sharp intakes of breath.

'Alessandro Rossetti,' Billings addressed him formally. 'You admit that you deliberately and with premeditation, set out to murder Ezra De Ruyter?'

'I have said so,' Rossetti growled.

'And you did this in cooperation with people in this room?' Billings continued.

'I speak only for myself.' Rossetti's colour had heightened, but he was now in tight control of himself.

I moved back to the table where Swift was furiously writing. I didn't want to condemn these people, and I doubted anyone else in this room did either – except for one. I took a breath. My task was to force the truth from that one person – the one behind it all. I knew who it was, it was the one who'd murdered Dickie Phillips, and I knew why.

'Clifton, what did you know?' I demanded.

'Nothing, initially.' His answer was succinct.

'It's true, he would have stopped us,' Lady Estelle said. 'I was careful to hide it from him.'

'You're no fool, Clifton.' I carried on as though Lady Estelle hadn't spoken. 'You suspected your wife was planning something. Wallace was spying for you. What did he discover?'

Clifton's eyes flicked to Wallace, who was studying his nails.

Sir Humphrey Stanford stood up. 'My wife and I have been married for thirty-eight years. Marina is not a secretive person, she is honest and open, and she is the joy of my life.' His voice broke over the words. 'I realised she and her sister were making plans and they involved De Ruyter. I asked Arthur to set Wallace to work, and some days later he reported that they intended to act on Ladies' Night.'

'Did you know about the tiara, and the source of the diamonds?' I pressed him.

He closed his eyes momentarily, as though in pain. 'Yes. Wallace informed Arthur and myself of the fact.' He glanced over at Clifton, who was expressionless.

'You lied, Lord Clifton,' I said. 'Three days ago you told me you had no inkling that your wife was involved in the plan to kill De Ruyter.'

'I would hardly tell you otherwise.' Clifton fixed me with a cold stare. 'I needed information from someone close to the police investigation and I hoped you may have been sympathetic to my cause.'

I didn't respond to that plea for solidarity. 'You knew your wife and her sister had planned to murder De Ruyter and you did nothing to stop them.'

'Why should I? My wife is an individual in her own right. I only wish she had confided in me first.'

'Oh, Arthur, really?' Estelle turned to him. 'Would you truly have helped?'

'Yes.' He reached for her hand. 'And I hang my head in shame that I didn't shoot De Ruyter myself.'

'As do I,' Sir Humphrey echoed his sentiment.

Lady Marina laughed. 'Oh, Humphrey, my dear, you wouldn't stamp on a bug, never mind shoot a man, even if it were that fiend De Ruyter.'

Their confessions seemed to lighten the atmosphere, despite the terrible stakes at play.

Browne stepped forward and bowed. 'Sir, I have arranged for refreshments to be made available for the ladies and gentlemen, if they require. May I take this opportunity to serve tea?'

I looked to Billings. He rolled his eyes but didn't refuse.

'Very well,' I agreed.

The tea trolley had been left outside the door by one of the staff; it must have been agreed before proceedings started. Browne wheeled it in, the cups rattling on their saucers. One of the police officers locked the door as Browne solicitously served each of us tea, or coffee, according to taste. Lillian Lamb made a fuss of demanding cream with her coffee. I opted for tea with two biscuits, as did most of the men. Rossetti refused to indulge.

I spoke quietly to Swift over a chocolate Bourbon. 'What are their chances in a court of law?'

He glanced about the room. 'I doubt a jury would convict, but a judge might instruct some sort of punishment.'

'Hanging?' I gave Foggy a piece of biscuit.

'No.' He shook his head. 'The only person at risk is the one who put the diamond dust in De Ruyter's custard.'

That had also been my conclusion. 'Browne, would you clear away now, please.'

He did so. Greggs helped in his ponderous manner. I think he wasn't enjoying the show as much as he'd expected, the emotions were too raw, and the risk of conviction too high.

'Sit down,' Billings shouted. 'Lennox, stop pussyfooting around.'

# CHAPTER 26

I went to stand in front of the fire. 'De Ruyter was murdered by diamond dust, it was poured over his custard—'

'Diamond dust?' Lillian Lamb broke in. 'Why the hell would anyone waste a diamond on that fat hog.'

That raised a few brows.

'You were his lover!' Gloria Thornton was astonished. 'You practically lived with him.'

'And I loved him,' Lillian Lamb snapped back. 'But my love died the day I found out where those diamonds came from.'

'You loved him?' Dr Moore leaned forward to wag a finger at Lillian Lamb. 'I don't believe that for a minute.'

'What would you know about it?' Lillian Lamb retorted with a curl to the lips. 'You lot have had your noses in the trough all of your lives; you haven't a clue what it's like to fight for every bloody crust.'

Her language raised a few brows, and lowered a few others.

'So you equate love with money?' Gloria was quick to notice the association.

'Oh, and you're different somehow,' Lillian Lamb snapped back.

'That's enough.' I slammed my hand on the table to shut them up. 'Who supplied the diamond dust?' I waited. No-one moved. 'You all know where it came from and who poured it into De Ruyter's dessert.' My gaze stopped at Dr Moore. 'Including you, Doctor.'

'Mea culpa,' he agreed with pride in his voice. 'I thought it an absolute corking plan. De Ruyter would die from his own greed.'

'Did Lady Estelle and her sister consult you with their idea?' I asked him.

'Of course they did; they know they can rely on me. I'm the soul of discretion.' He beamed, entirely unrepentant. 'I told them I was certain it would work, particularly given De Ruyter's ulcer…' His smile faded. 'But I was foolish not to think of the consequences. If he hadn't had the ulcer, he'd have died slowly from peritonitis, and the diamond dust may never have been found. As it was, he coughed up blood and the dust came with it. A post mortem risked revealing more.' He sighed. 'Ah well, better luck next time, I suppose.'

A few heads turned at that remark.

'Who provided the diamond?' I demanded, tired of waiting for the answer.

'Dickie Phillips did,' Gloria announced, with a degree of drama in her voice.

I was astonished. 'Dickie Phillips sacrificed a diamond to kill De Ruyter?'

'He loved Daphne.' She glanced at the Cliftons. 'He always loved her, and when her father manoeuvred him out of Daphne's affections, he became bitter and refused to paint any more portraits.'

I wondered if this was fanciful on her behalf, because Phillips had appeared an unlikely star-crossed lover.

'He was a lush,' Estelle broke in. 'And I was going to pay him the value of the diamond, as he was well aware. You should know better than talking such hokum in front of us, Gloria.'

Gloria was unabashed. 'You didn't see his sensitive side.'

'You mean his drunken ramblings.' Estelle was blunt.

'I don't want his reputation to be stained,' Gloria rebutted. 'He deserves to be remembered as a great artist, not a…a lush.'

'There's only us here.' Marina joined in support of her sister. 'Who's going to know what we say about him?'

'It's all being recorded.' Gloria pointed to Swift, who looked up from his note taking.

'Will you please explain why a small fortune was sacrificed to murder De Ruyter?' I raised my voice to quell the chatter.

Gloria rose to her feet to address the assembled. 'The diamond was the catalyst; it was the cause of it all. Ezra offered it to Dickie as an incentive to paint *her* portrait.' Gloria waved a ringed hand in Lillian Lamb's direction, who smirked in derogatory fashion. 'Dickie eventually accepted, because, as you said, it really was worth a fortune. And then he saw the tiara, she wore it to her sitting, and immediately realised where the diamonds had come from.' Gloria's sense of theatre took hold. 'He was beside himself. He convinced himself they were taken from the bodies – he even thought they may have been from Daphne's body...' She realised the pain her words were causing the Cliftons, and reigned herself in. 'Anyway, he said he'd told that woman,' she pointed again to Lillian Lamb, 'and she'd declared Ezra's actions sickened her and she was going to cut all contact with him. Dickie asked her if Ezra had ever admitted his guilt – she swore he hadn't, but she was beginning to believe it possible.'

Lillian Lamb broke in, her voice strident, the sleek veneer cracked. 'And I did confront him, but he wouldn't admit what he'd done. Using those diamonds for the tiara was evil, and I realised it meant he was capable of anything.'

'Thank you,' I said firmly, then turned to Billings. 'You interviewed the jewellers?'

'Yes.' Billings was leaning against the wall, his hands thrust into his pockets. 'De Ruyter approached Cadogan's in November last year and commissioned the tiara. He supplied the diamonds and told them to have it ready for Christmas.'

'Was there any reason for the urgency?' I asked, thinking it short notice for such an intricate piece of work.

Billings shrugged. 'He could afford to pay any price they asked.'

'He wouldn't consider it urgent,' Gloria Thornton called out. 'He was used to having what he wanted when he wanted it.'

There were angry murmurings from the Cliftons and Stanfords. I was surprised Gloria had spoken up; her words were causing old resentments to resurface.

'Dickie Phillips supplied the diamond,' I stated. 'Did he pulverise it?'

'Yes,' Estelle admitted. 'I had told him about Voltaire and the death of the Duchess, Henrietta. Humphrey had mentioned it one evening at dinner. He'd specifically said Voltaire was wrong, there were examples in history of murder by diamond dust, and it had stuck in my mind. I repeated it to Dickie and he agreed – we thought it the most fitting revenge.'

I turned to Rossetti. *'Revenge is a dish best served cold.* An Italian saying, isn't it? Did you sprinkle it when Lady Estelle caused a diversion?' I pivoted on my heel. 'Or was it you, Browne?' I stared him in the eye. 'You were the best placed of all – you wheeled the trolley in, and you served the desserts.'

He didn't flinch, his long face utterly passive. 'I'm pleased the man's dead,' he said in his Scottish accent.

I stalked to the centre of the room. 'Which one of you did it?'

Nobody answered, of course – this was a hanging matter; the culprit couldn't argue away premeditated murder. 'Which one of you put the diamond dust in the dessert?' I paced the floor in a circle, glaring at them, letting the tension rise.

'We all did.' Clifton stood up. 'We are all equally guilty, even if only by omission of action.'

Wallace was frantically signalling for him to shut up.

Sir Humphrey also rose to his feet. 'We are collectively guilty, that is the only admission we will offer. We are Spartacus!' he said with added drama. I understood the reference, it meant they would collectively take the blame, but it still sounded ridiculous.

'Tommy rot.' Billings straightened up, pulling his hands from his pockets. 'You didn't all pour the diamond dust into his pudding, only one of you did that. The guilty party should admit it.'

He was wasting his breath; they looked on in inimical silence.

'Phillips was poisoned.' I switched tack as Billings stepped back. 'Was it by the same hand? Did you all conspire to kill him, too?'

Marina jumped up. 'No, we'd never do such a thing.'

'Well someone did,' I cut her off. 'And those chocolates could have killed more than just Phillips. It was indiscriminate, and utterly ruthless.' I turned to Gloria Thornton. 'Were they meant for you, or did you add the cyanide?'

Her eyes flashed fury at me. 'Dickie was my friend. I would never do such a thing.'

I began slowly pacing again. 'Someone in here killed

Dickie Phillips. Is there one murderer in this room, or two?' They watched me, the tension notching higher; I could see it in their faces. 'And Miss Lamb's maid was attacked – was that part of your plan?' I made another circuit. 'Or has your criminal act of revenge unleashed a demon? Killing not once, not twice, but three times.' That last sentence felt a bit theatrical, but it had the desired effect.

'What do you mean, three?' Clifton was the first to speak, then they all began clamouring.

'Are you saying my maid has died?' Lillian Lamb demanded. 'Because I was told she's recovering and would be back at work today.'

There was a pause in the questioning as they waited for my explanation. 'Markov died,' I stated.

Billings and his men observed the reactions as acutely as Swift and I. None of them gave themselves away.

'Who is Markov?' Wallace asked, amongst others.

'Swift will explain.' I turned to him. I was in need of a drink and a quiet moment.

I retired to the corner with Greggs.

'This is becoming very exciting, sir,' Greggs whispered.

'Greggs, one way or the other this is going to end at the hangman's noose.' I spoke sharply, then added, 'A glass of something sustaining wouldn't go amiss.'

'Ah, indeed sir.' He slid a hand into his waistcoat and withdrew a silver hip flask. 'I filled it this morning,' he whispered as he passed it to me.

It contained Braeburn Malt, and was just what the doctor ordered.

'Greggs, how went it with Miss Fairchild?' I had to know.

He simpered. 'Ah, it was rather delicate, sir. You see, Miss Fairchild realised she too had been carried away by the occasion. She told me she was in trepidation of our outing and had been kept awake by concerns for my emotions. She was very considerate in her explanations.'

'Do you mean she cried off?' I cut through the circuitous discourse.

'Indeed I do, sir.' He grinned in happy fashion. 'And I was very sincere in my response.'

I raised the silver flask. 'Here's to your continuing bachelorhood, old chap.'

'Thank you, sir.' He beamed.

Swift had been expounding a precise explanation of Bronski, the tiara case, and Markov. He omitted our bout of fisticuffs, but relayed the startling news that Markov was probably the source of the explosives in the Birdcage. The assembled had listened in silence, broken only by the occasional gasp.

'How did you find Markov?' Wallace demanded.

'Your operative's notes helped,' Swift replied. 'He followed De Ruyter and Miss Lamb to the Chequers Tavern.'

'You what?' Lillian Lamb leapt to her feet. 'You had someone following me? You bloody sneak,' she yelled at him. He looked inclined to argue, but Billings cut in with a bellow.

'That's enough. Sit down.'

She was furious, but did as she was bade.

Swift continued. 'The outing to a tradesmen's tavern seemed out of character, and Lennox recognised Bronski's name on the clasp. Bronski specialised in reloading rifle cartridges; Lennox recognised the potential connection.'

Wallace glanced over to me in appraising fashion. 'It's nothing more than a hunch.'

'Really?' Billings stepped forward. 'In my book it's good detective work. That tiara case was deliberately chosen, and the name could have been the reason. Killers are known to collect mementoes of their work, it's a way of gloating over their victims. We spoke to the jewellers: both De Ruyter and Lamb decided on that specific case.' He glared at Lillian Lamb. 'Why was that?'

She laughed in his face. 'Ezra chose it, I didn't. It was just a stupid case. I didn't even like it.' That was the second time she'd changed her story, to my knowledge.

'Can you prove the connection between De Ruyter and Markov?' Clifton demanded.

'Not yet,' Billings admitted. 'He left the country after meeting De Ruyter in December 1914, and returned a very rich man two years ago. We are making further enquiries.'

There were more questions, but nothing concrete to add. I walked slowly back into the centre of the room.

'Markov was tortured and killed last night,' I stated quietly, then turned to face Rossetti. 'You ordered Pinner to spy on us during our stay. He reported our discussion regarding Markov to you.'

Rossetti didn't reply, he merely nodded his head in a stiff-necked manner.

'You knew what Markov had done, and Pinner told you his address,' I continued. 'You went there and beat the truth out of him with an iron bar.'

The Master regarded me coldly and without expression. 'That man did not deserve life.'

'Many men do not deserve life,' I lost my temper and shouted. 'But that doesn't give you the right to torture them to death.'

'You admit you killed him?' Billings stepped forward. I held a hand up to stop him.

'You'll hang, Rossetti,' I warned him.

'It is of no matter,' he replied.

'Please, please tell us what you learned,' Lady Marina called out.

'Did he do it? Did that devil pay him to plant the explosives? Were we right?' Lady Estelle joined her. They left their places and approached with hands outstretched.

'We've waited so long for the truth,' Lady Marina implored him.

The room froze in silence as we waited for Rossetti to speak. He bit his lips tightly together.

'You can prove who was behind the Birdcage murders once and for all,' I told him. 'Give these people the peace they haven't known for twelve years.'

Rossetti looked away, his eyes glistening with unspilled tears.

'I did it.' Browne's voice was gruff. 'I wasn't going to

let that monster get away with it, and I wanted the truth.' His tone hardened. 'My girl was murdered for money, for greed, an innocent wee lass who'd never hurt anyone. I beat that savage until he told me what he'd done, and I'd do it again and gladly.'

A gasp shot about the room. The shock of the confession was quickly replaced by the craving to hear the truth.

'What did he tell you?' Clifton had joined his wife, as had Stanford; they stood together in a tight group.

'De Ruyter paid him to prepare the bomb and plant it in the Birdcage.' Browne was almost animated, probably relieved to share the terrible secret. 'Markov was paid with diamonds stolen by Reynolds at De Ruyter's instruction. Twenty-five of them were replaced with paste. They knew it could never be proved because the explosion would destroy the evidence.'

'Oh Lord... oh dear Lord.' Marina was rocking on her feet, her husband at her side. 'Estelle we did right. Thank God, we did right.' They both burst into tears.

I hadn't finished. 'De Ruyter wasn't the brains behind the murders, was he?' I addressed Browne.

'No sir, he wasn't,' he answered calmly.

'It was Lillian Lamb, wasn't it?' I said.

'It was, sir,' Browne replied.

A scream of rage erupted behind me. It was Gloria Thornton. 'Harlot. You scheming, murdering harlot. I knew it, I knew she was evil—' Billings grabbed her by the waist as she flung herself at Lillian Lamb, her fingers raking the air as she fought to reach her quarry.

'That's enough, now. Calm down.' Billings tried to quieten her. His men moved to help but he frowned them away.

'Arrest her.' Swift swept into action, pointing at Lillian Lamb. 'She conspired with De Ruyter—'

'Wait.' I called a stop to the mayhem and approached the woman. 'You devised it all, didn't you? The explosion, the death of De Ruyter's uncle and cousin so that he would inherit their fortune. You realised you could live off Ezra, because he could never escape what you knew. Did you demand the tiara as a present from him? Knowing it could be the final straw that propelled the bereaved into action?' I berated her to her face. 'Did you choose Dickie Phillips as your stooge, knowing how close he was to Gloria Thornton? Calculating that she'd be bound to tell Lady Estelle and her sister? And when they devised their plan, you killed Dickie Phillips because he might guess how he was duped…'

She laughed in my face. 'Evidence, you dolt. You can't touch me without evidence.'

'Markov told Browne you were involved.' Swift was at my side. 'He'll swear to it.'

'I will.' Browne stepped forward. 'I'll swear to what he told me.'

'They'll hang you for it, Calum.' Rossetti spoke to his friend with sorrow in his voice.

'It is of no matter,' Browne replied, his solemnity returned.

'Markov's dead – you admitted you tortured him,' Lillian Lamb sneered. 'Your word means nothing.'

Browne looked to Billings. 'Is that the truth?'

'Yes, she's right.' Billings was holding on to Gloria's arm to stop her striking out again. 'A court of law requires indisputable proof to convict a murderer.'

'You don't need to worry about that,' Browne said. He was almost smiling. 'She's not going to answer to any court of law; she's going to answer to her maker.'

The sneer on Lillian Lamb's face faltered. 'What are you talking about, you stupid old man?'

'I didn't give all the diamond dust to De Ruyter. I saved some in case I needed it.' Browne leaned toward her. 'And I knew I'd need it today after what that savage, Markov, told me.' His lips curled. 'I put it in your coffee.'

Lillian Lamb blanched. 'No, no, I didn't have sugar, I don't…you can't…'

'It was in the cream, just like I put it in your lover's cream and poured it over the custard. It mixes well and slips down a treat, and there's nothing you can do now, lassie. It's going to eat through your mortal flesh, and you're going to die in agony.' Browne was close enough to see the growing realisation in her beautiful violet eyes.

'No,' she shrieked, and stumbled backwards, hands over her mouth. 'No…' And the room froze in horror as she screamed and screamed in terror.

# CHAPTER 27

She was still screaming when they escorted her out and through the garden. It sent a chill down my spine to think of what was to become of her.

'Major Lennox.' Clifton had walked to my side. 'How did you know Lillian Lamb was responsible for Phillips' murder?'

'It was indiscriminate,' I replied. 'The same mind must have been behind both killings, and Ezra De Ruyter was dead.'

'Do you believe Browne really did put diamond dust in her cream?' Lady Estelle had come to join us.

I glanced over at the steward. He was surrounded by detectives. Billings was firing questions at him. Browne appeared utterly sanguine; there was a grim smile of satisfaction on his lips. 'Yes, I believe he did.'

'We have to set Wallace on this, Arthur,' Lady Estelle told her husband, her face creased with concern. 'We must save Browne.'

'I believe Wallace will have a great deal of work on all

our own behalves, my dear,' Clifton answered her gravely. 'But I agree. We will do what we are able.'

'Estelle, I'm sorry, I'm so sorry.' Marina came to join us, tears streaming from her eyes. 'I betrayed you. I never should have said a word, but I couldn't lie any more, I just couldn't bring myself to do it.' She clasped her sister's hands.

'Marina, you never could keep a secret,' Estelle said, then threw her arms around her.

Sir Humphrey was almost as distraught, his face drooping and filled with sadness. 'Dear girl, do not cry, we have overcome worse…'

'I know.' Marina wiped tears from her eyes with an embroidered handkerchief.

I turned to Lady Estelle. 'May I ask why you gave us your invitation?' That action had puzzled me; it seemed rash.

'Because I wanted the truth, and that's all I ever wanted.' She regarded me steadily. 'I had lost all faith in the police. I didn't think they'd even guess what we'd done, but then I saw that that detective was real serious.' She indicated Billings. 'And then you boys came along, and I just decided that between you all, you might finally uncover the truth of what that Devil had done.'

'But you risked everything.' I was astonished.

'I figured that was a risk worth taking.' She suddenly smiled. 'And you just proved me right.'

'My wife is a clever and complex woman, Major

Lennox,' Clifton said, then gently took her hand. 'Come along, Estelle, we will return home.'

'Will they allow us to leave, Arthur?' She looked up at him.

'I don't believe they can prevent us.' Clifton led her away.

Sir Humphrey placed his arm about Lady Marina and they followed quietly. The policeman at the garden door seemed uncertain, but Billings looked over to him and gave the nod.

Swift came over. He was shaken, but trying to remain businesslike. 'He'll hang, and I don't think there's anything anyone can do to prevent it.'

I swore quietly. 'He deserves a medal.'

'Perhaps, but that's not the way the law works.'

'What about justice? Lillian Lamb would have walked free if it weren't for Browne's confession.'

'He fed her diamond dust, Lennox.'

'Yes, and justice was served, Swift, but the law failed.'

He glanced at me, then looked away.

Dr Moore wandered over. He seemed rather lost. 'They'll not execute him, will they?'

'It's too soon to say.' Swift was noncommittal.

'Poor show if they do.' Moore turned toward the officers around Browne. 'Still don't know what happened to the maid. Why was she attacked?'

'It was an accident,' Swift answered. 'I just heard Browne confess. He was the only killer amongst the bereaved; he knew none of you had murdered Phillips, and Gloria couldn't have done it because she was in jail. That only left Lillian Lamb. He went to her house to confront her, but was disturbed by the maid.'

'So, he didn't intend to harm the girl.' Moore seemed relieved. 'Lillian Lamb was behind everything, wasn't she? She designed it all, she wound us up like automatons, inciting us to kill De Ruyter by having those diamonds set into the tiara. We were full of fury and impotence, waiting for justice all these years. All she had to do was light the touch-paper, then sit back and watch us do her dirty work for her.'

'It was clever.' Gloria Thornton had come to join us, her face taut with shock. 'And so very evil.'

'She was the brains behind the Birdcage explosion.' Moore took a crumpled handkerchief from his pocket and raised it to his eyes. 'She probably manipulated De Ruyter, just like she did with us.'

Gloria Thornton nodded. 'Ezra was greedy, but he wasn't terribly intelligent.' She sighed. 'I couldn't believe he would have done such a thing, but now I see how he was led into it.'

'Will the diamond dust really kill Lillian Lamb?' Swift asked Dr Moore.

'Oh, yes, I'm certain of it,' he said, then blew his nose loudly. 'And she will suffer her last days in torment.'

'Can't they wash it out of her stomach?' I asked.

'No, trying to remove it would merely cause more damage. There's no way out for her now. She'll welcome death when it comes,' Dr Moore said with some satisfaction.

'It wasn't in De Ruyter's custard.' Swift seemed upset by the fact. 'We all assumed it was, and we were wrong, it was in the cream.'

'Does it matter?' I asked.

'Yes, we relied on an assumption, of course it matters. Policing is about method, and rigour.'

Personally, I thought it about people and their fallibility, and the assumption about the custard merely proved the point.

Billings began snapping orders. The police were preparing to escort Browne to Scotland Yard. Rossetti was at Browne's side and insisting on accompanying him. Wallace joined in, officious and obstructive. Voices were raised, and I decided I'd had enough.

'Swift, I'm going to telephone Persi.'

'Lennox, we'll need to make statements,' he objected.

'Then we'll go to the Yard and do it,' I told him. 'And then I'm going home.'

'Right.' He cheered up at the thought of going to the Yard again. 'I'll go and call Florence, erm…I'll just inform Billings what we're planning to do.'

'Fine,' I said, then headed for Greggs.

It was mid-afternoon before the luggage, passengers, and pets were loaded into the car; we were parked outside Brundles with the engine thrumming. We'd spent hours at Scotland Yard being questioned, despite them already having the answers. There had only been tea and sandwiches for lunch. The bread was stale. I was not in the best of moods.

'Right, ready?' I said as I revved the engine.

George advanced from the front step and held his hand up. 'Major Lennox, I have something. I wouldn't want you to go without it.'

'Ah, yes.' I'd almost forgotten amid the chaos. I let go the throttle.

'Wait just one moment, would you,' he told me, and retreated back into the club. A moment later he reappeared with a cloth covered object. 'There you go, sir.' He handed it to Greggs, who was looking bemused.

'Sir?' Greggs asked as he placed it on his lap.

'What is it?' Swift turned around in his seat.

'It's a present for Persi,' I told him. 'Let's have a look, Greggs.'

Greggs pulled back the cover from a willow cage enclosing a cockerel, which blinked at us in surprise. He was a splendid fellow with glossy chestnut brown plumage, bright red wattles, and a flamboyant green tail. Greggs looked askance.

'He's to keep the chickens in order,' I explained.

'Indeed sir, and he has come in his very own Birdcage…'

# EPILOGUE

'I didn't say his name was George,' I tried to explain, yet again. 'I said George found him for me...'

'It doesn't matter, sir, it's a jolly good name, and he's learned it now,' Tommy replied.

'Nonsense, chickens don't recognise names.'

'He does, sir, he's dead clever and he's really bossy with the hens, but m'lady says that's what they need or they'll carry on fighting with each other. And when they fight they run off in different directions instead of going in the henhouse to lay eggs, like they're supposed to...' Tommy was in full flow. We were watching the chickens in the walled garden; it was a bright sunny day radiant with the promise of spring.

He passed a sack to me. 'Now, you feed them, sir, and I'll go in and check the nests. What you have to do is throw the corn in one direction, then George and all the girls will run after it, and then when they're pecking at it, you throw another handful to Hoppy, 'cause she can't run.'

'Yes, I understand, Tommy,' I told him firmly because he seemed to think I was having difficulty grasping the principle. The black hen had recovered from Tommy and Brendan's ministrations and could use the stump of her leg to hobble about the garden. She mostly went around in circles, but seemed happy enough.

Upon my return home, we'd taken the cockerel and freed him near to the little flock. He'd headed straight for them and instantly begun strutting his magnificence in avian splendour. This ruffled the feathers of the matriarch, who'd puffed herself up in defiance. George had set back his head, flapped his wings at full stretch, and crowed mightily. The matriarch had cast him an appraising eye, turned bashful, or as bashful as a chicken can be, and clucked her approval. The rest of the girls had immediately followed her lead. Chickens are really very uncomplicated creatures.

Tommy crept into the henhouse while the flock were occupied pecking corn.

'How many eggs are there?' I called to him.

'Four, sir.' He had taken the basket with him. 'I don't think it will be enough.'

'There are only two people coming.'

He left the henhouse and secured the door carefully behind him. 'It's the vicar and his wife, sir, and m'lady said we had to lay on a proper afternoon tea. Aunty's making scones, and we're supposed to give them egg and cress sandwiches.'

'I'll have ham.' We walked back toward the house. Fogg was at my heels. It had taken a week of training to drum it into him not to chase the chickens, but I still didn't trust him.

Tommy closed the gate to the walled garden, the straw-filled egg basket under his arm. 'The fete's goin' to be magic, sir. I can't wait, but we're goin' to have to do a lot more work in the garden and—'

'What fete?' I cut in.

'The one the vicar's coming to discuss, sir. He was talking about it to m'lady after church yesterday. You must have heard what they said, you were standing right behind them.'

'I was watching crows building nests in the trees…' I began, then realised it was too damn late to say anything.

'It'll be super fun, sir.' Tommy continued chattering. 'There'll be cake stalls, and hoopla, and all sorts. And m'lady said there's going to be a dog show, and the vicar said Foggy was bound to win because he was the nicest dog around.'

'Hm, a dog show…' That threw a different light on the matter. A dog show might be quite entertaining.

'Even Mr Greggs thought it was a good idea.' Tommy opened the door as we arrived at the house. 'Now you give me the chicken food, sir, and I'll take the eggs to the kitchen.'

I duly handed the bag over.

Greggs arrived from the rear. 'Ah, sir. M'lady is helping Cook in the kitchen. The telephone rang while you were in the garden; it was Inspector Swift.' His tone was solemn.

'Right, thank you Greggs.' I strode across the hall to the apparatus. We'd been expecting news, and the old fellow's face suggested it was of a cheerless nature.

The operator put me through to the Scottish highlands and the call was picked up almost immediately.

'Swift?' I spoke loudly over a poor line.

'Lennox, she died this morning.'

I knew he meant Lillian Lamb; we'd all been waiting for it.

'Did she confess?'

'Yes, to everything.' He was having to speak above the crackling, then suddenly the interference dropped out and I could hear him quite clearly. 'She was proud of herself. She'd put the Birdcage plan into Ezra De Ruyter's head right at the very beginning, and she knew Markov from Whitechapel – she set it all up.'

'Good Lord, she was only seventeen,' I uttered.

'The back streets of London can be a tough environment, Lennox,' he replied, then sighed. 'Lamb identified Reynolds as being gullible, and became friendly with him. She organised it, and De Ruyter was fully complicit.'

'How were the explosives secreted into the Birdcage?' I asked the question that had been puzzling me.

'Reynolds provided a schematic drawing of the inside workings of the cage. Lamb took it to Markov and he prepared the bomb so that it would fit easily around the mechanism,' he explained. 'They had it all planned. On the night the cage was transported across London, Lamb drove a bicycle in front of the horses to frighten them, giving Markov the opportunity to climb in the back. He only had to unscrew the base, insert the explosive and attach the detonator, then screw the base together again. It didn't take long and he slipped out just before the carriage arrived in Chester Square.'

I nodded. It was much as we'd imagined. 'I assume De Ruyter paid Reynolds and Markov with the swapped diamonds?'

'He did. He wasn't certain he was going to inherit and wanted enough to live comfortably on. He gave one diamond each to the men and promised one more if he was granted his uncle's fortune. Once he received it, he and Lamb met Markov in the Chequers Tavern and paid him off. Markov was supposed to disappear; he went to Constantinople during the war, but he couldn't resist coming back to London and flaunting his wealth. Lillian said she would have killed him once she'd realised he'd returned.'

'She had no compunction to murder,' I stated, feeling a sense of revulsion. 'I assume she insisted De Ruyter have the tiara designed with the diamonds.'

'She did, and demanded Phillips paint her portrait. She planned it all, including his death.'

'Did Phillips really have to die – had he guessed what she had done?' I asked.

'No, it was to confuse the investigation.' Swift explained. 'She thought we might unravel Estelle and Marina's plan, and a random death would muddy the water.'

'So she didn't care who lived or died,' I said.

'No.'

'What about Ezra, why did she want him killed?' I asked the question that had puzzled me from the beginning.

'He'd grown fat and boring, and she couldn't escape.' Swift sounded as disturbed by the revelations as I was. 'They were bound together by the Birdcage murders, neither truly trusting the other. She could only be free once he was dead, so she siphoned a fortune away, and planned his murder.'

'They'd built their cage...'

'Ironically, yes, and trapped themselves in it,' he said.

'Did it have to be by such elaborate means?' I asked.

'Billings thought it was her idea of entertainment; inciting the high-born lords and ladies to kill her lover.'

'She really hated them, didn't she?'

'She hated everyone, Lennox. The world had dealt her a cruel hand and she lashed out against it.'

I was sick of discussing Lillian Lamb. 'What's happening with Browne?'

'Wallace is trying everything he can, including diminished responsibility, but Browne is determined to stand his ground. He won't withdraw his confession, and he won't admit remorse. He knows how it will end and he's reconciled to it.'

'And the rest?'

'Rossetti appears resigned to Browne's decision. Brundles are supporting them both; they want Rossetti to remain as Master.' Swift broke off to sneeze. 'Sorry, we're in the middle of a cold snap here. Wallace is proving a bit of a hero, actually, it seems likely the Cliftons and Stanfords will receive suspended sentences, and Gloria Thornton has nothing to answer for. She was on the periphery, as was Moore. Neither will appear in court.'

That was something, at least. 'Billings must be content.'

'Billings isn't the sort to be content,' Swift said dryly. 'But apparently he's been seen with Gloria Thornton. They had dinner together.'

That made me smile. 'Who told you that?'

'Greggs, when I spoke to him earlier. Miss Fairchild wrote to him with all the news.'

I shouldn't have been surprised. Greggs always knew what was going on before I did. I switched to happier topics. 'Persi is organising a garden fete with the vicar. You should come, and bring the family.'

'Florence has already accepted. Persi invited us last week.'

'What!' I exclaimed. 'Why am I always the last to be told anything…'

I do hope you enjoyed this book. Would you like to take a look at the Heathcliff Lennox website? As a member of the Readers Club, you'll receive the FREE short story, 'Heathcliff Lennox – France 1918' and access to the 'World of Lennox' page, where you can view portraits of Lennox, Swift, Greggs, Foggy, Tubbs, Persi and Tommy Jenkins.

There are also 'inspirations' for the books, plus occasional newsletters with updates and free giveaways.

You can find the Heathcliff Lennox Readers Club, and more, at https://karenmenuhin.com/

* * *

Here's the full Heathcliff Lennox series list. You can find each book on Amazon.

Book 1: Murder at Melrose Court
Book 2: The Black Cat Murders
Book 3: The Curse of Braeburn Castle
Book 4: Death in Damascus
Book 5: The Monks Hood Murders
Book 6: The Tomb of the Chatelaine
Book 7: The Mystery of Montague Morgan
Book 8: The Birdcage Murders
Book 9: A Wreath of Red Roses – available for pre-order. Previewed date of publication, February 2023 (or earlier)

All the series can be found on Amazon and all good book stores.

And there are Audible versions read by Sam Dewhurst-Phillips, who is superb, he reads all the voices, and it's just as if listening to a radio play. These can be found on Amazon, Audible and Apple Books.

## A little about Karen Baugh Menuhin

1920s, Cozy crime, Traditional Detectives, Downton Abbey – I love them! Along with my family, my dog and my cat.

At 60 I decided to write, I don't know why but suddenly the stories came pouring out, along with the characters. Eccentric Uncles, stalwart butlers, idiosyncratic servants, machinating Countesses, and the hapless Major Heathcliff Lennox. A whole world built itself upon the page and I just followed along...

An itinerate traveller all my life. I grew up in the military, often on RAF bases but preferring to be in the countryside when we could. I adore whodunnits.

I have two amazing sons – Jonathan and Sam Baugh, and his wife, Wendy, and five grandchildren, Charlie, Joshua, Isabella-Rose, Scarlett and Hugo.

I am married to Krov, my wonderful husband, who is a retired film maker and eldest son of the violinist, Lord Yehudi Menuhin. We live in the Cotswolds.

For more information my address is:
karenmenuhinauthor@littledogpublishing.com

Karen Baugh Menuhin is a member of
The Crime Writers Association

Printed in Great Britain
by Amazon